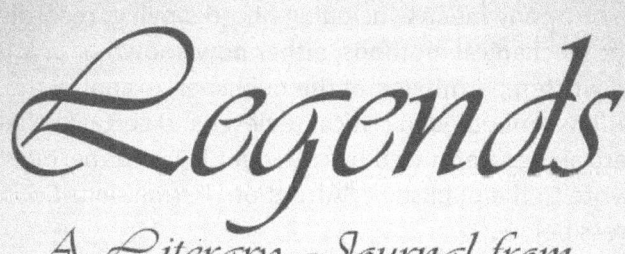

Legends

A Literary Journal from
Grey Wolfe Publishing

Passion Pages 2017

Edited by
Lisa M. Wolfe

Grey Wolfe Publishing, LLC
145 East Fourteen Mile Road
Clawson, Michigan 48017

© 2017 Grey Wolfe Publishing
Published by Grey Wolfe Publishing, LLC
www.GreyWolfePublishing.com
All Rights Reserved

Print Edition ISBN: 978-1628281941
Ebook Edition ISBN: 978-1628281965
Library of Congress Control Number: 2017963723

Grey Wolfe Publishing LLC
Ni bóna na coróin

Legends

A Literary Journal from
Grey Wolfe Publishing
Passion Pages 2017

Edited by Lisa M. Wolfe

Legends is an annual literary journal produced by Grey Wolfe Publishing.

Each a year, talented writers from around the globe lend their work to this showcase of short stories, essays and poems for your reading enjoyment.

Some of the stories and poems within these pages may help you revisit memories you thought you'd forgotten. Others may reawaken emotions long dormant. And still others may reacquaint you with the laughter of young love. Regardless of which piece of poetry or prose you find most appealing, we are certain that these authors will quickly become some of your new favorites.

Grey Wolfe Publishing is an independent publishing house, headquartered in Clawson, Michigan. We are committed to walking through the paths of the publishing forest with our authors as equals; never leading, never following... always side-by-side, with the strength and confidence of the Pack.

Ni Bóna Na Coróin.

Acknowledgements

The production of this book each quarter could not be accomplished without the expertise, literary passion and dedication of our amazing Pack. Each is a writer as well as a company team member; and each lends their unique perspective to serve both the company and our authors with integrity and creativity. We are grateful for their daily contributions to the growth of the Pack.

Contents

A Cup of Coffee

Susan Burdorf

Every day Jeff Klein would stop in at the Cuppa Joe Diner with his co-workers. They liked to sit at the old-fashioned style counter with the red-topped round silver backless seats that spun around like a top. He would smile at Wendy, the girl who stood behind the counter and grew old with him as the years passed and the cups of coffee grew to numbers so high they couldn't be counted anymore.

Every day Wendy gave him the same smile, the wrinkles increasing with age, the hair going gray, or in his case, disappearing altogether to be replaced with a red baseball cap that he always took off in her presence before she poured out his morning cup of coffee.

Like clockwork he and his construction crew buddies would bustle in at opening time, 6am, and wait for her to flash them her famous smile. She never disappointed them.

She was always happy to hear about his son, his wife, and his job. It was amazing what they could talk about in the thirty minutes each day before he and the guys would head off to work. And the routine continued, for Jeff anyway, even after his retirement.

Wendy heard about his son's first home run, graduations from high school and college. She commiserated with him when his wife got cancer and passed away after a long battle. She rejoiced with him when it was warranted and cried with him when life was hard, and through it all she kept the coffee coming, never asking for anything from him and always giving so much.

Jeff always expected her to be there, and she always was.

Until last Wednesday. That is when he walked in to the diner with a big list of things he needed to talk to Wendy about, but instead found a young pretty brunette. No wrinkles on that girl's baby face he noticed right away.

And no smile either. At least not for him. But she sure did smile for the young men who came in on their way to work. He waited ten minutes before she broke away from her conversation to ask what he wanted.

Her smile was as lukewarm as her coffee. In no time at all Jeff realized he was not going to be coming back to the diner. It just wasn't the same without Wendy.

When he paid for his cup of coffee he asked the owner where Wendy had gone. He held his breath fearing the man would tell him she'd gone south to retire, or passed away, or wouldn't answer him at all.

"Oh, she decided it was time to retire. I sure hate to lose her. That girl was wonderful. Always knew how to make the customers happy. All that one wants to do," he nodded his head in the direction of the pretty brunette, "is flirt with the young men. I'm getting complaints from the regulars."

Jeff turned then called out to Pete, "Hey, so where does Wendy live anyway? I think she told me she walks to work every day so I know she's nearby. I have something for her to thank her for all those years of coffee and conversation."

The owner stared at Jeff considering his question. Jeff didn't realize he'd been holding his breath until the owner asked him to wait a minute. Jeff let it out in a big *whoosh* that made his head dizzy.

In a minute the owner came back and handed Jeff a piece of paper saying, "You tell Wendy that if she wants her job back she can have it. Deal?"

Jeff nodded and took the paper. Reading the address, he smiled. Only a few blocks away and it was a beautiful day for a walk.

Along the way, whistling while he walked, he stopped at a florist and picked up a bouquet of brightly colored flowers. Then he saw a simple necklace with a heart on it in a shop window and stopped to get that too.

A few minutes later he was standing outside the building that matched the address the owner had given him. All of a sudden, he felt really dizzy and pretty foolish.

What if Wendy didn't want to see him? What if she was married? He suddenly realized he knew very little about her. All these years he'd talked on and on and drank all the wonderful coffee she'd made for him, and he knew almost nothing about her. She'd always avoided his attempts to glean details about her life by telling him she had nothing to tell.

Turning on his heel he almost walked away until he heard a voice say in surprise, "Why Jeff, what are you doing here?"

It was Wendy, in a light blue sweater decorated with large flowers in a variety of colors. She looked very festive and welcoming, just like he remembered. The big smile she wore on her face convinced him she was happy to see him, and he relaxed. In her hand she held a leash attached to a tiny dog staring at him with eyes full of suspicion.

He reached down, without realizing he was doing it, and petted the dog who promptly licked him while growling and wagging its tail.

She invited him to walk with them and he accepted. They walked a little slow, but that was okay, gave them plenty of time to talk. He told her he missed her at the diner, and she smiled, but didn't say anything else.

When the conversation got a little quiet, he told jokes just so he could hear her laugh.

After walking the dog, she accepted the flowers with a very sweet smile—Jeff kept the other gift for later. They returned to her house and she invited him in.

Stepping inside he was not surprised to find her house as warm and friendly as she was. When they sat at her kitchen table sipping coffee that tasted like the coffee she had always made for him, and not like the sludge he had drunk that morning at the café, he learned all he had ever needed to know about Wendy.

"This is the best coffee ever, thank you," he complimented her. "I stopped at the diner today and the coffee that new waitress served was horrible."

Wendy just smiled.

"What is your secret? You had best teach it to that new girl or they will be losing customers left and right. It was awful." he told her. Taking a deep whiff of the coffee, she had set in front of him he sighed in contentment.

"Oh, I never served you the diner coffee," Wendy confessed leaning in with twinkling eyes, "I always brought a special blend for you."

Jeff looked at her as the realization hit him; no one else ever got her "special blend".

Now, every morning, Jeff gets his coffee just the way he likes it. And he never has to leave his house. Wendy's love spoke to him with every cup of coffee she had ever served him and would serve him in the future.

A Love Extinguished
Michael Noder

Woe is the banefilled existence of the unworthy and unloved.
Destined to be alone in the solitude of their singularity.
Alas, the end draws nigh, harkened forth by the Heralds of
Doom and dismay.

Its arrival is like the drawing of a nightshade
Extinguishing the brilliance of the day.
Ne'er to be raised again upon the marrow.
Leaving only darkness, sadness
Pain, and sorrow.

A Russian Romance
Mark Hudson

(Inspiration: A stolen heart, then Prison, Source; U.S.A Today,
Chicago Sun-Times 1-1-17 Page 26)

Lyudmila Khacatryan was born in 1929, New Year's Eve,
and her whole story is rather difficult to believe.
Born in Russia, the only child of a family in the military,
she now celebrates her eighty-seventh birthday this January.

When she was seventeen, she met her first lover,
a Yugoslav soldier, they had to meet "undercover."
They married in secret, she didn't tell her mother,
But the marriage in Russia would soon be discovered.

Because of Tito and Stalin's relationship at the time,
communicating with Yugoslavians was a crime.
Lyudmila was detained by the Russian police,
put in the Gulag camps with a long wait for release.

She cried in her prison cell, while soldiers tormented,
an impossible work load to her was presented.
She was shipped to arctic regions, working non-stop,
with little sleep or food, supervised by their cops.

She was able to transfer somehow into theatre to entertain,
still as a prisoner, with too much to comprehend in her brain.
By the time she got out, they blamed her Yugoslav husband,
and she was never reunited with him, ever again.

She married twice since she was separated from her first,
but parts of her past she remembers as feeling rather cursed.
She finally got courage to write her first husband, his first bride,
the letter arrived two weeks after the Yugoslavian man died.

Love is a strong emotion, but can it conquer hate?
Can love save us all, before it is too late?
Love has no boundaries, but the ones we create,
and sometimes we lose loved ones as part of fate.

Love survived in Russia, maybe not in political ways,
but everyday people will fall in love till the end of all days.

Affianced, At Last
Nidhi Singh

"Show them the love, Humpty Dumpty. Wrench it up from the guts and whack them on the head with it, if need be. Scream from the rooftops, or cry from the sidewalks – let them know what love is," said lovely, insanely lovable Alessandra, flicking off stardust from her damask cheek as she primed her beau to seek her parents" blessings for marriage.

Humbert Lambert, junior barrister's clerk with Messrs. Sapper, Suckett, and Siphonandra, at the Inns of Court, with a modest salary for now, but with the vague promise of an immodest bonus in a few years, fumbled at his tie knot and quivered. "I wish you would stop calling me that – it hardly inspires a man about to look a lion in the eye in his lair and ask him to part with his flesh and blood."

"Don't sketch papa like that—once you get to know him, you'll see what a cuddly bear he is," she replied, stroking his hand, and getting him all twitter-pated.

Bear or lion, it was all the same to Humbert. Percival Wallace, her father, with the demeanor of a dark lord, with business interests ranging from trout to baked beans to single malts, and with an eye out for a nomination to the Upper House, hardly motivated a suitor to shed his comforting coat of armor and drape him in close embrace.

"It's very well of you to say so," Humbert observed, trying not to chew the end of his tie in anxiety. "But fathers are dry-eyed seasoned auditors ever ready with an antidote for the barbs of a pining heart. Pray, what must I tell him when he asks about my salary?"

"Simple," his enchantress said, drugging him with her sweet, delirious breath, "lie to him."

"That is out of the question, I cannot speak an untruth. And a man like him is certain to have made inquiries—he probably knows me better than I do myself already."

"What's a lawyer that can't tell a convincing lie?"

"Well, that's me. I will tackle the man anyhow—leave it to Hump—Humbert." He crossed and uncrossed his legs; his words seemed to waft like strange tidings from afar.

"Tackle as you will, Humpty, but don't be late. And don't take no for an answer. Ta da," she said, brushing his cheek lightly with her bee-stung lips and tearing off after the 3:20 to her Fine Arts class. Humbert loosened his collar, and oblivious to the sunshine and summer cheer on the sidewalk cafe, wondered how the meek lamb might prevail over the tiger burning brightly in the forests of the night.

****

It wasn't then a knight in shining armor on horseback that came knocking the next day at the castle gates to claim the hand of his fair lady: Humbert felt more like a little schoolboy in knickerbockers at the headmaster's office asking for his answer sheets to be reevaluated. Standing under Greek pillars at the Belgrave Square home, Humbert walloped a large brass knocker on a lavishly decorated, stained oak-paneled door, and then promptly jumped at the resulting thunderclap.

A tall, bald man opened the gate almost immediately as if he'd been lurking all day behind it in wait; and fixing Humbert with a saurian gaze, he half bent at the waist contemptuously.

"Ahem," mourned the cheerless manservant in the usual bib and tucker of white wing-collar dress shirt, pocket-watch, gray striped trousers and white gloves, making Humbert feel lucky he'd been allowed till the doorstep without being collared out. Humbert was sure the man had never smoked pot in his life or shared tea with a parlor maid.

"Hump… Humbert Lambert," he announced his arrival, straightening up somewhat, to match the minions' expectations.

"Aha! A Mr. Lambert is expected indeed," the Butler declared, not believing himself. "Would that thing be yours," he asked, raising himself on his toes and looking over Hubert's shoulders at the cheap Renault parked in the driveway. "You could leave the keys here, we'll get it hauled to the back. Master wouldn't have that thing parked where visitors can see it."

Pocketing the keys, he led Humbert through a marbled hall with recessed lights and picture frames with a gold-leaf finish, to the study. Helena Wallace sat on a large, leather Montague sofa with rolled paneled arms, while Percival took up a place next to the carved mantelpiece, casting a grim eye upon him, as his battle-ready ancestors might once have done, from the projecting battlements of Flodden Fort, at the enemy armada landing below.

Humbert was certain he'd seen Helena's face on the Tattler magazine – she probably ran an advice column warning young girls of poor suitors. Or was she the head of some secret coven whose name he couldn't recall; else, she was definitely involved to some extent in eleemosynary activities involving an African-American child's life.

"Well," said Humbert, rubbing his sweaty hands.

"Well," said Percival, twirling his mustache.

"Well," said Helena in a drawn-out, emphasized voice that was very cold and creaky.

"Ahem," added the butler, who'd brought in a silver tray with tea and buttered toast. After he'd served and left, Humbert cleared his throat and began, "Lissy and I... I mean Alessandra and I were together at Cambridge..."

"Can't help who you rub shoulders with in college these days," Helena observed to her husband. "I believe now you have rice eaters there, people who live on fiery curries."

"They are some of the brainiest and hardest working folks out there...." muttered Humbert.

"And what are your folks," Percival asked, keeping a comforting hand on Helena's shoulder—she'd crinkled up her nose as if the whole house smelt of boiled rice, asafetida and smoking chilies.

"They're from Ashburn. Dad has a small farm, and he tends to sheep, chicken, and pigs. Mom retired from the post office," Humbert said proudly.

"See, I told you so." Helena looked up at her husband accusingly.

"I work at—" Humbert started; he felt an insight into his own standing might clear things up a bit.

"I know, I know," said Percival, looking at his gold pocket watch, and tapping his foot impatiently on the Turkish carpet. "What is it that you want from us?"

"I want... we want... I was thinking... Lissy asked me to..."

"Alessandra is a dreamy kid. She's an artist—she has these make-believe notions from another world. Don't take her too seriously—shell soon get over it. I know she takes up these projects—she has a thing or two about the underdog and the downtrodden. Long shopping lists and creature comforts soon push affairs of the heart on the back foot—remember that.

Now—can I write a reference for you, or advance you a spot of a loan or something?" Percival said, reaching into his breast pocket for the checkbook.

"Certainly not, Sir!" Humbert rose to his full height, his jaw set. "I have come here to ask for Alessandria's hand in marriage, Sir, not compensation!" He bowed stiffly, his British manners, and strict upbringing stretched to the straining limits.

Helena cupped her hands to her mouth and looked faint. Percival's sideburns bristled as he grabbed Hubert's arm and led him out of the room. "You, Sir, are out of your mind," he said, banging the door in Hubert's face.

The smirking butler stood in the hallway trying hard to compose himself. "Follow me please," he said, showing Humbert into the balmy sunlight of Belgrave Square.

Humbert was sure he'd heard a wry chuckle as the oak doors creaked shut on him.

****

The Regent's Park was awash in a ruckus of colors and chirping and the sunshine, but the pensive young man on the white bench remained oblivious to the charms of the quiet lake and the sculptures park nearby, or the black swans and bolshie squirrels that gamboled over there, or the thorns on the rose stem that he so moodily twirled in his fingers. Lissy snuggled up close to Humbert and weaved her artistic fingers through his mop of red hair.

"Why are you so mad—what happened," she asked again.

"And why weren't you there? Leaving me alone with them... puffed up... scoffers."

"Aunt Rhadamanthine was out of sorts. At the last minute, I was bundled into a car and asked to keep her company – my parents would have none of my protesting."

"And was she?"

"No. She was hale and hearty, wagging fingers at the menials. Forget her—tell me what happened? Did they agree—did you tackle papa like you said?"

"The question of tackling arises when one is allowed into the field—I was collared and heave-hoed before I could spit in my hands and say hut-hut. I tried to get back into the game, but then it was like maneuvering your ball in a field of very agile attackers with no one to pass to."

Lissy chuckled like a cow that has discovered sweet cake mix in her feed.

"It all started with the hound dog on pork chops you've got at the gates. He relieved me of my car and snuck it six blocks away—he said the master would be ashamed of it!"

"What a dear... oh what a..." Lissy hastily changed to "...bear," as Humbert turned to her in pain. "Then?" she shook his coat sleeve eagerly.

"Your dad said I was a project; that you were in love with the idea of love! Why he even offered me some money!"

"Really? I hope you took it! We could go shopping," Lissy said, doubling up with laughter.

"That was another thing he said about you – the long shopping lists!" Humbert rose in a huff. "So, they do know you properly – and I've been blind! I'm the standup comic around here, and you're quite the chuckle bunny today, aren't you? You're going to be getting over it soon, aren't you… the sad little project? Do you ever take anything seriously, Lissy? The joke is on me, isn't it?" he said and stormed off.

"Wait," she cried and ran after him. "Humpty—hold up!"

"I'm not Humpty!" He paused to waggle a finger at her, and then continued on his way.

"Yes, you are," she yelled and sprinted after him. When she caught up she leaped on his back and held fast. Humbert tripped, and they rolled to the ground. Humbert tried to break free, but she wouldn't let go.

"You are a determined woman, aren't you?" he said finally. She didn't say anything but just wrapped her long legs around him tighter. "And I am your project?"

"No, you aren't—never say that again." She turned up his chin and looked deep into his eyes. A tear had stolen to the brim of her eyes and hung there bravely.

Humbert realized he was being a fool. "I'm sorry. I was taking my frustration out on you," he said. "I was such a miserable failure. I love you so—I couldn't bear the thought of losing you."

"I love you too." She bent down and pressed her lips against his for a long blissful spell. "Now the important thing is," she asked, leaning on an elbow and tickling him in the ear with a grass stalk," what are you going to do."

Humbert crossed his hands under his head and looked for an answer in the fluffy clouds floating lazily overhead, their white plumes outstretched.

"Let us elope," she cried out.

"Please, Lissy. I wouldn't steal you from yourself. I won't have it without the parent's consent—you would always be looking over your shoulders. You pretend to be tough—I know you chew rusty nails—but I know you love them too well to let them down. And deep down, we're all too British to do anything rash."

"The consent is not coming unless you become a Lord or a tycoon or something—and knowing you—that's not happening anytime soon." She giggled, and then cupped her mouth just when the hurt-puppy look began to flicker across his face again. "I could ask Papa to get you a promising position?"

"Never! That wouldn't be the right honorable thing to do. Just leave it to Hump—Humbert, darling."

"If I leave it to Humpty again I'll turn gray and wrinkly before I float down that aisle. What happened to that drunk, rich uncle of yours? Any chance of his copping it and leaving you the hidden loot?"

"No chance—the wine seems to be agreeing with the old primate. I can swear the man is getting younger by the day—I won't be surprised if he outlives me!"

"Then I will have to think of something," she said and lay back, thoughtfully chewing on a rose petal.

****

Nothing much changed for the next couple of days. Except that Lissy received a call from Ursula, her American roommate, and soul mate from Willingham-Boarding-School-days. Ursula happened to be flying back from a business trip to Germany on a hopping flight to Canada, where she'd moved with her family. She'd wondered if Lissy could take time out to meet at Bentleys" Oyster Bar & Grille at Piccadilly and catch up on old times. It was always a delirious delight to meet Ursula, so Lissy had readily agreed.

Now, Ursula was not one, but a twelve-hugs-a-day person who'd headed a Laughter Club in school, and taught people how to activate sullen solar plexus *chakras* in their body by spreading the love. She was like a flower that wilted without a comforting cuddle, peck – and a firm back rub if possible. Accordingly, the old friends rendezvoused at the grill one sunny afternoon before her flight.

It was a chic place done in pastels and gold with mirrored walls and leather banquettes, with artwork of the chef proudly displayed on the broad white pillars with Corinthian caps. The girls tucked into complimentary canapés and coffee and began to chat animatedly about boys—out of old habit.

"What's the family strength now," Lissy asked. "Is Robby still the Italian Stallion?" Ursula had gone ahead and married right after school.

"He's called the Italian Stallion, not because he runs fast!" Ursula laughed, squeezing Lissy's hand tightly—in fact, she hadn't stopped stroking it all afternoon. "I had to put the brakes at number four—mothball the birthing cannon, as it were—else the entire neighborhood would have been run down by the offspring. And what about you? Has the lawyer boy perked up enough nerve to face the old Grouch?"

"I had to put him up to it at gunpoint—ooh, the silly oaf makes me go so weak in the knees! But it went very badly, I believe. It provoked even the sad Butler into drollness."

"Oh, my poor babe." Ursula, always one to embrace other's miseries, reached forward and pecked Lissy and curled her fingers into her hands again.

"Can I," Lissy asked, gesturing towards one hand, wanting it back so that she could tuck into the Bouillabaisse with Seared Squid.

"Oh, sure," Ursula shrugged and reluctantly let go of one hand.

From the corner of her eye, Lissy noticed two old ladies sitting beyond the broad pillars in the far corner, glaring continuously over pince-nez at her, their mouths agape. "That's so rude," she thought. She leaned back in the wing couch slightly so that they couldn't see her. As she turned her head slowly in their direction, she saw it was Aunt Rhadamanthine, with another old lady, a fellow coven member perhaps. Lissy's first instinct was to walk over to them and say a loud Hello and thwack them on their backs—see if she could thump their fake dentures out, but something made her decide against it.

She pushed aside her soup bowl and crawled her hand back into Ursula's tentacles, which coiled themselves gratefully around once more. "Have you checked out Chanel's vanilla hand serum? It's awesome!" She dangled her hands in Ursula's face who couldn't resist rubbing her snout appreciatively on them, rolling her eyes, and moaning softly. Lissy giggled, it felt so ticklish.

"My, it's yummy!" Ursula said, rising halfway, and like a sniffer dog nuzzling all the way to her shoulders. "I'll make sure to pick some up at the duty-free shop. Canada is so cold and dry; my main problem is frizzy hair. But yours are so luxuriant – what do you use on them?"

"Russian Amber Imperial Conditioning Crème by Philip B – no less—the best of the best! Feel them?"

"Sure!" Ursula leaned in and cupping her wavy mop of hair, inhaled deeply. "Umm! And what's that delicious scent you're wearing?" Her face encircled Lissy's neck and lingered at the hollow of her neck, inhaling deeply of Chanel No 3. "Like old times, eh? Lord, how we used to love it back then. But I am famished now," she said and returned to her seat to winkle out the grilled halibut with peach and pepper sauce, and quell the growls of the healthy appetite of a mother of four.

"Oh my God," Ursula screamed later as Pineapple Carpaccio and Sicilian Citrus Sorbet were placed before her to round off the perfectly gourmet meal.

Lissy, realizing the peaking distress of the old ladies, who were now leaning in and jabbering animatedly, decided to serve up a piece de resistance herself. "My feet are killing me – would you," she asked, shaking off her heels and putting a foot on the edge of Ursula's chair, between her knees.

"Why not, child." Ursula, trained masseur who could induce burps in the most stubborn of babies at her knee, began to good-naturedly knead Lissy's toes with one hand and digging into the dessert with the other, enjoying the sweet dish thoroughly with unbridled expressions of loud "oohs-and-aahs".

The Maître De seemed embarrassed with all the brouhaha the growing, unbecoming intimacy, and public display of unwarranted passion between the two ladies was causing, but remembering who Lissy was, decided to look the other way.

But the old women, who had seen what seemed enough unchristian sin through their failing eyesight from afar in the darkled hall, got up and striking the Chef Sous deftly with the leather-bound bill, stormed off, their umbrella tips sharp as snicker-snees pointing straight ahead of them.

****

Lissy came back home to find Aunt Rhadamanthine leaving the house. Lissy's full-throated "Yo, Grumpy," met with a cold shoulder and icy silence. She went upstairs and plunked on her bed. She gazed at Hubert's picture frame for a while, sighing ever and anon, wondering when the twain shall meet and become one. While daydreaming of him kissing her among the amorous white blossoms, now red with love's wounds, she fell into carefree asleep. Awakened by a soft knock at the door just before supper, she was informed by her handmaiden the Ancients" desire to see her at once in the Study – the Bema seat of Judgment.

****

Mother looked like she'd been caught in a sudden downpour without an umbrella—she swayed slightly in the wing chair, while Father hung on to the mantelpiece for support, fortifying himself with scotch and soda.

"Hello parents," Lissy piped.

"Where have you been," the Pater asked, his finger, like an accusing compass needle pointing straight at her.

"School—sketching. In fact, we were drawing nudes today."

"What—men I hope?" Mother was rapidly deteriorating into the arena of delirium. She looked discomposed and awesomely unwell. "O Lord, what am I saying?"

"No—women." Lissy, with a carefully constructed cool demeanor, began to leaf through a copy of "Country Homes for the Rich."

"And no doubt, you treated one of them to lunch today?" Father asked; his hand already half-raised to hammer down the "guilty" verdict.

"Now that you mention it—yay—I do recall taking one of them out today—though I can't remember if it was the same one as yesterday or different."

"You were seen in the bar—you were being watched." Her father's voice shook as he absentmindedly plucked hair from his sideburns.

"Everything?" Lissy allowed her hand holding the magazine to quiver, nay shudder so that everyone could see it.

"Everything," her father thundered. He wiped his brow in slow motion, and then changed tack. In a much gentler, coaxing voice he said, "look we all know you are a bold... adventurous girl— it runs in the family, alas. But that's no reason to get a rash on the rebound. A little emotional setback doesn't mean we should let our youthful passions... our hot-bloodedness... the fires in our belly run amok, and we start playing against nature's course."

"This is what becomes of little girls when you send them to girls-only convents. O Percival, I told you so! My little baby," Mother moaned and looked like she was about to keel over and capsize.

With another great heave, Percival continued, "What happened to that Humturd who drifted in that day—you aren't still seeing him, are you?"

"Hump- Humbert Lambert, Papa. With his movie star looks... heart of pure gold—and he was on rugby scholarship in college—fat chance! I guess he must have moved on. He never tried to contact me after the way he was treated here. And I can't find any match—in men at least—who can show him dull in comparison."

"In retrospect, it seems we were a tad crisp with the boy. He didn't get the hearing he deserved."

"You bet, papa. He was hunting for his car all evening."

"Yes, yes, the servants do tend to read a little too enthusiastically into their orders—I shall have to talk to them about it—I say. But the boy has promise—why in a few years, Siphonandra assures me she will be ready to pick him as a partner. You must remember we give them good business each year, and I do have stocks—and a say in that company."

"He'll never let you influence his standing papa – he's a very proud, self-made man."

"Yes—what a pity—an affliction rather. I do wish they'd pay him better, though—our Lissy is used to a certain style."

"There is nothing a fat dowry cannot correct—no man may object to what parents wish to bestow upon their daughter," said Mother. "But what of his status—his standing in society?"

"He has an uncle, with a drinking habit," Percival said, carefully avoiding Lissy's eyes. "In deep debt—a pecuniary condition carefully guised from society. His estates could be purchased, and a title of "Lord of the Manor" could be transferred to this Huppert."

Mother suddenly became bright eyed and bushy tailed like a squirrel that has discovered a chest of hickory nuts under the tamped snow. "How nice – being mother-in-law to a Lord of the Manor – whatever that might mean."

"What say, Lissy," Percival asked, looking from mother to the only daughter. "Should we call the man, and settle for a date – the earliest possible?"

"What can a girl—who is not financially independent say, Papa dear, when her parents have already thought out everything for her. I know you mean the best for me—so I will go along with anything you folks say," she said, trying very hard to look the coy, demure wife-to-be, and not let the firecrackers bursting inside show.

Alice's Love Story
Linda Tyler

A week ago, Alice joined a creative writing class.   Now, her husband was at work, the boys were going after school to a friend's house for tea and she had the rest of the afternoon to herself.   She would start on her first assignment.   Alice made a mug of coffee, carried it through to the dining room and settled herself in front of the computer.

Your story can be about anything, the creative writing tutor had told the class; the important thing is to express yourself.   Alice stared at the blank screen.   Easier said than done.   She gazed out of the window, but the garden with its neat and colourful bedding plants produced no inspiration.   What on earth could she write about?   Gritty stories are what readers want these days, someone had told Alice, but she knew she couldn't write about murder and the like.

In the silence, the clock ticked.   She needed to make a start.

Alice looked down at the keyboard, her fingers hovering over the letters.   She would write a romance, set in an exotic location, with thrilling, passionate characters.

First, a hero was required.   Alice pictured him immediately. Tall, about her age, his loose white shirt open at the neck to reveal a manly throat.   He wore black baggy trousers and in the wide leather belt at his waist was tucked a cutlass.   As he was clearly a pirate, she gave him a small moustache.   She smiled at him and he smiled back, a wickedly charming grin.   He needed a name; he looked like a Marcos.

Alice positioned her fingers on the keys, took a breath and typed.

From the prow of his pirate ship as it sailed across the sparkling blue Mediterranean, Marcos spied the white sails of another ship gleaming on the horizon.

Alice saw the shimmering sea, felt the warm breeze on her face, tasted the salt on her lips. She typed on.

Silhouetted against the sky, he lifted his spyglass and brought the enemy into focus. His eyes shone. The flag of a French merchant ship – a valuable prize. Marcos's black curls were wet with spray, and he laughed as he shook off the droplets.

Alice knew there would be precious jewels and wonderful fabrics on board the merchant vessel; rubies the colour of blood and velvets as soft as peach skin.

After it, men! shouted Marcus. And into position on deck!

Of course, the merchant sailors wouldn't let Marcos take their ship without a fight. It was inevitable some men would be hurt in the battle, but there would be only minor injuries.

The crew ran to their positions as their ship flew over the waves. The highly varnished wood of the hull glistened in the sunlight. Through the portholes in the enemy's hull gleamed the muzzles of cannons. Wisps of smoke drifted from them. The cannoneers were at their posts, ready to light the fuses.

The captain of the other ship gave the order. Fire! Each of the three big starboard cannons recoiled on their tracks from the shock of discharging its load. Their boom echoed across the sea. Alice felt a temporary deafening and the smell of powder tickled her nostrils.

When the smoke cleared, she was relieved to see Marcus' ship had not been hit. Rough-looking men with cutlasses lined the gunwale, their oaths mixing with the sound of the waves.

On board, the French ship there was someone who was not like the others. Alice strained to see. It was a woman; her blonde hair shone, her slim figure barely covered in a dress of pale green silk. She looked alluring and in need of male protection.

Alice frowned. That wouldn't do. She wondered how to divert Marcos's attention, but he and his men had already boarded the other ship. The clash of metal blades and the fierce curses of sailors and pirates filled the air. Alice was able to pick out Marcos in the swarm of fighting men as he was the tallest and his shirt the whitest. He had already reached the fragile blonde and was clasping her to his broad chest. She was smiling up at him in a simpering kind of way.

Thank you, the blonde whispered, for protecting me from your uncouth men.

It is my pleasure, Marcos said, white teeth gleaming in his tanned face.

Alice could see where this was going, and she had to do something. As if from nowhere a storm came up. The mast creaked, wind screamed in the rigging, the ship rose and fell through the crashing waves. Around them stretched the open sea, terrible and mysterious. Alice pushed the blonde in green silk overboard and stepped into Marcos's embrace.

You are beautiful, he said softly; a more perfect prize than any treasure. Come back with me to Spain, where I will take care of you. He bent his head and gently kissed her neck.

The storm dropped, the sun blazed, the sea was a dazzling blue. With the captured sailors secure below deck, and a small crew of Marcos's men to sail it, the French ship beat its way through the sparkling waves.

Come with me. Marcos took Alice's hand and led her to his cabin. Motes of dust danced in the shafts of sunlight through the porthole.

I am yours, she murmured.

Marcus kicked the door shut and drew her down onto the couch. A languid sigh escaped her. Alice closed her eyelids and raised eager lips—

"Are you okay?"

She opened her eyes and saw her husband standing in the doorway.

Alice flushed. "I'm working on my writing assignment."

"I'd love to see it," he said, coming into the room. He undid his tie and threw it on a chair. "But first, what's for tea?"

Alice clicked on save and closed the file. "I feel in the mood for fish tonight."

She turned and watched as her husband undid the top button of his shirt. He looked smart as usual in his white shirt and black trousers, but there was something different about his face. Was that a shadow on his upper lip?

"Are you growing a moustache?" she asked.

"I thought you'd like it." He smiled.

She returned his smile. "Oh, I do, Mark."

An Inquiry into Mount Agape, January 2017
Michael D. Jones

Why do you think, she asks, they
named the mountain that? Is it
for the numerous gaps and fissures
near its base that one must cross
before beginning a true assent?
Good question, I say; I don't know.
Perhaps, (deconstructing the linguistic
elements, which I suppose is fair
although all language is in translation
until it is as dead as stone, like Latin)
the "A" does peak like a mountain
and mountain "gap" is a real thing
in the English language, my simile
thinning like mountain air as I reach
letting us both know I don't know
and have a long way to go.

Why do you, she asks, think they
named the mountain that? Is it
for the awe inspired wonder and
majesty of mountains; the creative
energy that raised them up to
touch the sky; how they say, Here
is as high as you alone can travel
and there is still more air above?
I lazily say, No, that's very poetic
and I don't know about all that
but I have a long way to go.
Why, she asks, do you think they

named the mountain that? Is it
a person's name, a place or a thing?
There are many different places
near, around, and on this mountain
each wonderful, each beautifully peopled
so to name it for one of many
magnificent people or places would
diminish all, diminish the mountain
reduce the grandeur, the massive nature
fields, forests, fissures, and faces
the streams and rivulets descending
from ice caps, rock and falling rock
tumbled down as the mountain rises.

I don't know, however I think
they named the mountain that
because in Latin it is Love, or
better still, a divine sort of Love
the highest form of Love; of man
for God and of God for man
acquired from the Greek originally
a familial or brotherly type of love
which is as firm as mountain rock
so I think they named Mount Agape
because our love is a mountain
(I could indulge this metaphor Ad
Nauseam, except I love poetry)
good both in the ascent and descent.
Your opinion, she says. I know.
Yes, we have a long way to go.

Art and Falling Irretrievably In Love
J. J. Steinfeld

At the waning dinner party
long past the unrhythmic discussions
of family, films, books, world events, and politics,
of investments, infidelities, and sexual fantasies,
a guidance counsellor at a local high school
who had earlier revealed a long-ago nervous breakdown
and a proclivity for blindfolded experimentation
in a lively voice asks everyone left
if they were to die in a room alone
bare except for a single painting
from the history of painting
cave drawings to the most modern
including postmodern splashes of concept,
she describes like an almost-drunk art historian—
what would they like that painting to be?
Then she has another drink, now fully drunk,
and the answers from those remaining
leap forth, a romp through the history of art
until an elegant woman who had spoken little all evening
points to a kitchen wall with an oversized clock
and says in a single breath with the confidence of a person
who has vanquished both boredom and trepidation,
"Hieronymus Bosch's *The Garden of Earthly Delights*
the panel dealing with the imagined congestion of Hell,"
and a man who has the most colourful tattoo
anyone at the dinner party has ever seen
asks why that painting of all paintings.
"Because I wanted to see what awaits me,"
she says with measured words bereft of irony
and he falls irretrievably in love.

At the Beginning of Unending Love
J. J. Steinfeld

I want to own loneliness
the woman with the slight but threatening stutter
tells me after the loudest thunderclap
either of us has ever heard.
I want to possess aloneness
she adds as the night sky
lights up with a sinister brightness.
Loneliness and aloneness
I say as if the two words
are meant to mate
and remain forever together.
I neglected to mention
we are strangers at a bus stop
that had been recently painted
a colour neither one of us
can describe accurately.
We wait for an hour
that turns into a night
of hours and mischievous thoughts
for the bus to arrive
and finally I turn my head
toward my inadvertent companion
and see the woman
I had been waiting for
all my life
at a thousand bus stops
no two the same
in colour or in location.
Why does the bus not arrive?
she asks an instant
before I say the same words.

Are we the last two left on Earth
fated to be eternally waiting
for a bus to arrive?
Yes, I say as convincingly as I can,
and we both start to laugh
like lonely and alone deities
before our imaginations
take us elsewhere.

Awakened Angel
Gavin Meggs

My angel that lay undisturbed
For years in a transient state
Have I woken you love?
Unbroken your dream
Have I opened your view
Of the stars?

Did you fall to that place
Or were you placed there with care?
Did tears fall upon you?
Were they your last sensation?

I did not see your youth
Feel the excitement of your maturity
But I can imagine its originality
And its verve

The buds of your wings
As they were developing
The envy of the stars
Symbols of your mortality

Then somehow a peace
Befell you and you slept
In a place that was timeless

If I am responsible for
Finding you then I am pleased
For you to soar and to shine again

To feel the rain upon your face in awakening
To count the stars you thought had gone
To taste life's reality upon your lips
To live, to roam, to love, to own

To cherish, to be, to wonder

Beauty Beatitude
Sandeep Kumar Mishra

Beauty is blessedness, euphoria
When life unveils her holy face;
A soft whisperings, speak in our spirit,
The eternity gazing itself in a mirror,
It glows with pure tints of varying hues;
It shall rise with the dawn from the east,
A lock of angels forever in flight;
Exulting beauty descends from centered
And from errant sphere;
Balmy nectar glows,
Its enchantment entices the bosom;
Come! See the breezy dome of groves,
At its fountain quench the thirst
Of magic thrall

Becky
Moshe Sonnheim

Becky was not pretty. Her nose was a bit sharp. Her lips were a bit thick. Her cheeks were a bit puffy. Her left leg dragged a bit behind her right leg. And she had a slight figure fault in her back. Her brown eyes, however, exuded warmth. She was an only child. Her parents loved her as best they could. Her days were drab; her nights lonely. She had no friends. She was a sweet, lovely child, helping her parents as best she could. Excelling at school, she helped her classmates with their studies, but they deserted her when they succeeded.

In High School, her loneliness intensified. As her body developed, other feelings began to emerge in her. Boys, however, were not drawn to her. She took dance lessons, but no one invited her to dance at class parties. She stood as prominently as she could, with inviting eyes, but she was invisible to those around her. The Senior Prom was approaching, and Becky had no hope of being invited. Her gentle heart ached with sadness. Her parents, too, were filled with sadness mixed with pity for their beautiful daughter. But unlike Becky, they were angry that no one saw her inner beauty.

The day before the Prom, Becky received a call from Izzie, one of the more popular boys in her class. He apologized for calling so late, but he wanted her to be his date for the Prom. Without question and hesitation, Becky replied happily that she would be pleased to be his date. The moment the call ended, Becky and her parents burst into frantic activity. Becky, who had good taste, bought a yellow dress which accented her brown eyes, and minimized her figure fault. She bought modest makeup which accentuated her slender lips and now softer cheeks. Her face as a whole radiated a gentle beauty. She was happy!

Izzie arrived promptly at eight o'clock with orchids for her wrist. In his white tuxedo, he cut a handsome figure. Tall, with a crop of black hair, and a Greco-Roman face, Izzie was a dream come true for Becky.

Faces turned when they arrived. The faces turned even more when Becky moved gracefully and confidently across the dance floor. Izzie seemed to enjoy her company, and they spent most of the evening together. He was, she thought, a perfect gentleman. As the Band played "Goodnight Irene" to signal Prom's end. Becky pressed close to him, nestling her head on his chest. He stiffened somewhat, but she seemed not to notice. When he brought her home, Izzie's parting kiss seemed a bit cool, while she touched his lips warmly. This day was not drab, nor was Becky's night lonely. She imagined his strong arms around her as they lay naked in bed.

But he did not call her again! Several days later, Becky understood why. She heard him telling his friends how Becky had "saved" him when his girlfriend was sick, and unable to accompany him to the Prom, even though they had made the date a month earlier. He said nothing about Becky's appearance or about her graceful dancing. He did, however, make some snide remarks about her awkward attempt to stimulate him sexually.

Humiliated, and angry with herself for being so naïve, Becky did not give Izzie the satisfaction of seeing her cry. She vowed, however, that she would never again be lonely. She spoke not a word to Izzie during the remainder of the school year. At Graduation, they went their separate ways, and she never saw him again.

Becky was accepted to a prestigious program for Physical Therapists, earning a Doctorate in Rehabilitation. She had turned into a lovely woman, whose external beauty reflected her inner beauty---warm, sensitive, and caring. She had no nasty bone in her body.

The boys, meanwhile, had grown into men. They found jobs, married, had children, and some went to war. Some returned healthy and whole. Some returned in coffins, with full military honors. And some returned with mangled bodies and souls

It was the latter group with whom Becky worked, in a VA Rehab Center. Others would be repelled by the burned bodies and missing limbs. Not Becky! Her sweet nature and tough professionalism made her an ideal and much sought-after Physical Therapist. She was often assigned the most difficult cases. One "Wounded Warrior," a Major, who had been badly burned by an IED, but with intact limbs, had difficulty moving and speaking. He was assigned to a team of Plastic Surgeon, Social Worker, Occupational Therapist, and Physical Therapist (Becky).

When she read his chart, Becky knew immediately that he was the same Izzie who had humiliated her so many years ago. His once-handsome face and muscular arms were raw with third-degree burns. There was a blank look in his eyes, and when she introduced herself as Becky, he did not recognize or remember her. Not one to bear animosity, feeling pity and compassion for this man-boy, Becky reminded him gently that she had been his Prom date. The look in his swollen eyes prompted her to add that she had enjoyed that evening very much.

Then, she set to work! For two and a half years, she encouraged and prodded him to do the exercises to strengthen his limbs and mobility. In the beginning, he found it difficult. Once, he cried from the pain, and Becky cradled his head in her arms. The other team members were doing their job as well. Numerous operations repaired Izzie's physical features as much as possible, though he would never again have the beauty of a Greco-Roman face. Izzie's emotional status continued to improve as the Social Worker, the Occupational Therapist, and Becky encouraged him to deal with his trauma and renew purpose in life.

Better Latte Than Never
Pamela Q. Fernandes

She could smell the freshly ground heaven and told herself everything got better with coffee. But when she sat down at the same table as she did every evening for the last year, she set down her cup and a wave of sadness enveloped her. The face of her latte had a wide smile, done by the barista; a genteel old woman who operated this cafe.

As she watched the traffic move outside, she saw Liv, her colleague, darting across the street. When she came in, she was huffing and Zara held her hand, forcing her to sit.

"Did you check Finn's FB status? He's engaged."

Both looked at her hand, there was no ring.

Liv continued, "To Cassie, is she the same childhood bestie you were talking about?"

Zara's voice was barely a whisper, "Yes."

"But Zara, I thought you said, he took you home to meet his parents."

"Yeah, but things changed after that."

A lot had changed. On that trip to Chicago, his parents were quite happy about her as well. But the evening they were due to leave, on her way to the local supermarket on Finn's insistence, she got mugged. When she was taken to the hospital, she confessed to him, she'd been sexually assaulted as well. Back in New York, he was cold and aloof, saying she needed to have her space. Now he was engaged. To someone else.

"How can it go wrong so soon? Did you say something, did you two have a fight or an argument?"

There was no one else in the coffee shop, save the barista and the guy who always took the same seat opposite her, with his back to her. Like her, he was always here in the evenings. But she was sure everyone could hear Liv.

"What happened Zara? Where did it go wrong?"

She scanned her tablet; he was indeed, engaged. Cassie was wearing the same ring, she had picked. He had taken her to the store and asked her what she'd prefer. She loved the emerald, a small single stone, in yellow gold. She hated the white look.

Now it seemed so silly, she'd picked another woman's ring. They looked happy, well matched. That was something he always complained about, her height. "You're a foot shorter than me, people don't naturally assume you're my girlfriend." And now she wasn't. Just like that. Could reality be this cruel? One minute you're committed and the next, you're a castoff.

Liv had to rush back home, and Zara sat at the coffee table, alone with her thoughts. Tears pricked her eyes and the barista came over, "Here love, I got you a hazelnut mocha, you need something extra."

Zara half smiled, how could she bear this?

The late evening crowd came in and Zara sat there, dazed as she scanned her tablet. He'd scrubbed every picture of hers, off his social media. Just like that she was erased. She felt erased, as if she didn't exist, as if no one could see her. No one really did. She didn't register the music now booming with R&B strains, the sound of the coffee grinder and the aroma of beans and chocolate wafting.

A shrill voice sounded, "Zara, wow, imagine meeting you here. Meet my friends, we all work together, in fact they work more directly with Finn."

At the mention of his name, she became queasy. Her coffee was travelling up her throat. One of the girls spoke up, "Hey haven't I seen you at the YMCA Centre for RAINN victims."

Suddenly the café was quiet, as necks craned, and people turned to see who the said victim was. Zara's lip trembled. Hushed whispers went around the small place and Zara glanced across the room, shame burning through her. They all saw her, the way Finn did, spoiled, tarnished.

Tears blinded her, and she stood up, fumbling with her things, spoon clattering to the floor and then she found a strong hand, picking up her bag and with a firm grip leading her outside the coffee shop. She didn't lift her head, her vision, blurred and he cradled her neck, letting her lean against him. She cried, and he hugged her close. He smelt of cloves and pine. He was warm, and she clung to him for dear life, sobs racking her.

After a while, she pulled away, snort, threading from her nose to his black polo. She didn't look up, as she wiped the front of his polo. "I'm sorry," she said, "I just…"

She couldn't get any words out, so she took her bag from his hand and darted home. The next day after work she didn't return for coffee. There was no way she could walk back there and pretend no one knew. They were regulars, they would remember, people always did remember these kinds of things. A whole week, she didn't and that was telling something. For a woman who could ask for coffee in six different languages, it surely did.

At work Liv asked, "What are you planning to do for your birthday?"

"Nothing, there's no reason to celebrate me getting closer to my death," she chucked her files on the desk.

"Don't be like that, it's twelve days away, we can do several things, plan a trip, go dancing, bar hopping, bowling. Come on, let's pick one thing, we'll make it a night to remember."

She kept quiet and Liv took the hint and left. After finishing the rest of the account work, she came home and was surprised to find, a cup of coffee, sitting outside her door. Written on it was, "Depresso—the feeling you get when you've run out of coffee." She scanned the corridor, no one was there. The cup had been signed, "O" and nothing else.

It was steaming and when she sipped, she moaned. It was just the way she liked it. Cream, two sugars and a load of vanilla.

At work the next day, she mentioned it to Liv, "Thanks for what you did yesterday, nice touch with the initial. It really made my night."

"What initial?"

Zara's mouth dropped, "Please tell me you're the one who sent me a cup of coffee, last night. You left it on my door!"

"Nah, wasn't me. Maybe it was your neighbour," Liv winked, "a very interested neighbor."

"My neighbors are out of town." She sat at her desk, chewing her pen. Whoever it was, knew her pretty well.

Liv came up with an idea, "Why don't you check the cup, you know, find out which café and ask the barista?"

"And what am I supposed to ask them, uhm, excuse me do you remember seeing this cup?"

By seven she was knackered, she didn't get up, choosing to work late. Pressing her hand to her neck, she stretched a little, when her tablet beeped, she checked the chat message, "Oh look, it's coffee o'clock."

She looked around at the office, no one was there, save the clean-up crew.

"How was the brew yesterday?" Another message came.

"Do I know you?"

"No, but I'm like your coffee, dark, strong and too hot for you."

Zara couldn't believe her eyes, he was flirting with her or maybe she was misreading things. "Well then, hello Darkness." She typed and there was no reply.

Shutting down her computer, she headed home, her cheeks were hot and her pulse was racing, maybe it was the bad coffee at work. But then, bad coffee was still better than no coffee.

The next day Liv asked her, "Any more coffee?"

"No," she bit her lip, keeping last night's chat a secret. The office coffee machine was alright, "Let me get a cup first, I'm sure I'll be nice after I've had my elixir."

Liv was more of a tea lover, " Why? So that you can be hyper aware of how little you're getting done today. Go ahead, get your drug."

By midday day her boss was breathing fire down her, "The budget had to be presented in a flattering manner Zara. This presentation is boring, you need inspiration."

She stormed out of his cabin, "I don't need bloody inspiration, what I need is a freaking cup of coffee."

At her desk, a small package, sat. She looked around. "Who put this on my desk?"

Liv rushed over, "It came via courier, go ahead, open it."

She carefully unwrapped the gift and Zara's eyebrows creased.

"It's a tote," Liv said, "read what's written on it. With coffee, all things are possible. O"

The girls broke into a smile, "What's with this guy and coffee? I mean first he sent you a cup, now he sends you a bag, just tell him to buy you a blinking café." Liv stopped, suddenly gasping, "Or maybe he's a barista?"

Well if anything, this guy knew her addiction to caffeine or rather its addiction to her. She laughed as she closed her eyes, whoever he was, he knew her blood type was coffee.

In the morning, she was about to leave for work, when she heard the knock on the door. No one was there. A pink box sat there, and she knew what was in it before she even opened them.

She carried it to the office, where Zara ate the salted caramel donut, and Liv devoured the other two chocolate covered ones.

Liv, read the card, "Man does not love on coffee alone, Have a Donut." Liv squealed, "Is this guy for real?"

"How do we know it's a guy?" Zara licked the chocolate off her fingers.

Liv's face pinched, her lips downturned, "Don't be such a Debbie downer, no chick would do all this for you and it's you were talking here. I'm the only girlfriend you have."

Her senior accountant came over, "Will you girls stop yakking and start working?"

Liv shuffled away quickly, but Zara was less than polite, "I will start working, when my coffee does."

At midday her office phone rang, "Hi there, coffee lover." Zara sucked in a breath, he was calling her. His voice was low, rich, timbered and reverberated right through her. Was he a guy with a beard or clean shaven, what color were his eyes and why the heck was he calling her, better yet who was calling her?

"I hear no answer, maybe I should call after you have your cup."

She looked about the office, her half-finished coffee was still at her desk.

"I'm done with my cup, why are you calling me?"

He laughed, a low rumble and her hair stood on head. She felt giddy and she couldn't wipe the smile off her face. "Why aren't you hanging up?"

Her smile reached her ears. He was flirting. "I like people who make me think, make me smile and make me coffee, not necessarily in that order."

"Girl after my own heart, I'm glad I can do those things for you. It's been my pleasure."

She licked her lips, "My pleasure, ooh, how else do you expect to pleasure me, pray tell."

He chuckled again, he dropped his voice another octave, "Most definitely like your coffee, warm, strong and keeping you up all night I suppose."

She sucked in breath, as he laughed. Her skin prickled, and her lips trembled, she clutched her phone tighter.

"Until later," he said and hung up.

Zara felt hot and bothered. At the end of the day when the office line rang, she didn't even check who it was, she just answered it, "Hello there."

"Zara, you're sounding pretty upbeat." Her heart sank, when she realized it was Finn. He asked her to meet him at the same coffee shop. Her favorite one.

She deliberately turned up late and saw his nostrils flaring, fists clenched as she approached her usual table.

"I wanted to see you, to tell you about Cassie and me," he said.

"After you got engaged. I guess you're here to hand me a wedding invitation."

"Zara please, having you home made me realize a few things, how out of place you were with my folks, how wrong we were for each other." He pushed a cup toward her. "I ordered you a pumpkin spice latte."

She snickered at the small cup.

"So, what happened to me had nothing to do with your decision?"

He nodded quickly. "Of course, not Zara. Besides, let's face it, you're a small-town girl, who has no clue how some of us in the upper classes live."

Her blood was now coming to her simmer, add to the fact, that he didn't even order her favorite brew. Without thinking, she took the cup and flung its cold contents in his lap.

"Don't ever call me again. And pumpkin spice? Really? I don't take my brew with pumpkin or cinnamon. I take it very, very seriously Finn."

The next morning as she walked to work, her cell phone rang, the caller ID blocked, "How are you this morning, coffee lover."

The way he said lover, made her heart soar. "How did you get my number?"

"Well, morning has broken and I'm guessing your coffee hasn't spoken. How was your day yesterday?"

She bit her lip, "It was awful, I wasted a perfectly good cup of coffee in a guy's lap."

"I know I was there. But then again, size does matter, the cup was pretty small."

Had he just casually mentioned he was at the café.

"Are you there?" His voice was unsteady.

She shook herself, "Why didn't you say something?"

"You seemed pretty chummy there, didn't want to bother you. Besides I figured you were on withdrawal."

She laughed and people around her turned to see if she was laughing at them. It was nice to be one of those people tethered to someone on the phone.

He didn't call her all day, except for late at night, when she was about to hit the bed.

"Hello there, ready to retire."

She smiled, her dimples showing. "With a good book and coffee in bed, can't beat that."

"Hmm, I like the sound of that." He said.

"When are we going to meet, or you plan on doing this forever?"

"Patience, my love."

God, he was driving her crazy with the endearments, she hadn't even seen the man.

"Well my patience is at the bottom of this cup, hang on while I can find it."

He laughed, "I've never met a girl like you."

She wanted to do a happy dance. "Tell me something, I mean I need a little something for my imagination, are you clean shaven?"

"No, I can't seem to get it permanently off my face, so I kept a trimmed beard, nothing grizzly, neat I promise."

"What about me? You've already seen me, haven't you?"

"I like big cups and I cannot lie."

She could feel him smile at the double entendre. "How can you be so trusting?"

"How can I not be? I'll leave you to your book and brew, goodnight lover."

She sucked in a breath, lover. Oh my, indeed. She could do with some loving.

****

"Five days more for your birthday? Are we doing anything?"

Zara smiled, "He called, rang me up, last night."

"Where, when, details and hurry?" Liv was quite happy, "This sounds straight from a Nicholas Sparks novel."

"I know right, I mean he's so dreamy and the things he says."

Liv grew quiet, "Zara I hope you're not making this something bigger than it is. Maybe he's fooling around. Don't expect too much, you're just getting out of a bad breakup. This is rebound, and you know what they say, if it's too good to be true, it probably ain't."

Her words rang through her the whole day and because of that, she let her phone go to voicemail throughout. Her boss was at her throat, Liv was pessimistic, and she was running on low. She just wanted to fill the sink with coffee, dunk her head in it and suck. She didn't even answer her cell phone and let it buzz. Over and over and over.

In the morning, she noticed someone had left another brew on her door, this time her door had been chalked, "How I wish, I was this cup that kissed your sleepy lips. May your burdens be light, and your coffee be strong." Again, he signed his initial "O."

She sipped the brew and even showed it to Liv.

"Just be careful," she said.

At the office, she sighed. Her email list was long, but one caught her eye. The subject was: I'm cream to your coffee.

"I have blue eyes, am five eleven and thirty-four. No, I've never done this before, never been married, separated or divorced. A coffee and you that's all I want. Now don't kill yourself, just have your coffee."

This guy was really something. The thought of him and all the little things he said and did, put her on cloud nine. For a man to take two minutes of his day and think of her, made thousand minutes of hers fantastic. She did have an amazing day and by the end of it went to her RAINN meetings. For the first time, in a long time, she felt strong, empowered and appreciated. And it had nothing to do with the counselling.

She liked the way it was turning out. At work the next day, she was surprised again. Pinned to her soft board was a small silver chain, with a weird pendant, a coffee cup.

A post it attached to the gift said, "Coffee is our love language." Without thinking, she put it on and the whole day she was floating on a cloud. Several people remarked about the pendant and it made her soar higher.

She wondered if the real thing would stand for this. What if he was a shy guy with crooked teeth and gangly legs? What if he was a serial killer? Real men weren't like this; thoughtful, anticipatory or even this keen. Finn hadn't been, he was always measured, cynical and calculating, always doing stuff that she'd have to repay in kind.

That night when she went to bed, she did get a call. Expecting it to be him, she picked up in haste.

"It's Cassie, I hope it's not too late. But I thought I'd give you a call. Look I know what happened to you Zara, but I don't understand why you need to make Finn feel guilty about it. He's been a wreck ever since."

"He wasn't supposed to tell anyone," Zara bit her lip.

"I know but were partners now, so he had to. Besides, I think you should't be meeting him."

She gasped. "Stop preaching to me sister. And what do you mean not his fault, he was the one who insisted that I travel to Chicago, meet his parents at home, then go buy them a stupid farewell present. If it weren't for him, I wouldn't have even been at that damn store. So, if he's feeling guilty, let him. He should be. Now do me a favor and don't me again. I've had enough of the both of you."

"You know you're a real piece of work Zara, I'm not surprised this happened to you. Well, I'm glad it happened, because you deserved everything you got. Finn is mine, you were way out of his league anyway, a classless country girl trying to ingratiate herself with the likes of us. Well got knocked down, didn't you?"

Zara banged the phone, her breaths came fast, and she picked up the coffee mug on her table and flung it against the mirror, causing it to crash into a million pieces. All the pieces now scattered across her floor.

She didn't get out of bed in the morning and informed Liv she wasn't coming in.

A message came in on her phone, "Rise and Grind. O"

She smiled, he was still keeping this up. She didn't reply, and she wasn't up to waking up, besides it would be a world of pain before she could make a first cup. Then her eyes fell on the shattered mug on the floor and winced. She'd let her anger get the better of her.

Then she thought about the phone call. How could women be so cruel to other women? Finally, she scanned his message and his initial.

"O," what did that stand for, Oliver? Othello? She laughed, Odin. She didn't know many names that began with O.

Then she kicked off the covers and made a coffee so strong, it would wake up the neighbors.

Liv texted, "Four days for birthday, what are we doing?"

She didn't know what she was doing, not today, not now. She sat at her table and her phone rang. Again, Caller Id blocked.

"Did you know that coffee drinkers make better lovers?"

She smiled a little, "Are you listing your qualifications or asking me mine?"

"I'm a very good lover, that I can guarantee you, like your cuppa, I like it hot."

Her skin tingled. His rockstar voice made her shiver.

"Listen Mr. O, I've liked all these games and it's been fun, but there's a lot about me you don't know. And if you did know a few things about my past, you wouldn't be," she gulped, "... this forward."

"Zara, I don't care about your past. I want you now. It's the moments that make the years and I want your moments. If it's not coffee on your brain, then it has to be me. I want to be your drug, your habit, your addiction, just like your brew. I could love you more than you love your first cup of coffee."

"How much longer?" She asked him, hoping she didn't sound desperate.

"Let's make a deal. You have until your birthday, if you want to continue this."

"How do you know my birthday?"

"Zara, in four days it's up to you whether you want to see me or not. I'm giving you time, because I know you're on the rebound. The last thing I want is for you to feel rushed into this. For now, you're in a committed relationship with your coffee and I quite like that. But with me there's no out. I want to possess you, no withdrawal, no hangovers, nothing."

When she put down the phone, she finally took a deep breath. She didn't even know She'd been holding it so long. He was like a maelstrom. Every time, she encountered him, he whorled through her life, her thoughts and her entire being.

The next morning, she knew it was one of those days where even her coffee needed a coffee. That's what happens when you play hooky. He didn't call her at work or at home. When she did retire for the night, he messaged her, "Are you like my coffee? Wet and warm."

She sucked in a breath. "I'm awake, and that text has now left me wide awake, I'm off to make another cup."

Her phone beeped again, "Babe, no amount of coffee will keep you awake like I do." He was driving her crazy and the effect his words had on her. It was like making out with him without actually doing it. He was getting it on with her in her brain. How much more stimulatory would he be in the flesh? She just hoped he hadn't been released from prison or something.

Three days were left, and he sent her a gift at work. It was a tee shirt. "I want you to wear it on your birthday. O."

It had a tick mark with the words, "Just Brew It."

She tried it at home. He rang her late into the evening, "Did it fit?"

"What's happening on my birthday?"

He laughed. She loved hearing it. "We're going to do the Java jive babe, trust me I'm going to blow your mind."

"I've seen it all Mr. O. I don't think you can, but we'll see, for all I know you maybe mama's boy hiding in a basement, hacking into my stuff and getting details about me. Remind me why I didn't report you to the cops."

"Because you love your men like your coffee, strong and rich." He laughed. "A couple of day's lover. Just you wait. I hope I sound enticing enough."

The next day was the penultimate. He sent a morning cup of her favorite brew. It was a grand gesture. A barista came in, complete with his hair net and apron, and set a cup on her table and then poured the frothing milk into her cup right in front of her, leaving a message in it. It read, "Date Me. O"

Liv and her supervisor, and even some of her colleagues from the other cubicles watched him do his little stunt. Some of them even clapped when he was done.

"My goodness. This man does have a flair for drama."

"He certainly does," she said, her eyes slightly misty, hands clasped to her chest.

In the night, he rang her, "What say you?"

"I say yes."

"You sure," he sounded unsure, a pause in his voice, "I'm not sure what you're expecting Zara. I'm afraid, I must confess, I might not meet your expectations."

"I'm resigned to thinking that you can't possibly be worse than the man I just broke up with. If you're a drug dealer, then I'd understand. I have an addiction too." She laughed, trying to sound casual. "Any other red flags, we'll cross that bridge when we get there."

"Fine then," he sounded more sure, "meet me at the coffee shop, in your usual spot by the window. I'll see you at sixish, in the evening."

She smiled. Tomorrow was D-day.

When she went to the coffee shop in the evening, she wore the tee over the snuggest pair of jeans she owned. With kohl rimmed eyes, and a light gloss on her lips, she let the coffee cup shaped pendant fall outside her collar. She licked her lips and threaded her fingers, her stomach a rolling boil of emotions.

The crowd was sparse, but most of the regulars were seated, all bent over their laptops and tablets. Her hands were clammy, and she kept swallowing her fear. The lady behind the counter smiled, "Happy birthday Zara," she said and placed a cake in front of her, after she sat in her usual spot. It was shaped like a coffee mug, with chocolate in the centre and a dollop of whipped cream. "Happy Birthday," had been written on the cup.

She looked out of the window. It was past six. Worry began to eat at her. Was she making a mistake? What if he showed up covered in tattoos, or in orange?

He messaged, "Are you there?"

She frowned.

"Why the face?" She heard his voice, crystal clear and she looked about.

"You look pretty," he said, and her eyes darted about the shop, until she realized, it was him. The guy who always sat with his back turned to her, at the next table.

He turned around. He'd worn a dark shirt, his raven black hair and trimmed beard, that brought out his blue eyes and his pale lips turned upwards. His fingers were long, and his skin was flushed. It was as if, everyone in the room faded and she couldn't keep her eyes off him. Tall, proud and confident, his eyes never left her. She couldn't hear the music, as her own heartbeat drummed in her ears. He was nothing like She'd imagined, because her imagination paled in front of the living, breathing, fine specimen of male standing before her.

He took a seat beside her. His trousers were dark, leather shoes shining, a gleaming, heavy silver watch and his hair short cropped. He was lean, and he smelt of pine and cloves. "You."

He had brought her out that day and at once she flushed and she was about to dart out. But he must have known. He put his hand over hers.

"I've waited a whole year, Zara. I've watched you ever since you walked into this café, asking for all that extra vanilla in your cup. And I've waited, while you dated and got engaged to that jerk. I always wanted you to be happy. But after what he did to you, I couldn't wait."

Tears bristled in her eyes. She didn't even know he was here. "So, you know?"

"All that there is to, yes."

She searched his face, a glint to them, his upturned lips, and his voice gentle, his grip strong on her hand.

"When did you know?"

He smiled, holding her gaze, flashing his small teeth, "I kept coming back to the shop and I've had better coffee." He stopped.

"So many blends, so little time," she said, trying to fill the awkward silence.

He laughed, his head thrown back and his eyes crinkled. It was wonderful watching him laugh.

"Two months later, I realized, I wasn't coming for the coffee. All the while I was coming back for you. Hearing your wit and folly, witnessing your joy and sadness, I came to know who you are, better than I would on a date."

"It's a lot of time wasted, for you I mean," she said, her voice hushed.

"Better Latte than never, my love."

She watched his eyes and leaned in. He pressed his lips to hers for a kiss. Starting at the edge, then licking her lower lip. Soft tentative and he tasted like her coffee, strong, dark and hot. His hand was still covering hers.

"What's your name?" She asked as she pulled away.

"Owen," he said. "It's Owen, coffee lover, I hope you're ready to do the java jive tonight." He kissed her hand.

"I'm more than ready lover."

Campsite 70
Shelby Curran

-Big Lagoon State Park, Pensacola, Florida

Our knuckles white
from holding kayaks
so that they won't slip
off the roof rack.
Four sunburnt elbows
hang out of car windows like red flags.

The SUV's tires
crush grained gravel
and the Labrador in my lap
fusses like a bear
awakening after winter hibernation.
His ears point forward,
hand of a compass
finding its way north.

Campsite 70,
a barren plot of dry land
between two patches of dense forestry.
You string hammocks
around the tree's chestnut arms,
the two least likely to let you fall
in nighttime.
Is that how you chose me?
with my strong arms and weak hands.

The air in the state park
is heavy with pollen
and travelers' whispered escape prayers.
The dog starts to piss on the fire pit.
I do not stop him.

Sun's rays are strong
striking like a warrior's arrows
on my freckly skin.
You ask me to help set up the tent.
I tie the Labrador to a post.
He immediately tangles his paws,
knotting himself in rope
for fear of being left behind.

I unfold red tarp on dusty ground
like a bed of squished red roses, happy to bleed
for sake of another
foreign in body and spirit to its design.

You slide plastic poles together,
Bending the hinges like knees of a child in prayer.
Plastic pieces obey you, always
and now the tent has learned to stand alone
like I did, after meeting your hands.
You have built the home without me.
I will stake the ground, because you taught me how.

Cast iron hearts burn from the outside in
like chicken cutlets cooking over fire.

We string lights through the tent's interior,
roof of dancing fireflies.
Echoes of a six-string seep into my skin
along with drops of humidity.
Sing me to sleep,
song of surrender and salvation.

In morning, we walk along the trail
a few miles outside of campgrounds
without following signs.
Blackened branches
and welded wooden stumps
are victims of wildfire.
Stench of fresh forest fire tells us
that this is the healthy way
to rebirth.

Come and Gone
Danial Francis

There's nothing like when space and time
stops within a smile,
There's something there when all That's mine
is hers for a while,
Alone within the breath we share
standing much too close,
Our wordless gestures in the air
as our distance grows,

Left to take a token part
never to return,
To live inside a broken heart
where a fire used to burn,
The will to be, the soul to pray
the right to carry on,
To live and dream another day
When love has come and gone.

Every House is a World
Christopher Woods

A Brief Two Character Play

Characters—A man; A woman

Scene—A man and woman in bed.

Time—The present

(As lights come up, we see a couple in bed. Wine glasses on a bedside table. The man is reading a newspaper. After a moment, the man puts the newspaper aside and clears his throat.)

MAN

It's getting late.

WOMAN

Do you realize, we haven't left the bed all day?

MAN

It's been a perfect day.

WOMAN

Yes, it has.

MAN

I've been thinking about us.

WOMAN

Oh?

MAN

If I had to describe us, we would be like an old cathedral. Lasting, you know.

(The woman thinks about this, smiles, then runs her fingers across his chest, then traces the line of hair down his stomach.)

WOMAN

Us, a church?

(They both laugh, she because of his statement, he because she has tickled him in a tender place.)

MAN

A physical cathedral. Nothing more than that.

(He takes her wandering hand in his own.)

It still amazes me, how lovely your hands are. And how they fit so nicely inside my own.

(He places his palm against hers. She laces her fingers around him. Together their fingers make a steeple.)

WOMAN

We aren't as stone cold as that. Like a dark old church. Not us. We still have fire inside us. This afternoon is proof of that.

MAN

I'll say.

WOMAN

A cathedral. Are you trying to tell me something? Maybe, something sad?

MAN

Shh.

(He runs his fingers across her lips, then leans over to kiss her.)

Don't you remember, when we went to visit the cathedral? How it had lasted? Supported from the outside?

WOMAN

Buttresses, you mean?

MAN

Right. Sturdy stuff. Moored in the earth.

WOMAN

(Relieved.) I see now.

MAN

Good, then. That's how it is, this thing between us.

(He puts his arm around her and draws her close. Her head rests on his chest. He plays with her hair.)

I have never felt this way before, with anyone. The rarity of it. The simply joy. I've never known a thing like it. Before now, I wasn't even alive.

WOMAN

(She takes his hand and places it palm to palm against his, and makes another steeple.)

Someday, all cathedrals will be like this. Rising up to the sky.

MAN

We don't need sky.

WOMAN

No?

MAN

Just earth. Sturdy. Solid. Something else might bring bad luck.

WOMAN

Then let's leave it the way it is.

MAN

Good.

(Without another word, he shifts his body, moving until she is beneath him. As the light begins to fade, they begin moving slowly, deliberately.)

BLACKOUT

Fragility
Gabriel Parker

The world collectively drew a breath. There she was, across the crowded street. She was shorter, only her blonde hair jutted out among the swarming mass of bodies. Right then Jack knew, from somewhere deep inside that she was the one. That she was meant for him whether by some supernatural power or the Universe or Fate. He knew that she was destined to be his and he was to be forever hers.

Making his way across the street, all other color faded from view. Glimpses of her magenta blouse became the only light in the color-dark world. His heart filled his chest, bumping around like a caged gorilla. Drawing on all the courage of whatever divine had set up his meeting, he tapped her on the shoulder.

"Hello, Miss? I really couldn't stop myself from coming over here, as soon as I saw you I thought, "You just have to go over and introduce yourself to that gorgeous lady." So here I am. My name is Jack by the way." The words seemed to trip over their own feet, but eventually they all fell out.

She had a cute little smile, if lopsided. It creeped up on the left side of her face, seemingly saying "I'll humor the poor soul." Then when she spoke, it was like a lilting melody—harmonious and something more. More than the words of a mere mortal, like the speech of a goddess. "Thank you for the compliment, though I have to warn you. You aren't the first, and I certainly hope you won't be the last, so what makes you so special, Slick?"

Her words, though calloused, fell on accepting ears and they seemed to clear the street. Suddenly, it felt as if there was no one else in the city, no one else in the world—only the girl. While his mind was still searching for a clever answer, his hands moved as if separate entities. They grasped her slender wrist and gently held it up to his chest. Finally, his mind was filled in on the plan and the words took shape, "Do you feel the beat, the thump of the universe? Fate, God, destiny, call it what you will, has taken control. I can feel it as surely as you can feel this beat. It has led me here, brought me to you. I am at its mercy, at your mercy."

For a brief second, her eyes flashed. Jack thought it was sorrow, deep consuming sorrow; but it was gone as quickly as it appeared. She drew her hand back to her side, slowly demurely. "What if I don't believe in fate or destiny? What if I don't believe in love?" Her tone had a playful mocking quality, egging him on.

Playing into the drama, he drew back with an exaggerated gasp. "A lovely girl such as yourself must believe in love. To disagree would be an injustice, like a rainbow without the pot of gold. The world is full of too much brokenness to not believe in love."

"Ah, but that is exactly why one wouldn't believe, is it not?" Her face never lost that playful smirk, full of mischief. "All the world is too broken for love to exist. The thorns have choked out the beautiful flower, the thief has stolen the pot of gold."

"Tell me you don't believe that, for love rests on a tender ledge. The slightest disbelief could topple the whole cup. For that push to come from such a beautiful person is too much to bear."

His thought plucked a nerve, its mournful pitch sounded behind her next words. "Sometimes love is crushed by beauty. Sometimes the broken world can't bear the imperfection and destroys the beauty in its futile search." Gone was the mocking tone, these words were cold, cracked, and true. The smile faded off her face and she turned away. In that moment the goddess became incarnate, the angel lost her wings. Gradually the sounds of the street returned, strangers passed on each side going their own ways.

Jack reached out and grasped her shoulder, "Wait. Don't go. What's your name?"

"Hope."

He Told Me
Jen Hughes

One word,
So overused it's clichéd
Can make this lonely girl's heart a sparkler.
Can give this electric eel the buzz
To live in the hub-blub of goldfish.

One casual
Combination of letters
Sent to her by a man with bright eyes
Can make her beam like the sun
Can send her dancing like an idiot
In her closet bedroom.

Tonight she was told she was beautiful

Home with You
Danial Francis

From a distance I can see
the place we met beneath the trees
a road removes me from my own
and takes me back where I belong
when I was young and not so me
I looked to places far beyond
indulging in my fantasies
they always bring me back to be
home with you, alone with me

The road still calls me fast away
when here I'd just as soon as stay
out of the way among the trees
needed freedom leads to dreams
repaid from days long betrayed
invading thoughts brought in haste
my mind at ease in memories
that always bring me back to be
home with you, alone with me

It Was Raining
Shayna Boisvert

It's raining...

I thought to myself as I stared out the window of my second story bedroom. Clothes were strewn across the carpet; fabrics colored in reds, blues, greens all mingled together to mock me. They whispered that I would not look good today, and I could almost hear them laughing at me. The candle in my room was burning low, releasing a warm vanilla scent that danced about the room. My paper lamp I had made as a child was fading from the years that had past. The covers of my blankets were neatly made, a stark contrast to the piles of clothes that were threatening to eat me alive.

I sighed and pushed open a window. A rush of cold air whipped across my body as I stood there in just my underwear. The rain sprinkled across my skin and it brought me to my senses.

"Today is the day," I whispered, the wind and rain almost drowning out my voice.

I glanced at my wrist. The gleaming red numbers depicted there were ticking down. They made no sound, and yet I felt as if they were mocking me as well. We all stared at our numbers on the wrists and were taught since nursery school what they meant. I still remember what my first-grade teacher had told us. "Remember children, always watch your clocks, for the second it hits zero, you will be looking into the eyes of your soulmate."

I remember all of us falling silent, staring at our clocks; some people had millions, even billions of minutes, while a select few had as few as a few million. One girl in my class had exactly 525,600 minutes. One year. I remember the day she came into class in a beautiful pink dress with rose appliqués, and her golden hair was pulled into a long braid down her back. A new boy entered our class that day, and his ticker fell to zero at the exact same time. They had been inseparable ever since.

Everyone's feelings changed after that and became one thing: want. You want this love. Not need, want. You watch everyone else's ticker go down and feel the pangs of jealousy. You don't actually need any of this, didn't ask for it, and in fact would probably be better off without it. But you want it, want him or her, want love, even if it's the worst thing in the world for you. And That's how it starts. The endless stares at your wrist, the math to find out the exact day. The days close to zero you can hardly pay attention to life. You just wonder who it will be and all the wondering eats away at your mind.

Only forty-eight minutes remained on my wrist. That was why clothes were strewn about the floor: I couldn't decide what to wear. Today I would meet him, my soul mate. Today would leave an imprint of me on his mind, just like when you drag your fingertips across the window and the streaks never truly go away. That is why my favorite blue dress suddenly looked too blue on me, and my red scarf seemed too distracting. I finally tore myself away from the window and grabbed a plain grey sweater and jeans to wear. The grey sweater made my eyes pop, but didn't seem like I was trying too hard.

Nine in the morning was when my ticker was supposed to reach zero. As I got dressed I wondered if it would be someone new or someone familiar. Maybe a classmate who I had seen before? Sometimes that happens. You know someone, see them every day, but never think to compare tickers until the time comes and... they're your soul mate. I should't have been so excited, but in reality, I was longing to meet that special person in my life.

Pulling myself away from my day dream, I grabbed my keys and headed to my car. I walked down the same steps I always walked, the wood worn creaking under my feet. Notches were carved there from the games I played with my dolls, despite my mother's warnings that I would scratch the fine wood. My feet landed on the plush Persian carpet and I pushed open the door, not even bothering to see if it locked behind me. I wasn't going to make it school on time; I'd have to speed. I couldn't meet my soulmate if I was stuck in a car.

How could I have been so careless? I thought desperately.

I got behind the wheel and backed my car out of the driveway, taking off down the road. Wet leaves rustled up into the air as my car blew them up. The black of my steering wheel made the crimson numbers on my wrist stick out even more. Only thirty-six minutes left and my school was about twenty-eight minutes away. I was cutting it really close. I slammed my hand on the steering wheel in frustration as my foot pressed down on the gas. I couldn't be late, I couldn't miss my soulmate, I had never heard of anyone doing that before. I wondered what could happen. It couldn't be good.

I should probably slow down, with all this rain... My car slipped back and forth but I hesitated to lift my foot off of the gas. It was my time for a happy ending, I couldn't stop here. As I caught a glimpse of myself in the rearview mirror, I wondered what he would think of me. I was very plain: long brown hair, pale skin, and blue eyes. Plenty of girls in the world looked like me. What if he's disappointed?

I looked at the dark clouds as my car sped down the road. I had to get myself out of this cloud of fear, so I turned on the music. A love song played through my speakers, one that my friends and I used to listen to while imagining our future soul mates. As I drove I wondered if he would have green or brown eyes; I hoped he would be about six-foot four, so that, despite my unusual height, I would still have to stretch to kiss him. I imagined he would be an old soul, but would be able to put up with my quirks. Picturing scenes with my soul mates was something I did often: the two of us talking, lying in bed together and reading. Leaning in and giving him a kiss. As long as we were together, no obstacle would be too big.

The glowing numbers on my wrist brought me back to reality: only nine minutes left! I could see the school in the distance. I wanted time to calm down and maybe fix my hair or something in the bathroom, so I pressed my foot down harder on the gas. 36 miles per hour... 42... 58... 60, my car began to shake, the rain started to hit the windshield so hard I couldn't see out of it. My wheel twisted out of my hands and it felt like I was on ice, but I kept going. Then my car began to hydroplane out of control. Helpless, I curled up in my seat and lifted my hands to block my face. The car hit the curb and I felt it lift off the ground, flipping so many times that I became disorientated. My body hit the dashboard, knocking the air out of my lungs with a whoosh. After that my vision flickered in and out and only sound that filled my ears was the cracking of glass.

Then suddenly, everything became light. Distantly I heard the rain echoing off of the pavement. I struggled and tried to look at my wrist, but I knew it was hopeless already; it felt like I had been out for hours. Which meant only one thing... I missed him.

Suddenly I heard someone coming closer. "Hello?" I heard a voice call. It sounded low and smooth as velvet. "Can you hear me?"

I tried to answer, but my throat felt like it was full of glass. Only a whisper escaped my throat. "Over here..."

I heard someone pulling on the door of the mangled car. My eyes opened slowly and I was momentarily blinded by the light. Then through my blurred vision I saw a young man, probably about twenty or so. "I'm going to get you out of here," he said. "I'm an

EMT. You're going to be okay." He glanced down at his wrist and let out a dry, humorless laugh. "Of course," I heard him mutter. My eyes managed to focus just in time to see the crimson numbers on his wrist: a bright red zero. Struggling to sit up, I tried turning my head to see my own wrist. I had to know if mine showed a zero too.

"Hey, hey, it's okay. You're going to hurt yourself," he cautioned, a hint of worry in his voice.

"My num... bers," I managed. "I think... they hit... zero."

His eyes widened in shock, his mouth going slack. "Quite a way to meet," he said after a moment, his surprised expression changing into a crooked smile. My whole body went numb at the realization. My soulmate.

After that everything went by so quickly. He must have deemed my situation to be a stable one, because he removed me quickly from the crash. My once pretty, grey car was now in pieces, and I realized how lucky I was to be alive. He laid me on the ground and began to further check me for injuries. He seemed to genuinely know what he was doing.

"I called 911 when I pulled off to the side of the road to get you, they should be here soon. Did you hit your head?"

"I think so," I mumbled. My head was pounding, and I remembered hitting the windshield before blacking out.

He tore a strip of fabric from his shirt and covered the cuts on my arm. They must have come from the glass. Then he tore off another piece and pressed it to my forehead. I must have looked like such a mess and I anxiously wanted to know what he thought of me.

"Your arm may be broken, you have a few cuts, and probably a concussion," he informed me. "You're lucky. This could have been so much worse..." I noticed that he was choking up. "I could have lost you," he said softly, his voice cracking.

I looked up at him and time seemed to slow around me. I had been waiting for this day my entire life and here it was. I focused on his face, taking in all of his features. He had reddish-blonde hair that stood up in all directions and bright blue eyes. I thought blue eyes were boring until I looked into his. The same blue shade as the sky on the first day of summer, yet they also lit up like a bolt of lightning. I couldn't take my eyes off them, the worry and fear coursing through them, just like the ocean before a storm. There was a whole other world in his eyes. And I realized then, that That's where I wanted to be. Warmth filled my body. I had been so worried about meeting my soul mate, but everyone was right; I knew he was the one for me. I couldn't explain it, but the tender expression on his face showed that he felt the same way.

The sounds of an ambulance flooded my ears then. EMTs rushed towards us. "Is this her, James?" one asked. He nodded and the EMT gave him a reassuring nod. "Don't worry, we will take care of her." They must have been friends, these must have been the people he worked with. They also gave me his name, which I hadn't even bothered to ask for yet with everything going on. James. It was a lovely name, and I kept repeating it in my head.

They loaded me on the stretcher and he stepped away. "James... don't leave... "I struggled to get out.

He looked shocked that I had called him by his name and followed me into the ambulance. James then grabbed my hand, his eyes watering. "You know my name, but I don't know yours," he said quietly. "What is it?"

"Rosalyn."

"Rosalyn..." he repeated. "I've been preparing to tell you something all day. I know the universe assigned us to be together, but know that I'm going to cherish every moment with you. As if you can be taken away from me anytime, which almost happened today. As if I'm sleeping and you're just a dream and that I someday will have to wake up. I'm going to love you as if the sun will never shine tomorrow, or the moon will no longer cast its light upon us. I will love you as if you're the last drop of water I would ever feel against my lips. That's how important you are to me. This is me saying I will love you until we disintegrate into stars in the night sky, until my heart beats its last beat. This is me saying, I don't want to lose you. Not now, not ever."

I looked up at him, and then down at the red zero on my wrist. He squeezed my hand, and I managed to smile up at him. He looked as if he wanted me to say something to his speech.

I knew exactly what to say. I too had thought about it for months as well. So, I gestured for him to come closer and whispered in his ear, "And I promise to love you until the fires diminish on this little thing we call life."

We just smiled at each other and continued to the hospital in silence, his hand firmly grasped in mine. I realized right then that I never wanted to let go. The numbers were right: I had found my soulmate.

Lady Margery
Lisa M. Scuderi-Burkimsher

Part I

Margery sat in her cold, damp castle bedroom waiting to hear news about her brother George. She looked up when she heard the old door creak open. Sir Joseph. Would he have news of George? She quickly stood, lost her footing, grabbed onto the wooden bedpost for support then straightened her gown. She tried to speak, but when she opened her mouth no words came out. She saw pity in Sir Joseph's eyes as he walked over to her.

"My Lady, let me help you." With Sir Joseph's hand around her waist, they walked over to Margery's writing desk and he pulled out her chair.

"I'm fine now, thank you. Have you come with news?" She shuddered when he kissed her hand and his lips touched her soft skin. She knew from his gentle kiss and somber look that the news wasn't good.

"I'm sorry. Your brother has been sentenced to death. He is to be beheaded tomorrow morning. I've made arrangements for you to see him tonight."

Margery's stomach churned.

"Thank you, Sir Joseph. Your kindness is appreciated." Margery curtsied and slowly closed the door behind him. She walked over to the castle window in her room. Her body trembled, hands numb as the guards brought out the block for her brother's execution. There was an indent where the neck of her brother would be placed. The sun shone brightly on that block. It turned Margery's stomach.

Margery decided she must speak to Her Grace, Queen Constance. She would try everything possible to help her. The queen showed Margery great respect for her loyal service as lady-in-waiting. Margery saved her life two years prior. Afternoon tea and rice pottage was Her Grace's favorite time of day she would frequently convey to Margery and her other ladies. She told them how she loved the sweet taste of cinnamon and raisins mixed in with the soft cooked rice. But she had a habit of overindulging and one afternoon she started to choke. The servants dumbfounded, stared wide-eyed at Queen Constance. Her Grace's face lost its color and turned white. She held her throat unable to make a sound. Margery stunned at the lack of help, lost her footing and nearly fell when she rushed to Her Majesty's side. With all her might, Margery smacked Queen Constance on the back several times, a raisin dislodged from her throat and landed on Her Majesty's lap. With both Margery's parents deceased, Margery wanted a safe haven. Once she saved the queen's life she was respected and considered a loyal confidant to Her Grace. Margery had the security she yearned for; a home at court and First-Lady-in-Waiting to the queen.

Margery skipped breakfast and excused herself from the other ladies. She went to see Queen Constance. The walk seemed to take forever down the long corridor. Her gown shuffled and brushed the white tiled floor as she picked up the pace. When she entered Their Majesty's great hall, Her Grace was sitting on her throne. Margery admired her velvet gown meticulously sewed by her other ladies. Her diamond crown beamed in the sunlight streaming through the stained-glass windows. Her sky-blue eyes matched the shade of blue in her gown. Margery greeted the queen with a curtsey.

"Lady Margery, I'm saddened for you at the news of your brother."

"Your Grace, I've come to beg you to ask His Majesty to spare my brother." She bent down close to Her Majesty and held both her royal hands in hers.

"He is accused of having impure contact with the king's sister. I pleaded with His Majesty for your sake, but he won't budge."

Margery loosened the grip of Her Grace's hands.

"Your Grace, he showed only kindness towards Her Lady." Margery quavered trying to hold back tears.

"He kissed Her Lady, Margery. Victoria is His Majesty's sister."

Margery stood. She looked directly into Her Grace's eyes and touched Her Grace gently on the shoulder. "I know, but I've spoken to Her Lady, Victoria and she advised me that my brother was a gentleman. He greeted her with casual conversation and a formal kiss on the hand that any noble gentlemen would give to a woman of her stature."

"Lady Margery, I admire and have a deep respect for you. I'm afraid His Majesty will not change his mind. Her Lady also pleaded with His Majesty on your brother's behalf, but she only angered him more. He sent her away to a nunnery until he decides, if ever, to forgive her and only then, can she return. She, at least, will live. Your brother George is tried for treason for improper contact with King Alfred's sister. Whether it is true or not, I'm not in a position to go against His Majesty. It was up to the king and His trusted advisors to decide. I wish there was something more I could do, but there isn't. I suggest you say your goodbyes to George." Margery curtsied, turned to walk away, but Her Majesty touched her shoulder, pulled her close, hugged Margery and whispered: "I will pray that God grant him peace."

Margery took a step back. She had a nagging pain in her neck and her head throbbed. She was going to see her brother for the last time.

"Thank you, Your Majesty." Margery curtsied and left the hall. She headed straight to the tower to see George. Her eyes watered, but she took a deep breath and composed herself. She didn't want George to see her upset. Margery asked the guard to unlock the tower door, per the queen's permission. Margery could tell from his shrewd grin that he recognized her as George's brother, and let her enter.

When Margery saw her brother, she was stunned. His thick black hair was matted and dirty. His tattered shirt sleeve exposed his arm to the cold air and his pants were frayed at the ankles. Her brother, once strong, was thin and frail. She managed to raise her lips into a smile.

"Margery, I'm so happy to see you."

Margery walked over, and they embraced. He was cold to the touch.

"I can't believe this happened. How could the king have you tried and sentenced to death when you did nothing improper?" Margery paced.

"I'm afraid it's more than that sister. I spoke out of line when the king advised us on his next move against Scotland. He wants to invade small villages and kill innocent people. He used my kind respect for his sister as an excuse to protect his pride."

"What were you thinking? This happened because you couldn't keep quiet?"

"Margery, I won't go to war, and kill innocent children. I would rather die than have their blood on my hands. I'm a knight, not a monster."

Margery hugged her brother tightly and didn't want to let go. Her arms fitted completely around his waist. Margery finally released him, took George by the hand, and told him she loved him.

When she turned to leave, he grabbed her by the arm. His weak hand struggled to hold the grip, so she turned back around to face him and he let go. Flabbergasted, her stomach churned at what the king had done to him.

"Margery, I want you to have this." In the palm of Margery's hand, he placed an emerald necklace.

Margery held it up to the sunlight through the barred window.

"Where did you get this? It's beautiful."

"Our father gave it to me before he died. It belonged to our mother. She wanted you to have it, but I insisted our father give it to me before he died. I held onto it every day to remind me of them. I want you to have it. I should've given it to you sooner, but I was selfish because it was all I had to remember them by." He pushed Margery's hair behind her ear and kissed her cheek gently. She held back tears.

Margery held the necklace tight in hand and thought of her parents. The grip was so tight that it made a mark on the inside of her palm. She kissed her brother one last time on his forehead and left the tower. As she walked back to court, she couldn't help but think of George. He was a sweet child, her best friend. They played together and made visits to the nearby villages to buy food. Her parents would give each of them a coin to buy an apple, but George would always give his coin to Margery. She would buy two apples and try to hand him one, but he would gently push her hand aside and tell her she should keep them both and save one for later. They spent many nights talking about what they would do when they grew older. George became a knight just as he wished. He beat the king himself at jousting and it earned him great respect. The king knighted him the next day. That same day George told Margery he would protect her from any danger. She never thought it would be him in danger. Soon he'll be gone like everyone else she loved. All she would have left to remember her family by was a necklace.

****

Margery couldn't bring herself to watch George's execution from the courtyard the next morning, but, she forced herself to look out from her window. She insisted the other ladies leave. She needed to be alone and not have them comforting her with words that He'd be at peace in God's hands.

The guards brought George out to the block. A priest was administering last rites. He made the sign of the cross, placed his hand on George's head and then backed away. George looked up at Margery and smiled. She touched the glass window. The glass was cold, but she kept her hand there.

The executioner tied the blindfold around her brother's eyes and leaned George's head down onto the block. As the crowd chanted, "Behead him," the executioner held the axe up in the air and with one quick motion brought it down onto George's neck. His head rolled to the ground. There was blood splattered all over the block and the area where his head finally rested. His limp body fell beside the block still.

She had a clear view of George's dismembered head and she thought his lips moved. She pounded on the glass and screamed her brother's name. The window shattered into pieces. Blood poured down from her hand under the sleeve of her gown. A strong hand pulled Margery away from the window and she struggled to break free, flaying her arms. Her body ached from the struggle and she screamed. She wanted to run back to the window, but the grip was too strong. She heard the crowd chant with excitement to feed George's head to the wolves; that distressed her more and made it difficult to breathe. One of the two servants said:

"I'll fetch Sir Joseph." In haste, he slammed the door shut and the bed rattled.

The other servant finally let go of Margery and she threw herself down onto the bed. She cried and gasped. A sharp pain shot through her chest and her hand ached from the glass that cut through her palm. She held her hand up and the blood poured down under her sleeve. Did George feel pain? She turned her body sideways, leaned back on the bed and blood soiled the sheets. When the servant opened the door Sir Joseph hurried inside.

"Please leave us," said Sir Joseph.

The servant bowed and left the room.

"Margery, let me wrap your hand."

Margery held out her bloody hand while Sir Joseph wrapped a cloth around her palm. She leaned in close to him and he put his arm around her waist. She rested her head on his shoulder and wept until Sir Joseph hugged her and gave her a soft kiss on the lips. Margery longed for him, but it was improper for a woman to court a man. She sensed an attraction between them, the way he looked into her eyes and complimented her beauty, but she waited for Sir Joseph to approach her.

"Margery, it hurts me to see you suffer, but you must realize you are not alone. You'll always have me."

Margery managed a smile and kissed him back. He pressed hard against Margery's lips. Her body shuddered with desire, but she pulled away and stood.

"George just died, I can't do this now. It's not proper." She paced the room, put her hands to her face and cried loudly. Her sobs echoed in the room. Margery looked up when Sir Joseph touched her shoulder. She wiped away the tears with her bloodied sleeve and straightened her gown.

"I'll be back tomorrow to check on you. Remember what I said, Margery."

He lifted her chin and kissed her forehead.

The next morning Queen Constance's servant brought a note to Margery. It said Margery could take however long she needed to mourn her brother. Margery handed the note back to the servant and told him to thank Her Grace for her kindness. Margery went to her castle window and hoped what happened was a dream, but the block was drenched in blood. Her brother's. She turned away and tried to get the image of George's head on the ground out of her mind, but she was sure his lips moved, and she trembled. That thought disappeared when she became distracted by a knock at the door. It was Sir Joseph.

"Margery, you look well rested considering what you've been through."

"He was the only family I had left. We grew up and came to court together, but there was nothing I could do to persuade His Majesty," Margery hesitated. "Why have you come this early to see me?"

"I spoke to Her Grace and I've arranged for you to go to Winchester. You will stay at my cottage. I know You'll like it. It has a garden full of sweet smells of jasmine and roses. You used to tell me on our walks through the queen's garden that you would like to have a garden of your own someday."

"Would I be living there alone?"

"I'll be going with you. I've asked the queen to grant me permission to be your husband. Her Majesty wants you to be happy. As do I."

Sir Joseph reached into his pocket and pulled out a deep blue sapphire ring. It matched the blue in her eyes. He bent down on one knee and held the ring up to her.

"I was hoping you'd accept this ring and take me as your husband. Her Grace has arranged for us to be married as soon as we arrive in Winchester. I've always loved you and I hope You'll say yes."

Margery held her hands up to her mouth and gasped with surprise at his proposal. A tear rolled down her cheek.

"I'd be honored to be your wife."

She saw Sir Joseph's big brown eyes widen with joy. He placed the ring on Margery's finger. She never saw such a big deep blue sapphire before. It felt heavy on her finger and weighed her hand down, but she didn't care. The man she loved was going to be her husband. She embraced him with a hug and kissed him passionately on the lips, their hands around each other's waist.

Although happy to marry Sir Joseph, the thought of George and her parents came to mind. They wouldn't be there for her wedding.

"As the king's advisor, I have a few things I need to take care of before we leave, but once I'm finished and your belongings are packed, the queen will have a carriage waiting for us. I should be done in a few days. Will you be ready by then?"

"Yes, I don't have much to pack."

"Good, meet me by the carriage in two days."

She gave Sir Joseph a warm smile and he left the room.

Margery was ready to meet Sir Joseph by the carriage, but there was something she needed to do before she left. She walked over to her chest. She opened it and pulled out the only thing left, the emerald green necklace George gave her. She held it close then placed the necklace back into the chest, closed the lid and pushed the chest against the wall. Margery didn't need a symbolic memory to remind her of her family. She closed the door behind her and headed off to start her new life.

Queen Margery and King Joseph
Part II

Margery sat on her bed and rubbed her protruding stomach. With each touch, she felt the baby kick. "Joseph, the baby's kicking!"

Joseph tripped and fell flat on his knees when he hurried to her. He pushed himself up and Margery laughed with him at his clumsiness.

"Come here and feel my stomach before you fall again." Margery chuckled.

The gentle rub of Joseph's hand across Margery's stomach soothed her. She closed her eyes and moaned with each gentle stroke; body tingled.

"I feel it! That's the baby doing that?"

"I'm not punching the inside of my stomach," Margery said.

She took Joseph's hand, gently squeezed it, leaned in and kissed him on his moist lips. A loud knock at the door startled her and she pulled away.

"You stay here and rest. I'll get it," Joseph said.

"No, I'm all right. I want to see who it is."

Margery knew Joseph wouldn't argue with her, so she followed him to the door. The constant loud knock hurt her ears and she was glad when Joseph answered it.

A knight from King Alfred's court stood at the door holding a letter. He was tall and dressed in armor. Was he going into battle?

"Sir Joseph." The knight bowed.

"The king sent you this letter and I'm to wait here while you read it."

Margery's face whitened in fear. What would the king want with Joseph?

Joseph looked straight at Margery after he read the letter.

"Why was I cursed with being cousin to the king?   He demands we return to court at once."

"We must go then. But what about the baby and me? I'm almost ready for my confinement." Margery was concerned about raising a baby at court, especially if he demanded much of Joseph's time.

"All preparations have been made for Lady Margery's confinement. The king has arranged for her midwife to come to court." The knight spoke before Joseph could answer Margery.

Joseph frowned, but bowed in agreement like a gentleman.

"No need to pack. The king has everything arranged for you at court." The knight bowed to Margery and Joseph.

The ride to Buckingwald Castle was brutal for Margery. With the bumpy road, they had to stop several times for her to vomit and the back of her throat burned from the acid. Joseph gave her a jug of water. She gulped it to rid the sour taste in her mouth. Finally, they arrived at court and she could rest.

"Before you settle in, you must go see His Majesty in the main hall," the knight instructed.

Being in Buckingwald castle again where George was beheaded, brought back tortuous memories for Margery. On the way to the main hall they walked passed a large window that she didn't remember being there from her days at court. It had a clear view of the execution yard where George was beheaded. It looked as if the same block was there, but cleaned and ready for the next execution. It sent chills down her back and she looked away.

When they reached the main hall, His Majesty was sitting on his throne; his red velvet robe covered the bottom of his chair. He wasn't the strong muscular king she remembered. Now frail, his hazel eyes were shadowed by dark circles.

"Cousin Joseph, it's good to see you again. I see your wife is with child. I'm pleased You'll have an heir. Much has happened since you've been away. I'm sure you've heard that Her Majesty has passed on."

"Yes, We're very sorry for your loss. Her Grace was a kind and well-loved queen."

"Yes, she was. On her deathbed, she asked me to bring you and Margery back to court. I haven't forgotten what your brother did Margery, but Her Grace was very fond of you."

Margery was unsettled, yet she bowed her head with respect.

"As you know, Her Grace died without leaving me an heir. My only sister who I forgave for her indiscretion with your brother George, Margery, was going to return to court, but became gravely ill with fever at the nunnery and has passed on as well. That leaves you, Joseph, my only surviving family. I'm not a young man and my time is limited. I haven't been well these past few months so I'm naming you my heir. You will be the next king. In the meantime, I'm giving you all the lands of Winchester. You are now Lord Joseph, Lord of Winchester and your wife Lady Margery of Winchester."

Margery's hands trembled as she clasped them together. Lord of Winchester? Joseph the next King of England?

"Your Majesty, I'm deeply honored you've chosen me."

Joseph kneeled before the king and kissed his hand. Margery snapped out of her shocked state and approached the king as well. She stood next to her husband and thanked His Majesty for his generous gift.

"I have maids to help you. Anything you need for yourself and the baby they will attend to."

"Your generosity is most appreciated." Margery lowered her head.

When Margery reached their quarters, she was delighted at how nice their room was. It had big picturesque windows overlooking the garden. Yellow roses were in full bloom.

"Joseph, look at the beautiful garden. Aside from Queen Constance, of course, the garden is the only part of court I've missed."

"You always loved gardens. I remember when we went for walks in the queen's garden and you said you wanted a garden of your own just like hers with bright red roses. Now you will have that."

Margery hugged Joseph and kissed him passionately on the lips. A quiver went through her body. She wanted to make love to him, but she didn't want to hurt the child inside her. She pulled away and started to unpack, leaving Joseph flushed.

"When the baby is born we'll be able to make love again."

"I hope I can wait," he said in desperation.

The next morning Joseph was summoned by the king.

"What do you think the king wants from you?"

"He has chosen me to be the next King of England so there's much to discuss."

"I hope he doesn't keep you away too long. I wanted to go for a walk in the garden like we used to."

"I hope not either, but I have no say in the matter."

Margery rubbed her fingers through Joseph's thick hair, kissed him and wished him well. He left the room with Margery alone wondering what the king would ask of him.

Margery passed the time stitching a white blanket for the baby. She pricked her finger when the bedroom door flung open and the king's guard burst in.

"Lord Joseph needs to see you at once. He is in the main hall with His Majesty."

When Margery walked down the corridor her legs wobbled. Her scalp tingled, and she thought she might faint, but she held her head high for Joseph's sake. She noticed little droplets of blood dripped on her blue velvet gown. She squeezed her finger and thumb together. Hopefully His Majesty won't notice.

Margery reached the main hall and curtsied. His Majesty sat on his throne. His eyes focused, face stern.

"Margery, His Majesty's advisors said that King Philip of France wants to take control of England and overthrow His Majesty. He has put together a great army and his ships are at sea as we speak. His ships shall arrive on land any week now. If he succeeds, many people will die, and he'll take over England. His Majesty has commanded me to lead the battle." Joseph spoke confident in His Majesty's presence.

Margery's face whitened.

"I know this is not the best time with our baby on the way, but war is upon us and I must do this for our country, our king and my honor." Joseph stood tall, his body still, while Margery stood emotionless.

"I won't pretend I'm not frightened, but I know men must support their country in times of war. Just be safe and come back to us." Margery rubbed her stomach.

"Let's discuss our plans," the king said.

Margery sat on the bed and waited for Joseph to return to their room. The door snapped her out of her daze and Joseph entered the room. She approached him with a loving embrace.

"Joseph, what kind of danger is the king putting you in?"

"His Majesty thinks that King Philip's men will try to break through the castle doors. I'm to lead the attack from the castle roof. We'll have archers and cannons ready for them. The king has arranged for the Duke of Lancaster to lead the attack. The king is quite ill. He's been coughing up blood and breathing very heavily. His private physician said he may not last much longer. I've insisted the king leave tomorrow morning and stay at his quarters in Winchester Castle. He'll be accompanied by his loyal advisors."

"Are you sure you're ready for this?" She took his hands in hers.

"This is an opportunity to become king. We will have everything, and our son or daughter will be raised to be the next king or queen of England. The thought of having an heir to the throne is one I never thought imaginable. Now it is going to become a reality. I am quite ready." Margery shook her head and touched his face.

"I love you and I'll pray for you and the king's men, but what about the people in this castle? Where will they go? Where will I go?"

"Beneath the castle grounds is a shelter. You and the others will be safe. I would never let any harm come to you or our baby. No outsider knows of this secret shelter."

Although Margery wasn't happy, she smiled, took Joseph's strong hands in hers, and embraced him.

Three weeks later, Margery was stitching with the other ladies when Joseph flung the door to their private room open and broke the latch. The latch landed on the floor and rolled under the bed. Margery dropped her needle work on the floor.

"Margery, you all must come with me to the shelter now. King Philip's ships are approaching."

Margery and her four ladies followed Joseph, but her lower back ached and her feet were swollen with water weight. She reached out her hand for her maid Margaret to help her along.

When they reached the shelter, the steps were steep, and Margery held onto her husband for support. With each footstep, the stairs creaked louder.

"Margery, I must leave you now to fight for England and the king. You and the others are to stay here for your safety. I or one of the king's men will come for you when it's over."

Margery touched Joseph's face. His whiskers tickled the palm of her hand.

"I love you. Please be safe." With her hands still on his face, she gave him a quick gentle kiss on the mouth. When she broke the embrace, he somberly walked up the stairs. When he shut the door behind him, she listened to his footsteps until they became faint and he was gone. Margery stared blankly at the ground. She rubbed her stomach to sooth her nerves and prayed to God to keep Joseph safe.

In the chaos Margery left her stitching behind, so she and the other ladies passed the time by telling stories. When each lady spoke, it was background noise to Margery, because her thoughts were concentrated on Joseph. She nodded pretending to listen, until she felt a sharp pain. She bent over holding her stomach, screamed and looked down to see she was standing in a pool of water.

****

Joseph's suit of armor was unbearably hot and heavy on his body as he assembled his men. He removed his gauntlet and the sweat dripped down his face. He took a bucket of water and poured it over his head before putting his gauntlet back on. It would've helped if the water wasn't hot from the heat, but it washed away the sweat.

"We need to prepare. Get the cannons and archers ready at my command."

Joseph saw fear in some of their eyes, while others joked. That worried him. When the king appointed Joseph as the next heir, he summoned The Duke of Lancaster to train Joseph for battle. Before the Duke's training, Joseph had no experience on a battlefield. He didn't want to disappoint the king. He had to show authority for his men to trust him. Joseph briskly strode over to the men, held his sword up high and preached:

"Men, gather yourselves together! We could all die today! I won't have you make fools of us. We are loyal subjects to King Alfred and we must show him we are ready to die for England." Joseph took a deep breath.

Joseph lowered his sword. The knights stood, straightened their armor and positioned themselves.

"Upon my command, fire the cannons. Until then, we wait."

Joseph felt the hours pass as the heat took its toll on him and the other men. He peered down the castle roof and in the near distance he saw men on horseback coming towards the castle.

"Men, it's almost time!"

Again, Joseph peered down the castle roof and waited for the Duke of Lancaster's signal. Once the Duke signaled to him with a wave, Joseph prepared his men.

"Fire the cannons!" Joseph shouted.

The enemy was almost over the bridge to the castle doors.

Joseph watched The Duke wave his men on and they charged straight ahead, while their horses" hoofs pounded on the bridge. The bridge shook from side to side from the weight and some of the men were thrown from their horses. The men got themselves up, ran on foot with swords and axes in hand and screamed, "For King Alfred, for England!" Joseph watched with envious eyes wishing he was down fighting with The Duke.

One of the Duke's men charged forward and swung his sword through King Philip's knight's neck. His head landed on the ground and red blood spilled out. His horse yelped and galloped in the other direction. The man screamed; "For England!" Joseph could see The Duke had control.

Joseph kept the cannons firing. A group of King Philip's men screamed as the force of the metal balls pushed them into midair, crushed their bodies, and killed them instantaneously. Joseph looked away for a brief moment, cringed and then composed himself.

One knight managed to barely escape. He ran back onto the bridge to jump into the water and put himself out of his misery. He flailed his arms in the air, jumped off the side of the bridge and hit the water face down. The height and the force killed him instantly. His head seeped deeper into the river with his arms sprawled outward. His lifeless body floated down the riverbank and disappeared out of sight. Joseph knew this was war, but the sight of mangled and dead bodies; even from his distant, was disturbing. His stomach was nauseous, and bile filled in his throat. He spit over the side of the roof.

Joseph knew it was difficult for the archers to make a direct hit from that high above, but they did their best.

Joseph swallowed hard when he saw The Duke got struck in the leg with a sword. The sword struck him deep, but that didn't stop The Duke. As he limped, and his blood spilled onto the hard surface of the ground, he swung his sword at the traitor's horse. The horse winced, and the knight fell to the ground. The Duke with his bloodied leg, kneeled on the ground, took out his knife, and raised his hands high in the air. With one swift movement downward, he stabbed the knight directly into his neck. The knight gasped for air as blood streamed out of his mouth. He then gasped his last breath. The Duke took his knife, cut through the knight's armor and removed it from his lifeless body. He tore his shirt off to wrap his injured leg. Joseph raised both hands in the air and roared at The Duke's victory.

Joseph sighed and put his hands to his face. He had a guilty conscience that the Duke and his men were in danger below. He endured an injured leg and lost many knights, while Joseph and his knights were safe high above. The king insisted that he lead the battle from the rooftop regardless of his training from The Duke. The king didn't want his next heir to the kingdom in direct danger. Joseph couldn't go against His Majesty, but it still bothered him that he couldn't fight side by side with the Duke. When he is king, if a war ensued he would put his talent to use and fight alongside his men. One of his men approached and disturbed Joseph's thoughts.

"Lord Joseph, look! King Philip's men have retreated. We outnumbered them."

The enemies, on their horses, galloped across the bridge with incredible speed leaving their injured on England's ground.

Joseph and his men helped the Duke tend to the injured and dispose of the dead. The foul stench made the men gag. Joseph instructed them to burn the corpses. Then he quickly walked to the shelter, even though it felt like an eternity. It was unusual for a husband to be with his wife during child birth, but Joseph pleaded with the king and he granted him permission. Joseph thought it was the king's way of making up for not letting him lead the battle with The Duke of Lancaster. But Joseph was elated to take part in his child's birth and be there for Margery.

She had to be okay. When he arrived, he heard a scream. He opened the door, ran down the stairs and missed a step. He fumbled and grabbed onto the wall to steady himself. Margery was surrounded by her ladies. She shrieked as they told her to bear down and push.

"Margery, I'm here."

Joseph squeezed his way through the ladies and knelt before Margery. He gently held her hand in his to comfort her.

"I knew you'd come," she said in between bouts of screams.

"Keep pushing, Lady Margery. I see the head."

She pushed down as hard as she could and let out a scream that deafened the room. Slowly she caught her breath and heard cries from her new born child.

"It's a boy," her trusted maid Margaret said.

Joseph's eyes widened with joy.

"We have a son."

Margaret asked Joseph for his knife to cut the umbilical cord.

"May I do it?"

Margaret handed him the knife and stepped aside. He gently cut the umbilical cord and placed the baby in Margery's arms. As Margery cradled their newborn son in her arms, Joseph rubbed his bald little head and the baby cooed.

"What shall we name him?" Joseph asked.

"George," she said.

"That's a strong name, Margery. George, it is."

Soon after the birth of baby Richard, His Majesty, King Alfred, passed away. On his deathbed, he signed over his title of King of England to Joseph. The following morning Joseph was crowned the next King of England. Joseph's golden crown glowed brightly throughout the room. He took hold of Margery's hand and she smiled. Then the Duke of Lancaster handed Margery the scepter and handed Joseph her crown. Joseph gently placed the crown on Margery's head and secured it with his fingers.

"Behold King Joseph and Queen Margery of England," The Duke shouted.

Joseph and Margery raised their hands up high and waved to the crowd.

King Philip lost many men and declared defeat. He vowed never to enter England again.

King Joseph and Queen Margery would rule England together and raise their son to be the next king.

Lengthening Days
Michael D. Jones
For Joanne

Have you noticed the seconds, my Love
Over your bowl of granola, or oatmeal
Against the cold on this winter morning
Where horizons of snow and night emerge
Or have the days begun to melt together
Their winter grey and starless slurry;
Have you noticed the seconds, my Love
As they recede, receding into night?

Do you look for your breath, my Love
When walking in half-light or under
The brilliant moon, casting its cold light;
Or have the nights become your solace
Since the days began to wane; has your
Love embraced the darkness, nights slow
Abatement into lengthening days?

I find my breath in darkness and in
Clear light of day, and in the in-between
The seconds we find along the way.
I notice the night that shortens, between
The dusk and dawn; and each moment
 As it passes, our breath both here and gone.

Let This Wineglass Be a Beacon
Billy Malanga

A wineglass was shimmering on the kitchen windowsill.
My wife asked me if I had ever donated blood, I said, "no."
She giggled. I watched her mood freeze over like Siberia.
She said, "Nobody wants my troubled blood."

The sunlight had caused the glass to panic like a fisherman
signaling me at sea. I snapped a picture of it, cupping its
sparkling radiance in my hands. I wanted to touch your face
and heal you, make your lymphocytes stop what they were doing.

I went upstairs to give you both. I knew it was not the best time,
early morning when things seem hasty. You sat quietly on the bed
and received it. You had other things on your mind: research
papers, a teenage daughter, grad students, dog shit in the hallway.

Dear Wife,
let the light that made its way through that wineglass be
your bonfire below the skin. Let it guide you through this
mysterious revolution in your bones and give you strength
to fight this savage beast.

Loathing
Kayla Simmons

I loathed that man. The way his eyes transfixed you into a single space. The way they saw right through your skin, past your skeleton, to the core of your person. I pulled at the hem of my skirt, crossing my legs beneath the expansive conference table, glancing between the segmented charts of numerals and the graphs projected on the wall beside him. I needed to focus. I gripped the fountain pen in my left hand tightly, balling my right hand into a fist as it lay across my lap. If I had learned anything working as a female Executive Assistant in the 1950s, it was to never give a man an excuse. Leverage was perhaps the only other item than fine aged Bourbon that intoxicated them more.

I swiveled my chair to face the presenter, felt the unusual chafe of my blazer at the nape of my neck. I pushed myself up in my seat, hoping to readjust the irritating feeling, but it wouldn't dissipate.

Damn it all to hell.

It was all his fault. This voltage that coursed through my veins, made my skin flush, and the room too stuffy—it was all centered around that man. He punctuated each movement with hand motions. His hands were attached to those fingertips I had delicately traced in my precious memory, when I had the innate pleasure to view their perfection in splotches of moonlight and shadows. His silver eyes scanned the faces of each executive member as he circled the conference table.

I felt his gaze linger on me. Felt his attention as he discussed banal terms like marketing strategies and public relations with various accounts and VIP clientele as a thin veil for his silent flirtation. His suit tailored to his tall frame so as not to make him appear gangly, but like a dapper lawyer. That suit, with its careful stitches and accurately trimmed waist line, could make a shark appear approachable. I knew better though.

The meeting adjourned at its usual time, and I quickly sprung to my feet, hoping to relieve myself of the stifling atmosphere pressurizing each mote of dust in the room. His voice, like the smooth satin of Frank Sinatra's purr pouring from a vinyl record, made me hesitate. "Violet, would you stay a moment?"

How could I say no? I ceased shuffling my ledgers, tugged at the bottom of my blazer, and laid one hand across the scraps of paper centered before me, as one by one the other executive members filed out of the glass bowl we were encased in, retreating to their glossy sanctuaries down the hall. I braced myself as I turned to face him.

"What can I do for you, Cameron?" He flashed a half-smile towards me, smoothly placing his hands into his pants" pockets as he swaggered to my side.

"Do you have plans for this evening?"

"Not at present. My brother should be arriving later this evening though."

Cameron's eyes fluttered, his mouth falling slightly agape. "I'm sorry, your brother? I didn't know you had a sibling."

"You never thought to ask. You just decided I was a convenience. How did you put it the other day? One helluva a good time, am I right?" Cameron took a step closer, pointedly glaring in the direction of the glass frame of the conference room.

"First of all, I never had the opportunity to ask. Second, this isn't the place to have this discussion."

"Well of course not. That would be unprofessional. A CEO being seen with a lowly executive assistant isn't picture perfect, obviously. Perhaps your wife could recommend somewhere more suitable." Cameron didn't blink, but I felt righteous in saying the words aloud. His reaction wasn't what mattered. I propped a hand on my hip, gesturing to the city skyline opposite us. "Perhaps we could have this conversation over dinner, someplace downtown?"

I crossed my arms over my chest, tapping my chin thoughtfully, "Or I hear there's a lovely Bed and Breakfast down past Coral Cove. Would that be a more suitable place for this discussion, Cameron?" He stiffened. I felt the pride well up in my chest. I turned towards my ledgers, gathered them into a neat pile, and held the stack close to my chest.

I turned to face Cameron, pushing the rim of my glasses onto the bridge of my nose. "What would you suggest, Cameron?" His eyes bored into me, the wisps of quaffed ebony hair shuddering in the stagnant air between us. I felt a shiver course down my spine. I wanted to reach out and pull him towards me, envelope myself in the scent that lingered in the air around him. Refinement and primal masculinity, wrapped with a leather bow-tie. I grinned.

"Perhaps you can send me a memo when you decide." I stalked past him, free at last of his oppressive atmosphere. I touted my confidence with each stride I took towards my cubicle, waving to Lindsay behind her secretary desk, casually pausing at Mitchell's office to ask about the next company retreat planning committee meeting. The atmosphere shifted behind me. I felt the hairs at the nape of my neck stand on end. As I jotted down the date and time, I felt him encroach.

Cameron's lofty hand—as beautiful as the marble that Michelangelo carved—encircled my elbow from behind. I twisted around to face him, almost sending my assortment of papers flying. His eyes gleamed at Mitchell, and he flashed that smile, one that garnered him a photogenic descriptor.

"Pardon the intrusion, but I have to steal this firecracker for a moment. Shall we go to my office, Violet?" He stared me down, challenged me to refuse him. My lungs seemed leaden. Mitchell, his large, ruddy cheeks sunken into his round face, was oblivious. He nodded his approval. I flashed a panicked glance at Cameron, but he was serene, his face stone. There was a glazed expression on Mitchell's face.

Damn it all to hell.

I shouldn't have expected any sort of reprieve with Mitchell. Cameron had dazzled Mitchell like he dazzled the clients, flashing that smile that showed the small dimple in the right side of his cheek, his eyes crinkling with the warmth of a charming young man. My pulse ricocheted. How could a creature like him even exist in this world made of chrome? He was flesh and blood, and as much as I loathed him, I was fascinated by the way the world shifted when he stood in a room. It no longer held sharp lines and edges, boundaries long ago drawn with chalk against the glass that separated the elite from the rest of us. With a toothy grin and a quipping remark, Cameron made them disappear. He coaxed all formality of professionalism free from their rusty chains and tossed it aside.

He placed his free hand at the small of my back, guiding me towards his office. Like the first day I had met him, he erased the rest of the world, and I no longer understood the rules of the game. Lest of all when he dared reach out to caress the irritation at the nape of my neck. As his hand glided across my shoulder blades, my stomach quivered. My blazer felt suffocating. I felt the need to remove it, let him drape it across his arm like he did that first night, leading me down the narrow passage to his office. We arrived at our destination soon enough. He led me inside, secured the door, and then turned to face me.

I didn't have time to react as he strode forward and shoved the papers out of my hands. I gasped, watching as they scattered across the floor, floating like down feathers onto the carpet. He backed me against the edge of his desk, his arms on either side of me, closing me in. His eyes gazed into my own, and I felt the air turn sticky with his hot breath so close to my lips.

"She left me, Violet, after I told her the truth." My mouth ran dry, my jaw falling agape.

"Pardon? You did what?"

"I'm not going to lie about my feelings. I care too much for you to tell myself, and anyone else for that matter, otherwise."

"Are you insane? Her father founded this company. Cameron, you'll lose everything!"

"From my perspective, I've already lost everything." Cameron reached into the pocket inside his jacket. I pressed both hands against his chest, my bangs falling in my eyes as I sagged against the desk.

"Don't!"

He rested his hand over my own. "Violet, let me do this."

"Absolutely not!" Cameron's eyes searched my face.

"I know about the test, Violet." Damn his eyes. Those stupefying orbs of grey; glossy, like moonlight dripping across the ocean. I was suddenly very aware of our bodies. His tall frame surrounding me, the heat emanating from his flesh. How exposed my whole body felt beneath the blue button-down as I stood in front of him, ensnared. I shut my eyes, leaning my forehead against his shoulder. His arms folded around me. "Did you think I wouldn't find out? Did you plan to hide it from me?"

"You know me better than that, Cam." His hands eased their way across my back, comforting and gentle. I felt the titanium band around his right hand, warm from his flesh, as he stroked the tension in my muscles.

"I want this life with you, Violet. Without it, I wouldn't be the same person." I bit my lip, my eyes brimming with tears.

"Which life, Cam? Because there's only one I'm willing to share with you. And according to that test, there's less than six months of it left for me." Cameron pulled away from me.

"I can think of a lot of things we could do with that much time." Cameron pulled the titanium band from his right hand. He brandished it in front of me. He placed it delicately on the desk. He flattened his palms against the glass top on either side of me once more.

"I only need this one life." I clenched my fists against my chest, my hands shaking.

"I can't ask that of you."

"So, you'd rather just be an affair? A matter of secrecy I keep locked in a closet?" I swallowed a sob.

"Cameron, this isn't just a run of the mill disease. It will consume me. It will consume everything around me. I'll never be able to give you the kind of life she can." I chewed the inside of my cheek, resisting the burning sensation behind my eyes. Afraid the emotions brimming behind them would erupt, I rushed forward, burying my face in his chest. He smelled like the sea, so open and inviting. At the same time, I felt suffocated. His world was ever expanding, and mine seemed to become narrower by the minute. The watch on my left wrist ticked away the seconds, each strike like a hammer against a nail, slowly forming my coffin.

He asked gently, "What do you mean when you say that?" I hesitated, trying to formulate in my mind the most convincing argument. Find a reason for him to place that band back on his right hand.

I could only manage a few scattered phrases. "A future. Children. A home." I couldn't bring myself to say the last word. There had to be a better, more articulate word than that to encompass what a world could look like between two individuals with infinity facing them. I rasped, "If I'm lucky, I might be able to stay here with the firm a little longer before anyone's able to catch on." There was a long pause.

I drew away from him, unclenching my fists. I rested my hands against his chest, my hands crumpling the silken material to hide their trembling. I couldn't relinquish my hands from his shirt. I gazed up to gauge his expression. His face had softened, that lopsided grin spreading across that face which I adored. "How can you possibly be smiling at a time like this?"

"Because you are perfect." I felt my cheeks grow red.

"I just told you I have less than six months left to live—how in the world does that make me perfect?" Cameron cupped the side of my cheek. His touch was feverish, and I craved its

warmth over my flesh. Felt the need for it down my spine, the ache for his gentle caresses across my abdomen.

"Do you remember the day I first met you?" Cameron's eyes softened, the flecks of blue in his gaze glittering like sea-foam erupting into the sky. He said, "You were fumbling in that briefcase—"

"It's called a purse, you idiot!"

"Tomato, tomatoe. Violet, I'd never seen a more beautiful woman. Intelligent, funny, and infuriating." I felt a lump form at the base of my throat. I tried to swallow it, but it was lodged there. He pulled the glasses from my face, folded them up, and placed them beside his ring on the glass desktop.

He smiled. "There you are." My eyes stung even more. I bit my lip, unable to tear my gaze away from Cameron's face.

He said, "At first, I did everything I could to push you away. But by the time that happened, I couldn't help myself." His fingers weaved into my hair, the tendrils like honey dribbled across his skin. "By then, you were this ghost haunting my every waking thought. Each tick of your pen, every gentle sigh, I wanted each moment to be something I could call my own."

"You have Leslie."

"She's a capable and lovely woman who will make a man someday very happy. A man worthy of her. I wished to God I hadn't drug her through this." My shoulders sagged. I squeezed my eyes shut.

"So, you do regret sleeping with me." Cameron seized my shoulders, his fingers trembling. My eyes flew open.

Cameron's expression was panicked as he gripped my shoulders and shook me. "Absolutely not! I'll never regret that weekend in Coral Cove. I'll never regret anything about you, Violet!" The muscle along his jawline jumped. He clenched his teeth, drawing his composure back, a lock of his hair falling across his forehead. I reached up to brush it back into place, my fingers trembling.

He reached up and wrapped his fingers around my palm. He drew it towards his mouth, his lips searing a kiss against it. His eyes settled on my face. He looked determined, even as I saw the unsettled swirl of his irises. Cameron let go of me long enough to reach into his jacket pocket. He withdrew two envelopes, and tossed them on his desk. I stared down at them, running my fingertips across each manila lapel.

"What are these?"

"One's my letter of resignation. The other one is yours." Cameron stepped back. I turned my back to him, pulling out the standardized pieces of parchment from each envelope, carefully reading the lines. I brushed my index finger near the bottom, the places where our signatures would be scrawled, the official seal of the corporate world which Cameron and I existed. I meticulously refolded each piece of stationary, returned it to its proper envelope, my eyes stinging. Cameron laid his hand on my shoulder, turning me around to face him. He trailed his fingers along my jaw line, his lips parting as he hesitantly kissed my forehead. He pulled me into his arms, his body enveloping me instantaneously.

He whispered, "Let's not a waste a second pretending we're something we're not." I felt my arms wrap around him, felt them quake as the tears fell from my eyes, hanging on the tips of my eyelashes.

"I can't ask this of you, Cameron." He held me an arm's length away. He reached onto the floor. Amidst the feathery ledgers around our feet, he shuffled them until he found my long-forgotten pen. He held it out to me. He motioned for me to take it. I didn't move. He stepped to the side, unsealed the first envelope, and signed his name at the bottom of his resignation letter. He turned towards me, the pen outstretched.

"You're not."

"I hate you," I said.

Cameron grinned. "I know."

Lost in Her
Ian Dixon

Those months in Queensland, animating the sheer spirit of the place, the warm dips at seven o'clock, avoiding the man-o-war jellyfish, the naked dips at night, the cast, bonded by laughter under the pandanus palms, mango and guava trees with hanging orbs of fruit, vines that hung like languid snakes about the rippling trees, pursuing the sensual, the golden sands and burning sunsets, vodkas on the balcony, crinkling noses up against reddened skin. And the rift inside me, my strange pining loss of Berenice, I put silently to one side, but, like an ex-con, I hankered after my prison.

And rehearsals: the magic of Shakespeare's text, the camaraderie, the ocker vileness and good-natured jibing, the muse within *A Midsummer Night's Dream* and Nina, at five-foot eleven, playing Helena, inventing her theatrical devices. And in the guise of Puck I would hook her lip on invisible thread and knock her out on the makeshift ply-wood palm trees, thus sending her into her love-trance for Demetrius. This woman, Nina, had both height and elegance: so self-possessed, but playing the neurotic, becoming the spaniel.

Puck, however, imbibed it all with polymorphous flair, wondering secretly at the sensual touch of this Nina. Puck was springing at these foolish mortals, taking the whipping from Oberon, but upstaging him at the last. Playing out the enchantment of wild thyme potions, the magic that commends us all to love—whilst all the time avoiding love.

Yet, what magic we allowed ourselves up here in Queensland. On exiting the theatre, the audience was greeted by the balmy, tropical night outside. Faeries surely made their way, trippingly, about the ferns and vines, the ever-present vegetation, among sounds of raucous bats and howling dogs, the gentle patter of warm rain.

****

Driving through Far North Queensland: we were somehow crazy on the fecundity of it all. Her confident hands on the steering wheel of her creaky station wagon: she espoused theories of art and the virtues of men, of disappointment and the vain star of hope, the wishes, the magic, the Superman theory, the parallels of antiquity in the modern world. We whisked past bushes that burned and smoked in the heat, past the intoxicated cane, lolloping about in acres and acres of itself. The wet dust red with life, the grizzled faces of locals, somehow resigned to the sheer, living captivation of the place. The fruits and cane-sugar, supped at the roadside, sure sent us a little troppo. I'd glance at her thighs as her foot pressed down on the accelerator, a lovely rippling of Aztec designs on her skirt: a promise, a hope.

Somewhere north of Townsville, we stayed at a beachside, wood-decked dream-house of an actress friend of Nina's who'd worked with Kenneth Branagh. We slept on two couches pushed together and found ourselves clinging to each other in the night, cuddled in each other's grasp, staving off the erotic. She had known men like me before, she'd said. We were rats in fairyland, oisterous for each other's simple graces, sublime in the merriment of caring for each other's emotional wounds, and knowing, yes knowing, that sex was too easy an option.

Nina was a bass-flute, a gust of breath in every note. The cosmos played like an overture at the edges of her vision, or so she chose to be perceived. She was a rare human though, a quality of British Raj, but softer, more sensual within that Amazonian hubris of hers, her breathy inquisitiveness and air of nonchalance.

She sat me down once, telling me she would never hurt me — trust was essential, and she would not abuse it, poor rakish peev that I was behind that mask of fearlessness I wore, she said. I felt vaguely touched. I was clearly getting away with behaviour only a postmodern rake could get away with: achieving his sneaky intent without seeming to.

Nightly, I grew, step-by-step in rapture with her. Usually, the interest of educated women in a "rat-bag" like me waned faster than a cardboard moon on strings. And so, jilted as we were by previous lovers who'd never seen the joy, the grimy pride, the adolescence trapped in us—two misfit neurotics approaching thirty — we set out stealthily on each other.

I congratulated her on the accolades She'd received in the press. We had just appeared in A Midsummer Night's Dream and Helena and Puck—simply appropriate casting on both accounts — both given praise by the critics. Which came as a welcome change compared to some things I'd had printed about me in plays back in Sydney and Melbourne: "White Trash" I'd been labelled, for a "bitter portrayal of intelligence perverted by abuse" (I liked that bit). But here in Queensland it was us—Helena and Puck—who'd been awarded the accolades of success. Now we were on the road—heading god knows where.

In Cairns, Nina got drunk and danced in leather sandals, strapped up to the knee, her clothes wet with foam-party detergent, clinging to those luscious thighs. She flapped her dress about in the night air in an attempt to dry it, then rested on my shoulder in the cool night air and pontificated on why she wasn't attracted to me and why She'd never abuse my delicate soul. But I needed her, needed her flesh, her wound, and wanted to be inside her. She was never shocked nor teased by this, nor found it a mirror too sharp to confront. I'd clasp her about that hourglass waist and wonder at the sheer sexual power and re-productivity of her. And though my hurdy-gurdy tears swam out, I smiled inside for the thrill of it all.

We sat upon a low, stone wall at the river in Cairns. I leant on her foam-wet dress and pressed my face up against her shoulder, imbibing the persimmon flavour of her. I stopped breathing against my tears as if choked. Dropping my head slightly, I stared down to the place where her body was hidden by the folds of dress. She knew what I was looking for and seemed somehow comfortable. I'd never try though – she was too implacable and hurt, and after all, I kept an appropriate distance knowing the flag was not flying for me.

Yet, why she stayed beside me that night, I never knew, nor for these losses, this sense of melancholia, nor again why she stayed at all, nor, for that matter, why she didn't pigeon-hole me as others had. I never knew why, but knew in my essence why she placed her hand like a blessing upon my head, its weight pulling me imperceptibly toward her, toward her sex. Yet if I moved just an inch toward her my own volition, she'd up and dance about the night-time streets singing "Lulu" hymns. I wish I could show you her dance, show you through my own cracked eyes, her flippy, knee-high sandal heels clipping on the asphalt, spinning as she did, as if she might ascend. She was churning in timeless seconds of absolute glee in the consciousness of being watched by someone she knew to be hers.

The whirling, proud, erotic lungful of her towered over me, my eyes retiring on a tide, all my longings drifting away. She was enrapturing: such ex-bornagain passion. This quasi-moral weirdness, teetered within our steaming horse-poo utterances of disguised desire whilst my hands avoided brushing over those lovely limbs, tentatively, like snail's eyes upon meeting an unannounced leaf.

On our rambles around the rainforests we occasionally veered into each other, linking arms, platonically, meandering along beside the fertile trees, rowdy with exotic birds. Her jaw protruded on some theory or another, a hybrid of the spiritual and statistical, a work of art, espousing, extrapolating, posing artfully woven ideas, extracted like a ribbon from the sheer oral satisfaction of her company. We wandered under low hanging bushes, caressing each other accidentally. Our haloes, our auras, ricocheting off the other's.

She stopped, glanced in my eyes as if in slo-mo. A pause, an incremental move forward, then, "I have to be alone, now," she announced, suddenly pulling short. "Do you mind?"

Of course, I did not, and so we parted ways and lost ourselves in private ruminations. A few paces on, I chanced upon a waterhole in the creek. I took off all my clothes and spilled into the thrill of the warm water. A flock of inquisitive parrots raised their crests. I dived, the water was luscious and promised to melt me, borne into my spiritual self with the clear-water voice of heart-openness. The song in me sang out a rhythm of longing as the waters washed my privacy. It had been so long since I had felt truly alone. Vines cascaded down the rocks and dangled in, their tip-ends swishing enervatedly in the ripples. A cassowary eyed me from side to side before padding away downstream. I relaxed on my back. Puck began to relax, and the fish swam around tasting me as I dissolved in the fluid womb of my waterhole.

Naked still, I sunned myself on a rock, stretching out like a cat in the warmth. I'd never be loving Nina, I thought. So I fell to the lure of Earth, flipping off my rock and pounding the red soil at the water's edge, digging like a thing possessed. I delved in the healing, grounding mud, slapped it about my shoulders and rubbed it in my hair, squelched its skreeking, clay-rich textures into palms and filled my chest with life, drawing red lines on my cheeks (as lost lovers had done in my past), grinding grass roots and honeyed earth into my drying skin, sluicing these gentle undulations of dirt into the valleys between muscles and palming great clods of it onto my thighs. Mud fell like tiny bombs of bliss back into the water, the swirls and diving shapes of a preternatural sky at dawn. Sunlight skip-hopped across the surface and surging with life I embraced it, the magnetism of mud caressing me – the good earth. I relished the place and sat cross-legged to meditate in the arms of Pagan Deities, trying to breathe those past lovers out of my system. The warm wind slithered as an eel amidst the cacophony of groaning trees. The creek water, clearer than eyesight, whipped about at my toes. I breathed in the spirit of the land, co-mingling with my prahnayana and taking me skyward in release. I felt alone and united with that great world of light, as on stage.

I don't remember where time went, nor how I found myself back on the trodden path again, solid walking-stick yoked across my shoulders like a coolie, nor where I'd left my clothes. I guess that made me vulnerable to discovery. And yes, someone came wading among the trees, way up ahead, appearing somewhat reddened in the skin. Though she was distant, I could see the whites of her eyes. She caught my gaze, calmly and evenly, as if in a telephoto lens. It was Nina, wet, her clothes bunched up in one hand. We both were clay-clad, both in ecstasies beyond the here and now, if ever now and here configured in this place.

She was prepossessed in the eyes, as if she too had meditated, and, it seemed, the very unfettering of the act was again drawing us together. Gliding toward me, innocent in the strong, frank sexuality of her proud surge forward. Her limbs were cracking off with newly dried mud and as she drew nearer, I saw for the first time, her native body, light in the limbs but so grounded, so fresh. Red earth-paint on her face, limbs criss-crossed with mud, tufts of grass in her hair, a miracle of tribal events sown in her being. As we drew together, we knew we'd both been called to some rite. And, as we laughed in wordless recognition, our caked faces crackled and stretched against the hold of the clay.

"Did you…?" I asked.

She nodded, gape-mouthed and notched up another perception about me, one that she seemed to like, so I didn't mind that she saw right though me. For two who believed in destiny, it was not hard to recognise that choices were being made for us – and it was impossible to know which way the dice would fall. For both of us—a wall of unstated wounding.

Further downstream, we found a way to float nakedly though a portal of delicate rapids. I watched her slender limbs, like Ophelia brought back to life. The slithering grace and malleable urges within her, water cascading over peaceful face as she exhaled lovingly. Slipping along the creek, her limbs as chocolate, melting in the cool: mine thrashed about at fear of drowning, graceless muscular slaps at water. How did she do it, sustain this magic in everything she did? I was constantly turned on and cooled in her presence. Her education spoke as much as silence, as much in words as in the pure vertigo of her. I looked to her as a way out of the labyrinth of me and in her silent eyes I saw her say: "It's okay".

Later that night, as the rains came down, we chanced on a shanty-shack full of local hippies who were good enough to share their mulled wine. It made life seem blissful, stowing dreams away in closets: bitch eyes closing on a dull, lurid green, forever at point of drowning. Yet it was erotic—titillating at least—and Nina seemed to be appraising me from her corner of the shack.

We found the car and Nina drove us back to her friend's house. She drove carefully, always telling some story, some quip, some sensible tale. I felt I could listen to her voice transported without any intervention beyond this. I knew my place in her art, I was an object of strenuous contemplation, held at bay. I watched her lips move.

The trees lifted their hemlines clear of the mud as we passed. Drizzle pattered about the car and loosened tensions within our stomachs. Her short hair fell like a man's about her features. Her jaw cocked a degree or two toward me, eyes still fixed on the undulating road as mine were on her vacillating face. The thought she stepped about and tinkered with was heaving into life:

"Hey… I'd like to kiss you, Andy Greenwood."

She always addressed me by my full name, as I did her, like strangers in some courtly dance, a pavan within formality itself, but desperately and coolly erotic. And here it was at last – an opening.

"Well… you do that, Nina Aldridge."

She swung her face toward me like a naughty cousin.

"Shall we?"

"Sure"

"Okay."

She steered the station wagon to the shoulder, slid for a moment in the mud before applying the gentle ratchet of the hand-brake.

We met each other's eyes and laughed, her giggle forming an appropriate "O". She sighed and tugged at my breath. She lifted herself toward me, then flopping lazy arms about my shoulders as I lightly stroked her, she opened up her peachy, wetted lips and introduced her mouth to mine. I loved taboos and this entanglement, albeit innocent, was somehow forbidden; why, we couldn't tell. Her tongue slipped up around my teeth and left a life-long impression there. Can we list our three best kisses? This was number one. Something casual in her chafed so lightly upon me, I was left the sweet-smelling tastes of wine, passed on a fresh wave of mustard in her lips. I let her pull away, as she let me. We laughed with joy. A kangaroo pad-hopped across the soaking road, arching up in the headlights to chew at the vision of us.

"Andy Greenwood," she offered, eased the handbrake off and rolled the car downhill, kicked the chugging engine into life by a clutch-start. We flowed like water home, where we slept in each other's grasp on our two couches pushed together. We slept in moveless sleep, neither one of us venturing on sex.

****

Nina, by informing me of my own vulnerability, had become of utmost poetic importance to me. Our trip was an endless progression of driving conversations coloured with bliss. Knowing, as I did, that the key to seduction is patience, that sitting by upon my honour, clamping the lid down on the incessant voice of libido, left the way open. Her rhythm, her Amazonian limb-walking, her keen poetic sensibilities were acting upon me as I acted upon her. And yet there was another sense. A wholesome touch. I'd been on stage with her and knew when she, as Helena in the swoon of magic, had feigned theatrical sleep at the base of that plywood tree that she was brilliant at feigning sleep — was this not the girl who would nest beside me for weeks after this, as I willed my passion to go away? On stage, I'd felt her spirit lie down before me as a "spaniel" does, while I, the ithyphallic Puck bestriding her body, turned out to the hushed audience and found myself arching back in exquisite joy, allowing me to feel, to sing in my spirit, to arch like an orgasming satyr and spill my sense of the great world of light upon the approving audience.

Out on the highway we laughed at this recent memory. There are some things laughter doesn't give away.

We drove into each other's hearts. Nina had no time for petty insecurities, she was descended from Britain's finest, after all. Wallowing sometimes in thoughtless reverie, a pastel shade of her, a winter's boat awash with riches lost on a summer sea, she would tempt me to think how life might be: how, if ever I could relinquish the notion of freedom, I might be free in her. That erotic space in my brain admitted a slide-show of dumb repentance, a pornographic film in which she was the star. And in her laughter, I saw her watch me watching her. I saw her approve of everything I thought and subtly condone it, as if tinkering with my vision, she might have her say inside me.

The silly, denied fertility of us both, the temptations we set for each other, the literature of our two-week life, the glory of exploiting each other's need not to exploit. In some other life I'd lift her to a starry riverbank, where strange herbs grow in the wildness of time and make love – but not here – it was somehow too precious to risk.

And then, the final night of our trip, on the pre-dawn highway, a Harley Davidson gang throttled past and left in their wake a silence in our parking car. I had something to tell her: It was my part in this losing game. She pulled on the handbrake even gentler than she had before—when she wanted me. When she wanted me to kiss her. Now, no openings left: the film in my mind disintegrated, burned off its sprockets. The vision of her great implied held out toward me, at the last, like offerings to a beggar. I lapped at its memory, lapped at imagination as the nearby waves lapped at the mauve sky of morning. The sun was not long off rising.

The chill air surfed on the squalls of seagulls" breath. Fish-scales strewn about this dirt-based car park – and no-one else – no soul lay hereabouts except the shadows of the departed, who had long since passed away. A whirring sigh of far off bushland as if wind through the bones of extinct monsters. The sea breath. The trees bending about holding hands. She looked out of the car window into the still, paling sky, her distorted reflection on the inside. The lapping lapped, as on a loop, as though no single thought or action advanced, prepared to meet its maker-less future. She knew. She knew when the male libido was surging. She turned back to look at me. This was the makeup of Nina, pink lips, blue eyes, blonde 1920s flop-about hair, a cultured courtesan inside her, a child lost in a stony inhospitable place, only her nouse could defend her.

But I'd been in this weird space before, where poetry was colour-dipped in blackness. Our breathing scooped out the last of our entrails, so she suggested, tentatively, a walk on the beach then moved to get out of the car. I caught her wrist as she set the other hand on the door handle, but gently, liberated in the move, the touch, the snow-white feel of her. I'd escaped a horrible thing. It was only then that I knew what I had to say:

"I have to be with you."

Christ, how ludicrous. Her mouth chanced on the familiar "O" shape. But she never baulked.

"Oh... Oh sure... Beach?"

We shivered as we stepped on the blackboard sand and pulled off our clothes. Light flecks through dark clouds peppered the flat pre-dawn horizon like Renaissance art. We both splashed in the cruel water and made poetics of each other. We both squatted down and she laundered ourselves with chill seawater. She twisted back to make sure she was acknowledged. She knew me for the animal I was. She drank me in, a composite of newfound friend; shades of Puck and potential itself.

She was, in those slipping seconds, a terribly smart girl who became a mere thing and beautiful in the acknowledgment of what was happening. She heaved her perfect limbs about in a state of entrancement and she hauled herself into that characteristic dance, spinning artfully. She sighed and reveled in movement itself, her nobility of shimmering flesh, her pillar of salt-fire joy. She shucked off the damned interlocutions on such timeless attraction. Her naked breasts, her legs, her limbs swung about and she hummed like a medium. The freedom to watch her, the license from someone who cared, who had not been seduced to the point when all potential was lost in coitus: so tortured those last few days in her presence, yet the poetry perfect. The sun was rising, bleaching in golden light as I found my place beside her and we danced spinning, hurling and splashing in the warm seawater. We'd always be distant friends, with a secret between us, after this.

The golden arcs of light revealed our clothes, strewn about and trampled in the sand. We hadn't the foresight to bring towels, so we helped each other up the foreshore where we discovered an abundance of toilet paper in the ladies" loos, whisked sheath by sheath from the dispenser as the wind through the free-standing toilet-block sang a beautiful lament to the nature of liberation. We circled slowly about each other like dogs in a dream of being human, wiping off the spots of salty water and freeing each other from the cold. That was glorious, you might say: to be intimate with each other's nakedness – the sting of taboo temporarily removed by this belated teenage ritual. We simply expressed deep regard by investigating each other's bodies with sexless vindication.

In the bluish light that fell from the overhead vent, the smell rendered inoffensive, a dripping, sheathing, shucking motion, one to another, dragged down by a curious lack of need, we went through the rituals of after-play.

This was the opposite of pornography: Regard for another soul, care and acknowledgment and love within this divine intervention of innocence. I lifted her sandy trousers up for her to step inside and guided her pearl-flushed legs in, as one might a child, stepping from a bath. We were whole in each other's parental care.

****

On our way to the airport, a blob of weight jolted against my face from the inside of my head and words dropped out like pheromones. I didn't want to leave her. I fell silent. She did too. I was alone again – that heady, naughty loosened feeling, as joyous, as porous and empty as an outgoing tide, yet somehow devoid of its former glory. In the departure lounge she slipped out a grin:

"You know, it just wouldn't work—you and me."

I accepted this as my karma, as proof she had never ventured on loving me, only thought of me as worthwhile loving for a brief while. I was in no position to protest this.

****

There was no sense in getting on that plane, but get on I did and with such regret—there was something I should have done, something left unsaid. Then the strangest thing: the plane was grounded, no reason, no excuse for such a coincidence—just the dumb announcement that there were issues with the fuel tank. Half an hour later we were shunted off the stilled plane and filed back through the airport somewhere between sober and disgruntled. Queuing through an airport little more than palm leaves and thatched rooves, sore and confused—until one sun-drenched face stood out from the rest. There behind the cordon rope stood Nina—her Aztec dress curiously cultured within the sea of banana and hibiscus shirts. There she stood as I ambled back into the airport—a kind of dumbness on her face, a whitewashed innocence—an apology. My heart fizzled inside my chest like sunstroke—my gestures of greeting left me gassing out words that lost their meaning and died in the air between us. She was perfect just then and her jaw chewed sideways in that curious hybrid of insecurity and pride. She seemed frail in her assured beauty. That persimmon aroma—reaching to me like a beckoning amidst the crowd and I wondered what she saw in that moment. She was still with pregnant expectation and silly with giddiness, but knowing her as I did, I knew she would hold it together in exemplary fashion. Then a hand lifted and flopped on my arm, the space where her smile should be as she announced: "You've got my car keys in your pocket."

I'm dumb. I'm stupid with exposure. There she is—that hand on my arm so light and assured. She is staring into my eyes as she bleeds out words like absent tears. She is not back here for me. She is back for her car keys.

The next plane leaves in four hours, so she sits with me in the bar, our feet propped up on the railing as we slump back on banana lounges. We laugh about the plane and how—if this were a love story the plot would be ludicrous. But there's a step away she's not taking—and neither am I. The hours tick down to a relevant few minutes and I touch her lips.

"We had fun," I announced.

It was more than fun—we both knew this, but heart-sickness to a pair of twenty-eight-year-old thespians was a pang We'd rather not feel. There's been enough pain in losing love and loving where we should not have. There's independence and proud intelligence and it all might be lost in the throw of a misplaced dice.

Yet, there is this magnet pulling at my heart, doubting, moving, stretching like a cat yawning: a gaping wordlessness in a vacillating cavern. She's still there. She hasn't stepped away. Her pretty, pretty face and the sounds of her bubbling thoughts. She's still there and it's fifteen minutes until the boarding call. I don't remember how she came to be weeping, I only know I questioned why I couldn't cry too. I was free in her gaze. I was something I had never been and the thought of walking away seemed a strangulation inside me, a rusty gunwale of water, and this time it was she who stepped forward.

"It won't work, you reckon?" I offered and offered still in the burning behind my eyes. She stopped in her tracks, fingering the car keys. She was still there. Teetering like a thing that knew me. She was still standing there as I missed the plane.

That night we slept on familiar couches pushed together – innocent as bookends and touching warily. A bubbling green-blue hue between us and the darking royal blue of a Queensland midnight in the skies. We kissed. We acknowledged.

"Worth a shot?" she asked.

My only answer, the hand I held to her heart, the flutter, flutter, flutter inside me and that look of hers where a tide of questions melted into confidence. I closed my eyes to feel her breath on my eyelids. She was perfect in my arms. We slept. I was lost in her. I still am.

Lover's Call
C. Flynt

In a town as small as Allenville, nestled deep in the Smith Patent mountains of the Virginia frontier, neighbors tend to run into each other. Whether they want to or not.

The bakery door opened unexpectedly as John Sawyer passed it carrying a four-foot square carved wall panel. The door slammed against his fingers, knocking the heavy panel from his grip. The panel landed on John's toes and knocked Ellaree Allen back into the bakery.

He cursed, more from surprise than pain, then glanced up and recognized the belle of Allenville.

"Pardon, miss. Didn't mean to offend your tender ears." He tapped his tricorne hat with one hand and steadied the panel with the other. His knuckles were scraped, but not bleeding.

She dipped the slightest of curtsies, "Could your words offend me more than your presence? You might try opening your eyes while you walk. If you could move your lumber, and yourself, out of my way, I could get my father's breakfast to him before it cools."

"I believe I can," he replied. "Let me flex my fingers after you flung open a door without checkin' to see who might be in front of it."

He made a show of flexing his strong, tanned hand, lifted the panel, took a step away from the door. He bowed her through and continued on his way.

John nodded politely as he passed Mistress Willadeen and Mother Nona on their way to the bakery.

It was proper to be polite to the two widows.

The circuit preacher administered to the village's spiritual needs. Mother Nona and Mistress Willadeen took care of the rest. They oversaw love, childbirth, illness and death, for both townsfolk and livestock.

Mother Nona was not older than the hills surrounding her cabin, despite what her neighbors said behind her back.

Mistress Willadeen was a handsome woman of uncertain years. She wore her bonnet high to display coal black hair with a brilliant white streak. Rumor said she buried a husband before moving into the hills. No one asked if he was dead at the time.

The two women met every Thursday after the full moon to share hot tea and gossip. When the gossip was hot enough, their tea got cold. After witnessing John and Ellaree, each woman allowed as how the two young folks would spice up today's gossip.

As usual, tea was served at Mistress Willadeen's home. She had a full set of Delft china teacups she carried all the way from Baltimore when she walked into the hills.

Mother Nona sipped her tea and observed, "Women in this town got too much pride and not enough good sense."

Mistress Willadeen considered this. "Perhaps some. The ones I talk to are weak-willed and easily led astray."

Mother Nona stared over her cup, peering through the steam. "Three young men come to me last month askin' if I couldn't see Ellaree Allen in their future. Said they'd kill themselves if she wasn't to be theirs. Took a pile of tea leaves afore I found something to cheer them up."

Mistress Willadeen carefully placed her cup on the saucer. Delft china is fragile and easily chipped. "Five women asked me for herbs to make their moon-cycle regular. We both know what that means."

Mother Nona nodded. "Men won't buy a cow when the milk is freely given."

"Not men. One man. John Sawyer has talented hands, a supple tongue and a healthy appetite."

"Hmph. He'd be better courting Ellaree than cursing her. She'd slow him down some." Mother Nona returned her cup to the saucer with less care than Mistress Willadeen liked.

The two women stared into each other's eyes. Those eyes held knowledge, understanding and no small amount of meddlesome pride.

"Perhaps he should." Mistress Willadeen smiled and picked up her cup. The tea was no longer steaming, but was still warm. "Once Ellaree is betrothed, her swains will scoop up the silly girls throwing themselves under John. Spring should be full of weddings, not heartbreaks."

Mother Nona dipped a finger into her tea, swirled it around and sucked the finger dry. "By midwinter, we'll be passin' out colic medicine and curing diaper rash. It's more fittin' than correctin' moon-cycles and seeing happy futures for heartbroke fools."

"So, how should John and Ellaree be joined?"

"How? Quickly. Afore some fool truly dies for love."

"Or the seamstress moves the stays on too many corsets." Mistress Willadeen noticed the untouched bun and broke off a tiny piece to nibble. "It won't be easy. Those two fell afoul of each other the day they met."

"Don't think I was around that day." Mother Nona took a healthy bite of her bun and chewed around her missing teeth.

Mistress Willadeen touched a fingertip to her chin. "Let's see, it was October last when the sawmill was ready, and John came to run it. Nobody thought We'd get a master carpenter up here in the hills. Miss Ellaree was already in Philadelphia, at the Women's Academy."

"I was here when he come. Brought a wagon of dry lumber all the way from Richmond with him. That don't "'splain nothing 'bout him an' Ellaree."

"Well, Ellaree came back in April. If she was proud when she went to Philadelphia, she was a peacock in a chicken coop when she returned. She wouldn't ride in a farm wagon. She hired a buggy to bring her up into the hills."

"Wastin' her daddy's money. Healthy girl like her could of walked," Mother Nona observed, licking the remnants of cinnamon and sugar off her fingers.

"Not in the dress she wore, or the pretty dancin' slippers. Everybody came out to watch her get out of that buggy."

"I was tendin' to Si Bellow's foalin'. Came out crosswise and took a lot o" work to save the mare and colt."

"You and Si were probably the only folks who didn't see her step out of the buggy with a dress that billowed out as far as she could reach. She couldn't even begin to see her feet," Mistress Willadeen took another dainty swallow," or the cow droppings she was steppin' into."

"An" didn't nobody try to stop her?"

"Nary a one. John laughed at her, and then so did everyone else. I never saw a pretty face so ugly-mad. Rumor is she told her daddy to hire someone to take John's place." Mistress Willadeen took a sip of her tea and frowned. "Not many master craftsmen are willing to trade the bottomlands for the hills."

"So, she hates him for laughin' at her, an" he hates her for tryin' to take away what he's worked for. I'll give him the right of it, but not by much."

"They each have a high opinion of themselves. He, because he earned it, working from apprentice to master as young as he is. She because she's always had it. Her family started this town. If those two to are to be joined, it will take careful work."

The women leaned their heads together. By the time they separated, the tea was too cold to drink. Mistress Willadeen poured hers back into the teapot and studied the bottom of her cup.

"I see a tree in my tea leaves," Mistress Willadeen intoned. "I shall speak with John."

Mother Nona sloshed a spoonful of tea into her saucer and studied it. "Looks like a Sunday bonnet. I'll see to Ellaree."

****

Next morning, Mistress Willadeen emptied her jewelry box and accidentally dropped it. Twice. She gathered the pieces and trotted to John Sawyer's woodshop.

John Sawyer's woodshop was a new building, made from his sawmill's planks, not rough-hewn logs like the older homes. It smelled of pine, maple and chestnut wood. His tools hung neatly from pegs in the back wall, except for the clutter where he was working.

John looked up from his workbench as Mistress Willadeen tiptoed in, mincing her way through wood shavings and sawdust to his front counter.

Mistress Willadeen smiled sweetly. "My jewelry box fell from the shelf and broke. Can you, maybe, fix it? Please?"

John studied the bent hinges and broken nails. "Ayuh, I can fix her. Have to replace the hinges. I've got bigger ones to cover the old nail holes. Then some new brass brads. She'll be nicer than she ever was."

He pulled a box of fittings from under the bench and set it in front of Mistress Willadeen.

"These brass hinges will suit her best," John told her. "Shipped up from Boston. Which do you like?"

Mistress Willadeen fluttered her eyes. "Oh, they're all so lovely. I can't decide. What do you think?"

John selected a pair of polished hinges. "This set. The rounded corners and curved sides will set off the grain. The polished brass will set off the walnut once I oil and polish it."

"Ooh, that sounds grand. You're so clever and insightful."

John shuffled his feet and had the good grace to look embarrassed.

"Kind of you to say so, ma'am."

"A man as clever as you, I'm surprised no woman has snapped you up!"

John grinned. "Well, I won't deny there's women who fancy me. But I'm not ready to join up with just one."

He smiled at Mistress Willadeen and she felt fifteen years younger. And ten years more naive.

She shook her head. "I'm surprised Ellaree hasn't paid attention to you. She's certainly worth settling for."

"Humph. Ellaree is as stuck-up as a wall panel." John gestured to a carving on his bench. "This panel is the last one for the new courthouse. I'll use four-penny nails and my best hide glue and it still won't be as stuck-up as Ellaree."

Mistress Willadeen grimaced. She wouldn't be able to convince John to speak with Ellaree, let alone court her.

"I see. Well, when will my box be ready?"

"Take a couple days. Got to finish the carving first, then she'll want a day to dry between fresh oil and waxing. You won't know this box when I give her back to you."

Mother Nona's morning wasn't going any better. After traipsing through town three times, she just happened to visit the bakery at the same time as Ellaree.

Ellaree nodded to Mother Nona as the older woman strode through the door, then returned her attention to the baker. "I'd like two of the breakfast buns and a loaf of bread, if it's fresh."

Mother Nona stepped next to her and asked, "Sharing breakfast with some young feller?"

"The finest man in town," Ellaree replied. "My father."

"Fine man," Mother Nona agreed. "A bit older'n I'd 'pect you to be courting. Ain't there a young man you'd like to share breakfast with?"

"Hardly. None worth speaking to, or speaking of."

"No? I hear John Sawyer is well thought of—"

Ellaree snorted at the suggestion. "Not just well thought of. Well handled. I never buy day-old bread, and I certainly don't court secondhand goods. Good day, mother."

She flounced out of the bakery in a swirl of skirts and petticoats. The baker watched her sway out the door, then acknowledged Mother Nona's unsubtle glare.

He cleared his throat and shuffled his feet. "And you, mother, what would you like?"

"You got some day-old bread? Something dry and crusty will suit me just fine."

****

Mistress Willadeen and Mother Nona never met on Saturdays. Therefore, the morning after her meeting with Ellaree, Mother Nona had a pot of hot tea waiting when Mistress Willadeen arrived.

Mistress Willadeen scowled at the red earthenware teapot. It was from Georgia, given to Mother Nona in payment for making sure a heifer was properly freshened.

"You did no better than I," Mistress Willadeen observed.

Mother Nona shrugged. "Couldn't hardly do worse, could I?"

They sat down and studied their teacups.

"Headstrong fools!" they said together.

They stared at the crosses in Mother Nona's drawn-thread tablecloth.

Mistress Willadeen spoke first. "He'd want her if he couldn't get her."

Mother Nona nodded. "If he were above her, she'd be a'courtin' him."

"He is too good for her. And she's too good for him."

"Shame they don't know it."

Again, their heads met over the teacups and the tea grew cold.

On Monday, Mistress Willadeen revisited John Sawyer's shop.

"Is my jewelry box ready?" she called sweetly as she wended her way between scraps of lumber.

John pulled a box from under the counter and placed it before her. She gasped and clutched her shawl. It had been years since the wood glowed like that--so rich and warm.

She couldn't help but smile at the box. "It's beautiful!"

John's grin was almost as broad as Mistress Willadeen's. A craftsman loves to have his work admired. "Just brought out the beauty in the wood. Your chest is a fine bit of work." He pulled his eyes back to her face. "But wood needs wax and oil, not just dusting."

She traced the new hinges with a delicate fingertip. "I love how you placed them to reflect the grain. These are the perfect hinges. This is the finest jewelry box in the village. Not even Ellaree has a box this beautiful."

"Hmph. Ellaree bought her box from a peddler. Been here twice for fixing. The day I don't craft better than that is the day after I died."

"Really? She says there's no man in town who can build such a fine box as hers. Came all the way from New York."

"Didn't come from no master joiner. Ellaree doesn't know good work when she trips over it. Not when she's fooled by bits of gingerbread glued over sloppy joints."

John held up the carved panel for the new courthouse wall. "This ain't my best, but it's quality work." The panel showed a handsome man striding along a river with a sheaf of grain in his arms and a musket slung over his shoulders. "A master craftsman knows that the wood is as important as the carving. See, I used the straight wood grain for flowing water, and the wild grain over here for a tree's leaves."

"Oh, my, that is exquisite. You can almost see the leaves flutter in the breeze. It's a shame Ellaree has never had anyone explain quality to her."

She left John studying a stack of scrap cherry and maple. No piece was large enough for a panel or cabinet, but with some clever joinery they would make a fine little jewelry box.

Mother Nona was leaving the bakery, clutching the last of the breakfast buns, when Ellaree arrived.

"Still courting your father?" Mother Nona asked.

Ellaree nodded. "Still the best man in town. My father's not fickle, so long as I bring him a fresh bun every day for his breakfast."

"Shame he'll get no bun today. I'm feeding an old friend and just bought the last two."

Ellaree's face fell. "Oh, dear. My father looks forward to his breakfast bun. I'll pay double what you paid for them if You'll sell them to me."

Mother Nona frowned. "I had other plans, but I reckon he can make do with white bread and peach preserves." She wiggled her eyebrow in a way a woman her age shouldn't. "Still, I'll not deprive your father. It don't matter who gets a bun first, what matters is who gets it last."

"I suppose..." Ellaree dug into her reticule and exchanged coins for the bag. Mother Nona smiled at her back as Ellaree meandered down the street, lost in thought.

It was a shame that the baker's last two buns sat on his shelf until they were stale. The birds enjoyed them.

****

A day later, Mistress Willadeen rose early to the sound of courting birds. She looked at her teapot and decided today would be a two-cup day.

Mother Nona arrived a few minutes later.

"'specting someone?" she asked as Mistress Willadeen poured two cups of tea and set the pot on a lace doily.

"Perhaps," Mistress Willadeen smiled demurely. She believed it never hurt to pretend to more knowledge than you have.

"I put a bug into Ellaree's ear yesterday," Mother Nona grinned into her teacup. "She needs another nudge."

Mistress Willadeen set her jewelry box on the table. "I predict John Sawyer is making a nicer box than this."

"Gong to be a fine box. Yours is nigh perfect."

"But Ellaree's will be grander. John does fine work."

The tea did not get cold this time. Before the sun was high Mother Nona left with a plan. She strode through town, then hobbled into John Sawyer's shop, shuffling her feet through the wood shavings and leaning heavily on her cane.

"I'm needing a new cane," Mother Nona called. "Can you make one?"

John set down a roll of silver wire and stood up from the small box he was working on. "I can make you the finest cane in the village. Let me see your hand."

She looped her cane over her left elbow and held out her right hand, shaking ever so slightly.

"You got a big, strong hand," John said. "You won't need a fancy grip, but it needs to fit right." He measured her palm, index finger and thumb, then he examined her cane.

"That hook handle ain't bad, but it's too small for your hand. You'll get cramps if you walk very far."

She nodded. She'd never walked far enough with the cane to get a cramp, but it could happen.

"Do you do good work?" Mother Nona waved her cane to point around the woodshop. "Show me something you made."

John stepped to his bench and picked up the box. Dark cherry framed light maple panels. The joints were highlighted with sliver wire. Even rough and unpolished it was gorgeous.

"Does this suit?"

"Well, That's certainly fine work. Any girl in the village would marry you for that box. That is, any girl except Ellaree. She's got her sights set higher. How much for my new cane?"

They haggled for several minutes and Mother Nona hobbled out of his shop. As soon as she turned the corner she looped her cane onto her elbow and strode home, head high and footsteps firm.

****

It is only proper for two women to chat when they meet by chance. Mistress Willadeen visited every shop in the village twice before she encountered Ellaree.

"That's a lovely brooch," she told Ellaree, admiring a distinctly plain cameo.

"This?" Ellaree replied. "It's just an everyday bauble. I keep the nice ones in my jewelry box. For Sundays, you know."

"They must be lovely. Speaking of jewelry boxes, I hear John Sawyer is making a fancy jewelry box."

"He can make what he will. I won't be buying it."

"Oh, he's not selling this one. He says he'll give it to the most beautiful girl in the village. It's a shame I won't get it. I'd love a new jewelry box. He's found a special stain for the cherry That's as deep a red as your hair."

"Humph. I don't care how much it looks like me. I'm still not interested in John's wares. Let him give it to the least beautiful girl in the village, for all I care."

"So, you think even I have a chance?" Mistress Willadeen asked, arching her eyebrows.

Ellaree gasped and lowered her eyes. "Oh, no Mistress, I didn't mean that. Drat that man. He causes trouble, even when he's not about!"

"No offense taken, Ellaree. When you get a spare moment, you might stop by his shop to look at the box. It's worth a gander." She turned on her heel. "Farewell," she called over her shoulder.

Mistress Willadeen sauntered down the street with more sway to her hips than she needed, while Ellaree wondered who would receive the box. She knew she was the most beautiful girl in town, but John would never give her a gift.

Ellaree did not visit John Sawyer's shop that afternoon. That evening, when John was known to be at the saloon, she just happened to walk by his shop. She peered through the wavy crown-glass pane in his door and admired the box sitting prominently on his front bench.

It would look lovely in her bedroom.

Next morning, Mother Nona bet the blacksmith's apprentice that he couldn't budge the ferrule on her new cane. That afternoon, she visited John's woodshop.

"Ferrule's come loose," she announced, dropping the cane on his counter. "This what you call quality work?"

He dropped his tools and grabbed the cane, sighting down the length and tapping the loose ferrule.

"I swear... Pardon ma'am. I..." John studied the cane closely. "I'll fix her right now. Never should have come loose. Shouldn't even be able to come loose. I'll put glue on the threads. This ferrule won't come loose again."

While he busied himself with clamps and hot hide glue, Mother Nona hummed tunelessly and admired how tightly the planks in his simple counter were joined.

"I hear Ellaree's got a new suitor," she offered, as he painted glue onto the ferrule's threads. "Some sort of English lord."

"Huh? Some dandy in a silk hat, swinging a cane he don't need?"

Mother Nona leaned onto the counter and shifted her feet. This sounded like a good description of the man She'd just made up. "Yes, just like that. Have you met him?"

Of course, he hadn't.

"Never seen him, but I know the type. Met a bunch like that when I apprenticed in Boston. I'm not surprised at Ellaree falling for some fancy foreign fool instead of a solid American man."

Mother Nona nodded in sympathy. "You're right. But, there's something "bout them British lords. They's educated and cultured. Not like our local boys."

"Educated and cultured! As if spoutin' Greek and Latin makes a man any better. On a cold day in January you want a man to swing an ax and build a fire. Not some dandy who says "caw't' instead of "cain't.""

"Might be something to what you say. That Ellaree, what with bei' schooled up to Philadelphia, she 'spects to marry better than some dirt farmer." She watched him loosen the clamp holding her cane. "You finished my cane yet?"

"Just now. You try this. The day that ferrule comes loose is the day I'll be best man for Ellaree's foreign feller."

"I'll tell 'er you're willin'. I sees her most mornings at the bakery when she's getting' breakfast buns for her special man."

She hobbled out of John's shop, trying to remember which foot she favored last time she visited.

While Mother Nona spoke with John, Mistress Willadeen walked through town visiting every shop. At each stop, she dawdled for a few minutes with questions, then moved on to the next.

She finally found Ellaree in the milliner's shop. Ellaree had a half dozen rolls of ribbon spread across the counter. As Mistress Willadeen entered, Ellaree picked up two rolls, compared them, set them back on the counter and picked up two others.

The clerk stepped away from Ellaree with a look of relief on his face. "Can I help you, Mistress?" he asked.

"Do you have any royal blue twisted silk thread?"

"I'll have to run in back to check."

"If you don't have royal, look to see what you've got in navy."

The clerk trotted away, into shelves. Mistress Willadeen waited until she heard him rummaging through boxes. Then she nodded to Ellaree and pointed to the ribbon Ellaree had been studying when she arrived.

"That one is my favorite. The red sets off your hair."

Ellaree picked up the ribbon She'd discarded and pulled a strand of hair to hold against it.

"Honestly? It's awfully blatant."

"Perhaps, but it catches the eye. You young girls should show off your pretty hair. I hear John is intending to give his jewelry box to Mary Callan. She has lovely hair."

"That primping hussy? Her hair comes from a bottle of henna and her complexion is mostly powder."

"I've heard that. But she is friendly."

"Very friendly. How many times has she bought your Moon Potion this year? I certainly understand what John sees in her."

Ellaree left the milline's shop in a flurry of skirts, leaving all the ribbons on the counter.

The clerk came back as the door slammed shut.

"I'm sorry, Mistress. We don't have any blue silk. I've got some nice blue stranded cotton that might do." He spread a handful of spools on the counter.

"Thank you, but I really need silk for this." She smiled at him and sailed out of the store.

****

The next morning John decided to have a fresh-baked bun for breakfast. By accident, he arrived at the bakery while Ellaree was buying buns.

"Mornin', Miss," he doffed his tricorne hat. "Lovely day, ain-- isn't it?"

She glanced past his shoulder, out the door. "It does appear to be pleasant. I hear you're making a chest."

"Ayuh, a lady's jewelry box. I had some wood scraps to use up."

"I'm sure someone will appreciate it." She picked up her sack.

"Enjoy your breakfast, ma'am," John offered. He held the door as she swept past him.

"We always do. The buns are delicious."

He watched her trim waist and swaying hips as she sashayed through the door. After she left, he turned to the baker and asked for a bun.

Behind his back, Ellaree squinted at him as the door closed. He had such broad shoulders and such narrow hips.

****

Five days, five breakfasts and five discussions of the weather later, Mother Nona and Mistress Willadeen were too frustrated to drink their tea.

"Don't those two know how to court?" Mistress Willadeen glared at the tea.

"Don't appear they do. They's too used to being courted. We got to turn them around by hand, like I did Si Bellow's foal."

Mistress Willadeen nodded. She attended to human births, not foals and calves, but a breech-birth was a breech-birth, regardless. If you didn't turn the infant, you'd lose both mother and baby. It was something you didn't try unless it was necessary, but best done early.

You only got one chance to make it right.

She glanced into her teacup. She'd already decided what She'd see in it.

"You took John last," she told Mother Nona, "this is my turn."

"Ellaree's at the bakery when the buns come out of the oven. You "tend to John at eight. Keep him busy while I learn her some courtship."

The sun was just over the trees, bright and cheery when Mistress Willadeen promenaded into John's woodshop. His tools were all racked and he was reaching for his hat when she called his name.

"John, I brought you some of my home-made breakfast buns to thank you for fixin" my jewelry box. They're best now, when they're hot."

She set a sweet reed basket on his bench and slid away a gingham cloth with tiny hearts embroidered in the squares. Steam rose into the air and the scent of cinnamon and cloves joined the pine and sweet cherry perfuming his woodshop.

"I was just heading for breakfast." His hand stayed on his hat as he glanced at the door and then smelled the fresh buns. "It's wicked fine of you to bring me some."

He left his hat on the hook.

Mistress Willadeen smiled at him and lowered her eyes. "I know a hard-working man has a big appetite, so I made plenty for you. I do hope it's enough."

John examined the basket. Three buns the size of his fist, dark with brown sugar, cinnamon and raisins begged for his attention.

"I calculate three is more than I could eat. Maybe you'd share one with me?"

"Thank you, kind sir. It makes a woman feel special when a man offers her a gift. Even a proud lady like Ellaree thinks kindly on the men that give her pretty little things."

She glanced at the jewelry box sitting on the bench.

The bakery was empty when Mother Nona arrived. She glanced about and asked the baker how he made his bread, where he got the yeast, how long he kept the starter, how to tell good flour, until his patience was worn thin.

"Look, would you like something, or are you just here to pester me?" he finally snapped at her.

"Well. I was intending to get one of your buns, but I can't decide "twixt the bun and the cinnamon bread-- Oh lookee, here's Ellaree. You take care of her while I make up my mind."

Ellaree stepped around Mother Nona and asked for two buns. While the baker was putting them in a bag, Mother Nona called. "Long as you're there, put one in a sack for me."

He handed the sacks to the two ladies, who handed him coins and left the bakery together.

Mother Nona nodded back to the door as it closed behind them. "You certainly know how to charm that baker."

"I do? I wasn't trying."

"Oh, yes. You flutter them long lashes and smile them dimples and you make a man pay 'tention to you. You want to tie a kerchief around your waist. Show off how slender it is. Menfolk like that in a girl." She linked an arm with Ellaree and took a step, forcing Ellaree to walk with her or be rude. "An" ask him questions about his work. Man loves to talk "bout what he knows best."

"If I ever need to please a man, I'll remember that," Ellaree glanced towards the woodworking shop.

"You do that." Mother Nona released the girl's arm, turned down a dirt trail and waved good-bye. "You just do that."

The next morning, John met Ellaree at the bakery. He had a wooden bookmark for her in his pocket. She thanked him with a dozen eye flutters and asked how He'd made such a fine piece of work.

When Mistress Willadeen and Mother Nona heard this gossip from the baker's niece they heaved a sigh of relief.

****

One cloudy afternoon, after two weeks of Mistress Willadeen tutoring John in the art of courtship and Mother Nona explaining men to Ellaree, there was a quiet knock at Mistress Willadeen's back door. This door was hidden by bushes, far from prying eyes. This door was most used by folks needing special favors from Mistress Willadeen.

"Why, Ellaree," Mistress Willadeen greeted her. "What a pleasant surprise. What brings you to visit me?"

"I need a potion."

Mistress Willadeen raised her eyebrows and Ellaree stuttered, "No, not that potion. I need something for love."

It wasn't the first time the Mistress Willadeen heard that plea. It wouldn't be the last. Every girl in the village visited her for a love charm at least once.

Ellaree never needed help. Except this time. Ellaree wasn't getting what she wanted, and she wasn't used to that. It was hard not to smile, so Mistress Willadeen frowned as she spoke.

"I've got to tell you, they don't always work. And more, calling a man's heart exacts a price on you."

"I don't care. What does it cost?"

"It will cost you a piece of your heart. Calling love works both ways. Making him want you will make you want him as well. Choose wisely. The man you ensnare will own a piece of you."

"I'll take the chance. I don't believe any man can own me."

"Then, here is what you must do..."

Mother Nona strode to the center of town, paused to grasp her cane firmly and hobbled into John Sawyer's shop. John was frowning at the most beautiful jewelry box She'd ever seen.

"Come to tell you that the ferrule ain"t come loose. I'll let folks know you do good work."

"Much obliged, ma'am. I take pride in my work." He glared at the box again and set it on the counter between them.

He stared over her shoulder at the wall behind her, then at the bench between them. "Mother, I..." He paused, took a breath and words rushed out. "I'm a solid, church going man and I don't believe tales I hear, and no offense intended, but..."

He studied his hands, wrapped around the box, avoiding Mother Nona's eyes. The box glowed in the afternoon sun, deep red cherry with bright silver inlay.

He took another breath. "This box. She needs more than simple oil and stain to finish her."

Mother Nona ran a finger along the edge. Smooth as silk. So smooth it felt soft under her fingers. "What's it got to hold, that it needs more than your skill gives it?"

"It should hold love." He looked over her shoulder, toward Ellaree's home.

"Eub in oil of rosemary. Wax it with fresh beeswax, still sweet with the scent of honey. Finally, polish it with lavender."

"Just rosemary, beeswax and lavender?"

"Do this under the light of a full moon, while you chant the name of the woman you want. Let me tell you. it ain't safe. You're putting yourself into the box. You give her that box and You'll give her a part of yourself."

John smiled. "I can spare a bit of me for all of her."

Two long weeks later, the moon rose bright and full.

An hour before midnight John was polishing the box and chanting the name of the woman He'd come to love.

At the other edge of the village, Ellaree crept from her father's home and snuck into the fields. For two hours she followe' the moon, first east, then south.

Finally, she found the grove with the fairy ring in it, just like She'd been told. Of course, this time of year, most fields had a fairy ring or two in them. But this one felt like the one she needed.

She shed her dress and petticoats at the edge of the clearing and stepped barefoot across the cold, dewy grass. She gasped when a toad hopped over her right foot as she stepped. She crouched, found the sage bush it had hopped from, and extracted three leaves from the top.

Three steps later, a snake slithered across her left foot. She crouched and gathered three strawberries she found buried under the leaves.

Another three steps, and a partridge exploded from underfoot, brushed against her and was gone, leaving three feathers fluttering against her chest. She plucked the three feathers from the air before they touched the ground and stepped to the edge of the fairy ring--nine gleaming white mushrooms in circle.

She laid a sage leaf on the first mushroom.

"A gift from me, a gift for you. Unasked, not owed. Please let me through."

She laid a strawberry on the second mushroom.

"A fruit to eat, a fruit so sweet. Freely given. Pass my feet."

On the third mushroom, she placed a bird feather.

"T'was given to me, now given to you. From one to next to pass me through."

A cloud covered the moon and a sudden breeze lifted the leaf and feather. They swirled into the air and were gone.

She glanced at her feet. The strawberry was gone, as well.

She stepped over the three mushrooms she had gifted and into the ring, facing the other six mushrooms.

"Three I gift, and six are mine. Grant my wish, and they'll be thine."

The moon reappeared.

She arched her back, letting her hair fall loose to her thighs. It glowed in the moonlight like silver netting. She spread her arms and stared at the moon.

"John," she called. "Give me John Sawyer."

A shooting star crossed the moon, pointing back to the village.

She placed the remaining sage leaves, strawberries and feathers on the other six mushrooms, walked across the chilly spring glade, gathered her damp clothes, dressed quickly and followed the shooting star home.

"I don't rightly believe in this," she whispered to herself. "It's just something girls do."

Early the next morning, John tapped gently on a cabin door.

"John, what a surprise." Loose hair fell about slender shoulders. In his eagerness, He'd arrived earlier than he should have.

"I... I brought you this box," he stuttered, holding his eyes above those white shoulders. "It's a gift."

"For me? I thought... I mean, it's lovely."

He handed her the box. It seemed to leap into her hands as she caressed it, marveling at the carving and inlay.

"It's beautiful. I shall treasure it."

"That's my hope, ma'am."

She stroked a finger across the lid.

"I got a bigger roast than I need. Come to dinner. Please."

"I can do that. Shame if good beef should go to waste."

He bowed himself away to prepare for the meal. He bought a brand new white shirt. Not a local homespun shirt. This came all the way from the new mills in Lowell, Massachusetts. Then he polished his black leather belt, took a dip in the river and finally rubbed himself dry with pine boughs and sage stalks.

That evening he was fed, entertained, enraptured and captured. He left with a smile on his face and a heart in his pocket.

Next morning, the preacher read the banns for Mistress Willadeen and Master John Sawyer.

A man old enough to be a master in his field is old enough to know the difference between a schoolgirl and a grown woman.

Miss Ellaree didn't hear the news. She was sick abed with the ague.

This happens to girls who go traipsing about cold dewy fields, stark naked, in their bare feet. By the time she recovered, all the single men in town had paired off with healthy young women with apple-red cheeks.

Mother Nona followed few rules, but one was that you don't meddle unless you intend to fix what you broke. The same week Ellaree left her bed, Mother Nona took in a boarder: a young man who walked with a cane, but had no limp. Rumor said he was son of an English lord.

Loving Mellifluous
Ian Dixon

Part One: Falling

I lay beside her, a privileged part of her. No girl I knew before her seemed quite so perfect as Melissa, as if this was her preferred or known state of being. I could almost see into her   as I felt her muscles, fatty deposits, her breath and breathlessness, the purity inside her lungs. I was closer to her in that moment than ever to any woman again. With Melissa, I was breathing again. Although I was part of this experience, it was the spirit of her that engulfed us: smelling so salty and milky, so very much of love. She was nineteen. I was twenty-two.

Melissa was like a confluence of anything human and liquid. She had already given birth to a baby boy – another man's child. I couldn't care less that this equation didn't fit with my past experience of what proper turn-ons were supposed to be: those crimplene girlfriends for whom affection wooed affection in return, the heady smell of their perfectly combed locks, the freckles, the bands of ribbon in decent hair, the way they stared out on the world, the flicker of perfect non-recognition with the decency to ignore any evidence of my being slightly odd. Melissa was not one of these: Melissa was a tidal wave. And I soaked her up like a needy animal.

Right then, just moments before I fell completely and utterly in love, she was everything—that oblique cupid's smile just an instant away on precious lips. Our few months together suddenly exploded like an epiphany between us: how right we were for each other, how a spell had descended within me. On that night, the night I first loved her completely, there were fluids I'd never known. Tears hung from her nose and mingled with salty snot, a pastel-green hankie soaked in eucalyptus oil, tied about her neck.

What a fetish this simple knot created. I pushed my palms up against her, feeling so privileged to draw this close to this thing of beauty. Another sniff as she softly cried. My mouth agape, my cupped hands sluicing sweat from her nymphet arms. Like glass, she was liquid with only the appearance of something solid.

She blew her nose and spat in a tissue, a quick "hang on" turfed my way. God, how I loved her for that ease: the only woman to tell me that I postured rather than loved—and who cured me of it. But not in this moment. She had emancipated this moment.

She had trained me in the art of surrender and when she tossed that snotty tissue aside, she returned to me. This, in all my years of subsequent adventures (of happily running away, from the thing I treasured most), was the only woman who could make a momentary pause, a complete shift in attention into an erotic moment by default, then gear-change and take the next left into a smile, a gasp, a mellifluous trance. For behind her tough working-class façade was a heart in gentle giving.

We drew breath in undiscovered places. Places rich with adventure. Places in the sun. Her breath was wet and smelled of eucalyptus and rose. She was liquid. I was aghast, fascinated. And my heart, for the first time in my life, opened. All her pools of flowing succulence flowed on and I was filled with her – in love. This was like a dream but powered by the tactile fact of her.

Love came with such ferocity, I barely recognised it. On what basis was I supposed to recognise something so alien? And yet, here I was in love: divine mystery, dwelling confusion, the questioning. When we kissed, she took my soul inside her.

God is the only concept as implosive and fathomless as love.

****

King William Street, Adelaide, early morning. We sank in the bucket seats of my stuttering Volkswagen, this ideal car, the only thing that was truly mine, except for Melissa—though I could not bring myself to own her yet. We relaxed as we swept around Victoria Square while the fountain turned like a calliope. The brolgas and swans of that seventies fountain strained against the taught muscles of indigenous men, snap—frozen in the granite, who would hold these escaping birds back from flight. The yellowy light was caught in droplets of the water. A few stragglers alighted from the last Glenelg tram.

When I was a boy, this park was full with Aboriginal people—until the Hilton hotel was built and the cops moved them all on—the free-settler tradition enshrined in this quaint diamond of grass.

The setting ochre moonlight dazzled as it spilled out in subtle refractions: the undrinkable water was said to be connected to the mystery of Adelaide—a mystery, which when flipped over, revealed a creature of a thousand legs, wriggling ineptly

on its back. Yet, outside the blinkered vision of the average Adelaidian, lay a gem so beautiful they need not name it to own it, to bask in its beams, the nightmare somehow seductive, the spell unbroken. Colonel Light's unwavering vision—from his pigeon-crapped statue up on Montefiore Hill, the dark clay disguising our founding father's unmentionable Malaysian colour? Like all the secrets of the past, Adelaide was slowly slipping by and rejecting me. Or rather, I rejected it, revving up for a clean break interstate. But, as yet still in the grasp of good ol' Adders, I found myself sinking wholesomely into this little city's fractured folds, drawing sustenance from her widened streets and ill-fitting manners, the coerciveness of her, the sin, the sheer purblind delight. There was healing here, if only we could find it.

The morning traffic parked itself around the back-lanes of the inner-city. Melissa rented the only house in Adelaide that could legitimately be called "inner-city".

Adelaide was its own disappointment; pumped up on the grape of its self-importance, clinging stoically and artily to the clay of its foundations. Some said it had been an ancient, Aboriginal burial ground and was rightly haunted because of this. Some said a sexual force, which rose from the earth, had preyed upon the eccentric Englishmen who, having escaped their transgressions under British law, settled here and evoked their perversions anew.

Adelaide—her sleepy charm and clean, wide streets beckoned lazily from her lost position on the Gulf. She gave us Mother's milk and smelled of lived-in houses with grand backyards and I had nestled in the comfort of her, my eyelids dragging downward, like all the shy, lost boys of Adelaide, with pleading eyes, insipid in the extreme and bridled with an abated sense of lust. "Give up," She'd cry, "don't run, stay here, where life is easy".

****

To be honest, I don't remember meeting Melissa—she was just there in my share-house as if she had always been there. At that stage, she was four months pregnant with her first child. I blustered though the double glass doors into the loungeroom en-route to the dining room with shopping in cellophane-plastic bags, disgruntled and hating all unexpected things in my way. But one of those unexpected things was

Melissa and she struck me like an axe to the head: unnoticed to all but the deeper sensitivities, those little chimes so easily ignored. There she was on the couch, pink and pregnant, mini-skirted and smiling.

It seems so ordinary, but something uncanny underpinned our meeting in this wood-darkened loungeroom in the centre of this share-house in leafy Wayville—something elusive and slippery. I was in motion, she was ever so still, and she laughed. I grimaced (covering). She sat with the ever fey, ever smiling, "lost princess" Wendy on our old couch, which smelled of stuffing and musty rosaries. My heart doubled its timpani beat and, can you believe, I hid from her. Well maybe this was the thing love and anxiety had in common. Even before she was my "everything", a little bell inside me went "ping". You'd like me to say it was her obvious sexual presence, her slender legs, her Sunday-market smell, the fecundity of her little egg-belly bearing child? Well it was all of these and none. She was quite simply arresting in her sweet beauty: a beauty made for me it seemed, perhaps before I was ripe enough to know. But she was min-to-be and though I despised the thought of possessive love, I had to admit, even for an instant, that I might have been wrong.

Maybe That's why I could not overcome the arrest of her. She was tripping up my preconceptions and stepping into my heart even then. Did she feel the same? My head was not staying for an answer. I tore myself away and stepped through into the dining room, shopping bags cutting into my fingers, and paused out of sight, pondering.

Next moment, Wendy bustled into the dining room, where I stood in the afternoon haze, dust motes floating about like little evils in mirth. She smirked at me, then swanned away announcing that Melissa preferred sensitive men.

Alone again, I risked another peep, leaning back on my heel, I peered through the double doors. I saw the prismatic shock of Melissa, broken up in the deco glass design—all eyes and wonder. She watched TV, but moved as if called from an Elvin world. Aware I was watching, she eased a little taller, smiled an increment more, her face in shards like a streamlined Picasso, a mauve phase of fractured loveliness. And then I realised this was her word: she was quite simply lovely, so very lovely. And I sighed. And somehow, over the drone of the television, she tuned in and turned. She faced me. Our eyes, as if under guidance, quelled amidst all wrong and watched each other a moment, in unaccustomed ease. The rainbows about her face arranged in neat lines, the kidne-pie era of my grandmother, the tocking of a clock somewhere about my soul. Her violet eyelashes, her pale blue eyes. And somewhere deep in that gaze, a soul that ticked in unison, a hurt, a pain, a need to unite. An announcement crept inside me. Note to self: this is she (under a fog of denial). Living water held up to the disappointment of my life. She was an elfin child, all ice-cream and silliness. I was a thunderous snake on bird feet. But there would always be those eyes.

Then Wendy crashed back through the banana leaves and hoity-tottered past me humming out her mocking objection. I heard the twitters of swallows rifling about the sky. I fought for my perception, as if I wanted to hear Melissa's breath from the next room and over the television. Then, as Wendy resettled on the couch, I heard them laugh. It's supposed to hurt just enough (I knew this game), but it did not. Not yet. There was delicacy poised on expectancy within me. Why would heart moments with Melissa always feel so ripe? I stepped away from the adjoining glass door and in my mind, I stepped right back in and embraced this perfect she. But in my reality, I could not cope with the blood-flow, so I retired with shopping bags to the kitchen.

Yet, there was another side to Melissa. A side my adoring gaze could not capture or predict.

In a trice, Melissa marched into the kitchen from the loungeroom, grabbed a banana from my shopping bag, which curiously fouled my mood again—shattering like glass inside me. She peeled the banana as if breaking the enemy's backbone and told me: "Just calm down, will ya, Andy?"

How did she know my name? This laughing, pregnant girl pointed out the more ludicrous aspects of my face and didn't give a shit when I stormed away. She laughed some more between banana-stickied teeth as she tossed out chunks of shopping onto the floor. I was shocked: foolish despite myself. Didn't she know there were rules? This was my share-house, dammit and I wasn't gonna take this lightly even if she was pregnant. But somehow her voice sounded familiar. This ritual of teasing. I knew it like I knew her. There seemed a witch's past in this, our meeting. Never had I felt a voice as mellifluous, as pugnacious as Melissa's, descend inside me. Her off-the-cuff words were resonating inside my chest, my diaphragm, which quivered with faint I love yous that I hadn't even thought yet, let alone said. I turned back to her, half losing my motivation, like a dream of being on the stage, fudging through poorly learned lines. I felt the sun stream in and strike my face. It seemed she didn't care to see me then. But I knew she was deeper than the game she played. Despite her intoxicating mirth, there was hurt in her. She was staving off a darkness She'd been thrust upon—a child undermined.

I drew a breath co-mingling dust and incense concealed somewhere about the house by some secretive flatmate. This scungy house was idyllic now and so, in that moment, was Melissa's skinny bottom. Her mini-skirt hitched up, her independent legs poised in a battle-stance ready for another attack on my shopping bag. She was an intruder here, but seemed as much at home as anywhere. Her breasts rubbed against those cellophane bags and sent a gentle crackle about the room, competing with the strains of violent pun-opera, which now blared out from Wendy's stereo, making it pale in comparison—like a migraine.

I felt my head tilt to one side to take her in, a quizzical dog whose brain had rolled to the left. Melissa was now putting away my shopping. Girls shouldn't do this, I thought. She wore burgundy that day, her smirking lipstick set to match, her red hair slightly clashing, her nose ring sparkling in the sun. The weeds that grew up onto our kitchen windows reached out to her limply, as I guess, in my own way, I was doing also.

****

The very next morning, early, I emerged from my own room. I saw her again. The light was frosted. The pad, pad of her feet on wooden floorboards. Slender legs propped up her nightie. Red hair tousled. Countless whispers in my head, fell silent.

Her weeny fists in eyes of morning wakelessness, were rubbing through the din of silence. A toilet flush. Silence. A steamy breeze. Melissa's puckered baby face. A little bud of pregnancy off-centring her. The "egg on legs" they called her: innocence.

****

I didn't know what this image was telling me, but I grew to deeply like her. I watched her. I began to laugh with her. When her child was due, I visited her in hospital and told her she was brave, knowing that I was not. I gazed at her and she, uncomfortably, even shyly gazed back a moment.

I cannot tell you why Melissa took the form she did. She was simply beautiful, a thing of marshmallow smiles and gawky, cherubic grace—despite her rough manners. She was intuitive where I was cerebral; brimming with life, where I was driven by will. And despite her being born into a family of takers, she had a natural moral compass, which saw her through rocky terrain with a beatific smile. I waited until her baby Julian was born. Three months after the birth, I snuck up to her and explained that I couldn't get her out of my head.

North Adelaid's overhung trees and nineteenth century bluestone homes formed a soporific quaintness. Friends were all heading out for a picnic in the sun, but I was struck with a gentle turbulence, a private longing for Melissa.

She was changing the baby in an en-suite bathroom, so I offered help. Sunshine slapped against the tiled walls. There was scent of rosy soap and the ever-present purple and green of Melissa, her Mona Lisa smile about her, her charming insecurity. I helped her with the baby and felt touched. I held his little cloth nappy together and eased the safety pin from her lips. A tiny "cluck" of release between her teeth. This simple ritual seemed to sit so perfectly in both our futures—just two Adelaide refugees finding rightness in each other and a third. Or so I hoped. The baby mewled and gazed like a Buddha, chubby hands seeking his tummy for comfort. A child smelling of sandwiches and teacups whose future was told in the leaves. And in this moment, my perfect love and I teased each other with little glances in the toothpaste splattered mirror. She batted away my appreciation with a scullery maid's wave. In the mirror, I looked to her as a concrete block descended inside me. I pleaded for this curse of bad to quell.

Voices called from downstairs. We had a picnic to attend. Then I blurted out: "I can't seem to... get you out of my head."

Her response? She smiled and ducked her head, but she offered no confirming glance. Her eyes flitted like daisies and fell inside her. Was there something I had missed? She was the tiniest morsel of sad, disowned inside. She rested a calming hand on her child's tummy and offered me a non-committal: "Well..." She hoicked her child up on her shoulder and said: "You're just kidding yourself, right?"

My jaw snicked shut. The traffic outside grew audible just then. The bar fridge in the bedroom scuttered and gave up. She swung her baby back and forth, patting his bum. Her sweet nineteen-year-old face understood that hers would not be a blissful life: a trench filled with the vanity of others, she could trust only herself.

Though as I played and joked and fell about the park that afternoon, I was caught in the slipstream of Melissa. That eucalyptus soaked fetish-knot seemed never untied.

Her image kept calling me, enticing me further into her mystery.

****

We'd all been somewhere—out with friends, I think. And home to the crusty share house—the place we had met. Melissa wore burgundy again that night and she was her irrepressible fun-self (such fun we had) and with that, she replaced all the everything I didn't want to face.

I don't remember where We'd been, but the laughing, working-class, boisterousness of her, such convincing cover for her delicacy, had been there entertaining us all. But here we were— dropped off in the front yard as tittering friends parked the car or put on cups of tea upstairs. I could smell the mulch of this overgrown front yard. I could smell her, her powdered face, though she didn't need powdering, her skin was flawless. The sticky lipstick (violet to match her skirt), her nylon stockings hoicked up her skinny legs and boot-heels that made her even slimmer.

Now this is where you will think me a fool. This is where the confusion of your narrator takes on a complexity you will not like. For despite her loveliness, I was relatively cool. I seemed to have forgotten her inside me. I seemed to be sharing her with the world of ill-wisdom. And she stopped me here against the alcove of the stairway. She pulled me to her with her breath and uttered a gentle "hey?" It was "hey?" in that Adelaide way, which seemed both apology and promise fused. That "hey?" I would hear her utter for so many years, and it chimed like a bell inside me, so soothing, so very much her. "Hey?" she said, and I knew in that second, the thing was coming close, the bad, the thing I could not avoid and in my heart, in that moment, I was running. I kept thinking, "not this, not this", to questions and answers un-forewarned. The distant night-time traffic stuck to the roads. The plovers owning the night with their beautiful sounds etching in and echoing about. And my heart echoed to a tune it had not learnt to sing. Melissa drew me in and I was scared. She said, "Hey. Been thinkin' about your offer, and… you wanna know, I'm considering…" Considering what, I thought. But I knew as young men know when entrapment approaches, that she was wending her way into my softening heart. I stood there in the dark, hoping the shadows would obscure me. I was trying to hide from her, hoping that she might not see the fear (this unnamed fear would take me decades of life lessons to overcome). But now, I was free to just be with her and even in that I was drawn in, held in stasis, like an ambivalence dream; too mesmerised to leave, too terrified to set foot in a trap. I was awakening in some weird way – like a rope thrown to a mire I didn't know I was in. She said it: "Thinkin' about your offer…" But she was not thinking about the offer, she had accepted the offer and now was testing the me she wondered whether she could trust.

The smell of her white face. The ripple of cool in the breeze. The promise of Melissa – the beauty and honesty in her face and accent, drawing me in. Yet, I was fighting with an enemy neither one of us could face. Her fingers toyed about my waist, like a ghost-train ghoul, but comforting. How strange, I was in doubt, such doubt – the doubt I knew as a dull blade held to my life. But still she stayed, her back against the alcove. And me? Was I stepping into her? Indeed, I was, and this would be the first step in compulsion, wounding me like a witch's fantasy. And within the battle, the cool, the sound of night, the easing light of alcohol, I pressed myself against her and our lips came together – so simple, so rewarding, a step into the unknown. The feel of her feminine face, the rightness, the ease, the curling, simplicity, the taste of lipstick easing onto my mouth, her little tongue so sweet, as if we knew each other.

This ritual, performed by so many first-time lovers: the kiss of the love of your life, all but unrecognised behind an unknowable fear. And then, it ended, and I was confused again. I found myself looking down to the garden, smelling the trees and hearing the susurrus of those night-moving leaves and wondering. Like a child opened to the experience of adulthood and not knowing why. And only now do I know. That what had crept inside me as a boy was something so powerfully wrong at the hands of adults, that I would never again trust the beautiful simplicity of this perfect thing called innocence. I was destroyed at an early age and here in my prom-night reward, I was attacked by doubt and under doubt stood fear and under fear was a desire wakened in an infant's confusion. And this thing would take me, would send me down a path a thousand times blackened. I drew a blank at the rightness-meeting-wrongness under that stairway alcove. Was it the touch of my natural lover's hand? Was it the cool breath uttered that drew me inside and warmed my heart again? Was I some sociopath devoid of the means to know themselves? This horror, this dissociation whisked away, as always, at the feel of her linking arm as she guided me upstairs. We drifted upward, her mouth turned up at the sides. She seemed happy and that comforted me.

We sat for hours with our friends that night, laughing, drinking more and stepping out to the loo, playing guitars and discussing music and theatre and justifying our position on the world. Then it was time for bed and I relinquished the pull of my heart, assuming Melissa would drift off into Wendy's room, but she did not. She clung to my side, her confidence waning under her determination to have what she felt she might lose. I was too male to be flattered, too feminine to be proud.

We stepped sidelong into my tiny, sloping-wood room on the second floor, where the only window was a door to nowhere and the mottled glass announced a not too distant morning. There were candles, a mirrored reflection of pale light, a warm glow in the gathering gloom, a darkness threatening to consume the burgeoning morning. How did her boots come off? How did this baby-free body, so milky and perfect and oh-my-God gift-like, stretched out on the pink mattress on the floor, come to me? The universal student room with clothes strewn about and guitar propped in the corner. Her slender, shapely body rolling out on the ruffled sheet and we made love, a landslide between kiss and consummation.

Now this was Melissa, easing honesty by honesty into the essence I would come to love: her gentle voice, the insecurity behind the bravado. I wanted her as if I was falling down and falling into her. A litany of thankyous, the memory of childhood church services, the sense of floating ritual (whether earned or predetermined) was calling me. We sank in fascination. She was my rightful lover, not just another fumbling attempt. Despite the newness of it all, we were two people knowing of the other, knowing the smell of breathy sighs, the rightness.

The pale, mottled morning lightening the window, the occasional flicker of draft on the candlelight, the smell of polished floorboards and incense. The sheer gentle of it all in the least likely source, this guffawing, confident working-class girl: the real her, the sweet everything of her, the totem knot of colour in her heart and then the most wonderful initiation into the world of her. There was no child here now and I felt at home in a world, which ought to have been mine: the world of woman, of motherhood and my uncanny place within it.

We slept well into morning. Our eyes opened on a new reality: the new "us" in this time, in this share house and beyond. The disgruntlement of the world, the fear within, seemed far away and shining. We were at the open-face of possibility.

****

Part Two: Breaking

"Beach. Melissa?" I blurted out.

I sensed a barbarous jag in the salty air. I stroked a patch of my skin, my tawdry presence announcing my dismay, stiff-jawed as a 2D Hollywood hero. Melissa whined a bit and jammed her coiling body a ready about on the balcony floor. She grabbed her two-year old baby Julian, a bucket and spade, and pushed past me to the beach.

Somewhere there was disjunct in me. Somewhere there was something else, something betraying the rubbish-chamber of feelings inside. At times like these, I felt shame, a pure, groundless shame, which undermined all angers and loves and spat out memories of a babysitter, her generous breasts, her ample flesh.

And here I was on the beach now, stepping up behind the woman who might have been my wife, feeling things I could not face. All strangling the true gift of Melissa: stepping away on birdie legs, my stinging heart gasping for her. I felt the sparkle of Adelaide sunshine on flattening waves, the lap and drag of seawater, the pull of tide under happy splash-about families. And here was Julian; his curious need for fathering became a stone inside me. Melissa all white and smiley, but face turned away knowingly, her strains of reddened hair wisping about in an essence of supple aching joy. I was down to the ankles in love with her. But then another vision.

The sight of Melissa's skinny body on the beach. The freedom-clogged self-disgust of me. I ached for her, but I was already gone, her presence an anachronism. Her son a wanting part of lives and genes not my own. I etched my voice-print one final time in his ears and he slipped his sticky fingers in her hand and pulled her close. His wizened face a sailor's, knowing of waves and swells and stories locked inside his salty-apple mind, just as he knew, before we knew, that Melissa and I were breaking up. The beach was white and strewn with seaweed. His spade dipped at sorrowful angles in the sand, inept in his thumby little hand as patchy clouds blew eastward through the Rorschach afternoon sky. In the streaming white sun of South Australia, beyond our personal midnight, the ill-feeling was palpable.

Our parting hung like languorous flesh. I sneezed and with it came a curse of badness. I knew what I must say, like solid facts set in jelly. The grappling tide gently wore away resolve, for what did I have to offer as reason? I was simply running. Running for escape. That something deep inside me, that impasse, could see no other course of action. Certainly not staying and facing the problem. What, and end up ordinary and disgruntled to the fragile core? Sediment washed away at my feet. It was then I suggested we might be better off apart.

Then I fell silent, protest and loss smashing against each other. And in her eyes, those honest eyes, a thing so terrible: "But, you know me", they said, a washing-day of pain. She did not blink, just watered, a clock in time. The ironed world shifted, her eyes soft and hard and straining. I reached to her, she stepped away, mesmerised by the inevitability of it all. I reached. One hand fell limp at her side, the other retightening on Julian's. Laughter all about, the sunshine bleached like Kodachrome snapshots. I felt dry and old.

She already hated me. Her skin and eyes turned brown and cancerous despite her pale neediness. I don't remember the words I said, but we broke up right then and there. The Hero-Melissa came to her own rescue and that of her son. She scooped him up, his bucket of sand upturned on my feet, somehow burying me there. I shook it off and sloughed in her wake to the seaside square, a tight "getting away with it" smile at the corners of my mouth. Crank bolts churned inside me. She pined. I felt it as one does their partner's orgasm: her disappointment, her heart-break. The tinkering thoughts pleaded within our mutual mind and whispered: please, take me back. But even in her obvious pain, I could not.

I needed to breathe above the salt level. From the beach to Henley Square we made our awkward way amongst the half-turned tables of alfresco diners, half-consumed in wine-basted dreamy conversation. The smells of kalamata olives, zatziki, tiramasalata and well-cured meat. The languid hope of bread soaked in olive oil and mopped about for answers, which would only come in symbols.

Bemused baby in one hand, Melissa plucked chairs from her path with the other, hell-bent on escape. The sandy feet and heady laughs of Neo-European diners, pushing their presence on the bay.

I pursued the wash of reddened hair before me. How ironic, that I was chasing her. She hurled the package of her son about her hip, patted his bum in agitation and stepped up to the roadway. Behind my male's simple view of What's to be done, I felt idly for her safety. Such adultery. Restaurateurs and diners ricked their telescoping necks to see the origin of that voice of hers as she bellowed for a taxi. She spun on her flat-footed sole and yelled at them: "Seen enough have you?!"

She jutted her jaw in that familiar manner as their heads crunched back in and claiming her proud place as a working-class girl, she stuck her ghastly finger up in my face and hissed. I instinctively reached for Julian. She jerked him away.

"Get away from my son."

Then the perennial cliché of break-ups: "I never want to see you again." Her resolve.

Clever minds at the tables behind us, pieced together faults and motives: "He's left her."

"No, no, she's leaving him."

Their minds hammered us as they filled their gobs with dip and wine as adjuncts to their sport. My lips hung from my face, my body suddenly globular with fat. My heart burrowed inside me for safety. An umbilical cord between us snapped as the taxi door slammed, leaving us raw wounds in an alien environment. With a cabby's acceleration, she was gone. I quick-stepped to one side, my knees sank in a quagmire. Somewhere, I knew what a terrifyingly bad choice I had made. I was an arbour of satisfied loss. I was the wentieth century drama drawing to a close. I was mortified. My face took in the revellers: the arty class here, the workers out there.

The black soot of a gear change plopped out on the esplanade as the taxi cab carried away the most important found object, the most unlikely, enriching happenstance of my life. A grey-blue sheen descended on the beach and wrapped its hands around my heart. Somewhere a murderer was gratified. I held my breath in bucketfuls.

Then a bored God announced: "this is Andy at twenty-four, alone on a crowded street, divided from his true hero". All the received ideas of masculine strength clattering loudly round about.

After the taxi had left that day, I stepped slowly up the sandy, Sunday stairs to where the other actors lay about. My crackling lips parched against the words I might have uttered. Here my memory stops: what was spoken into my pale face?

Who held out a hand or didn't, remains a mystery, a cliff-hanger at this ending episode. Stupid in my repose, I slumped inside memory. A wave crashed on the shore. Out on the jetty, a fisherman hooked a nibble – then it was gone. A kid choked on sea-water, then thrust on upward, swinging an impotent punch at the brother who'd dunked her. Down in the square a child in soiled undies soaked up his brother's indulgent care; one arm slung about his shoulder in abandon. The gabble of words from the restaurant below made love with itself. And the real Andy ended here.

If I'd known that ten years later after travelling the globe, acting on the international stage, I'd be sitting here wanting her back like no other, would I have made this same choice?

****

Part Three: Reconciling

Back in Adelaide, at Melissa's mantelpiece, twelve years after "us" and a decade of my burgeoning career interstate. The fire crackles light around in golden hues and bounces in tiny rivulets, the tyre track of dusty tears that have been, just now, on Melissa's face. The purple-gelled light still perched in her eyes. She has cried for the film I showed her, my film, which made a drama of an abused child. His plight speaks to her.

And she asks that question no one asks. She is shocked I never told her, never in all these years told her of the abuse my childhood bore.

"Why'd you never tell me?" she asks, fingering away another tear.

It just didn't seem important, I think. Why draw attention to a shame everyone else's silence relegated to bad taste? This is the way of life, I thought: beyond our pompous sense of redemption, at base, no one really cares.

She is alone in her questioning and in my eyes, she knows it, yet she takes me by the hand and holds hers to my heart. Like falling into a haystack, I trust. Her eyes a mess of "should I?" and "maybe nots". She waits, until my heart accepts. Then being careful not to twist an ankle on the building blocks still strewn in odd places on the rug, she leads me, she leads me to the bedroom. In essence of boronia and the warm purse of cottonseed oil she lays me on the bed and massages me – as if she knows this body, although a thousand years have passed since the last time she touched me in this way.

The angers, the divisions, her ex-husband who treated her as a porn object, the damaging burrs and burrowing minds of those who would obstruct our path. And now her childhood and mine pop up to join the list. Slowly, as if in giving meditation, she rounds my shoulders and presses into my spine. Her hands are guided like a Shaman's and the only sound in this bedroom I'm a stranger in are the sounds of her breath and mine. She is hoping, in that well-winded way, that she, that I... and I'm hoping too, hoping that hurt will not be the outcome. We are both so very broken.

And here in her bedroom, five years after her terrible marriage, twelve years after her roadside finger in my face, the untimely end of what might have been, I am back.

Her palms slide oil between them as she suggests I turn onto my back. That tiny salubrious smile, that in someone else might be considered supercilious, graces her soft lips. She draws her oily hands across my chest. The dog garumphs and trundles out of the room, the Hills hoist turns in the wind outside and twittering night birds flutter away at the sound of a passing truck. Her now-black hair falls about her face, her hands are circling gently round and round my stomach. She is listening to an urge that grows in a life between us. How mesmerizing – safe under the hands of someone I loved and trusted, someone against whom life has dealt blows and yet whose resilience has made her all the more caring. Her hands are moving lower and lower.

The Holland blind crepitates, a slow-gin love song meanders in from the loungeroom stereo. My eyes are closed. This was my wish: re-union.

I say, look at me, I'm yours, always have been, although Melissa belongs to another part of my life, Melissa is almost the universe to me right now. I reach for her hair, glad We're alone again, I lift her still slim form, where gravity has taken its toll and for a moment we are the subjects of a Tarkovsky film – turning in the air. We are here together, clearing the tragedies and disappointments of time.

I ask myself if I was wrong to leave her, ignoring the imperatives of love and flesh. Was this night so wrong? She is off in a world where she trusts me and I'm falling into her. She speaks from time to time as I do, in soft whispers and hallowed puffballs of affection, deep affection. What would our lives be if We'd stayed a couple? Would I still know her? Would I bestow this strange journey of leaving with the same sly determination? And then all thought becomes deed. The heat rises up and we are together, locked so lovingly in that figure eight: kissing the woman I have loved, a current between us. We are together, we are free.

****

I stay with Melissa for three days. Each morning another child returns until all three are present, playing Pokemon and constructing dinosaurs. I chat away to Julian, having not seen him since he was the grizzly babe in my stunted arms, we chat about girls at school and naughty things like bolt-bombs and wagging school.

When Mickey arrives one morning at Melissa's side of the bed, she sits up groggily, and their eyes meet. I see the question on his face: "Who is this man? Why is he here?" That familiar ducky-daddles look and Melissa rubbing her eyes in the morning fog, as She'd done so long ago, when the "egg onlegs" of her came to visit. I know nothing of her. I only see the salty smile of him as he kisses her breast. She hooks an arm about him and smiles that Mona Lisa smile as he goes through the motions of supping at her, just as he did before his weaning. His long blond hair bounces in a promise of the future. And Melissa speaks softly to the child. I'm touched. I wish I'd been more empathetic, all those years ago, then I might not have been so destitute as to not love her and baby Julian. I know there is no place for Father here (not in my shoes, at least), and know that is okay.

I draw a breath. I sink into the bed next to her cool thigh. I'm tired. Tired as I've never been before—as if I've been shaken by a thresher in my dreams. And when Melissa gets up and Mickey shoves his bottle back in his gob and totters out after her, I roll on my back and stare at the blank ceiling. Just as three days later I stare into her blank face, her tired thought-assembled face and see the beauty of a decade there. Her chin is pulled in to glance down at her nurses" watch and hear the time of years ticking over. She stands there, hands by sides and heart bereft. I'm asking myself: "Is she the one?" and no one answers.

She has to go to work now and plods about on sensible shoes. Her blue striped uniform shucking around and smoothing itself as if the passion of the moment were a good stiff ironing and, with a gentle open-mouthed kiss, she is gone.

I look after the boys until she returns, and when she does, the dog refuses to speak to her. It snuffles to itself, raising its nose from the tuckaway position in its thigh and whuffing out a curt protest, only tucking it in again when I attempt to pat him.

Next morning, early, the boys go to their Dad's place – and though I offer to carry them to the car, Melissa makes me stay out of sight, whilst her ex-husband collects them at the door – the farthest reach of his restraining order. This is no place for a man, I think, hiding like a frightened child. But, I know that this is the best thing I can do to protect her. And God knows I've never protected her before. I've been a coward in love and all things.

She watches me take a shower. I laugh, and sing hit tunes from the seventies—her favourites. I lather in the smell of her and rub her hippy shampoo in my hair. She is becoming an archetype. And she only speaks to ask me not to use all the hot water.

She slips into the bath, a beam of sunlight curling in amongst the steam, the smell of her warm flesh caressing me. She looks sideways at me, smirks, then sinks back into her warm reverie. She closes her eyes. I watch her face sink into resignation. I am going, leaving for Melbourne tomorrow. She drops below the waterline then raises herself up again, black hair combing itself across her cupid's scalp. Her eyelashes stick together, and the pale blue eyes shut down under clogged patches of mascara, two trails of black run down her softened cheeks, co-mingling with the water, swirling like the steam above and forming a slow pavan of loss and years and pain and years. She still looks sixteen in the soft light.

I kneel down at the bath-side. I think of heroes proposing. I run a finger under her eyes to clean her up. My own eyes, the only thing dry in this shrine of steam and liquid. Trickles of condensation run down the window. Outside the blustery sky peeks out between thrashes of angry trees. The leaves fall like an army surrendering.

And I have no tears, just silhouettes of loss and hardened eyes.

"I'm sorry," I offer. "I had everything in you. And threw it all away."

My God, the hypocrisy: I want to make it up to her. This sin of years past is dragged out into the soggy day.

"Melissa," I whisper, lowering my gaze and slightly cringing. My heart begins to pound against my ribs for escape. All the thrills of life were about to slip into reverse. I feel like a surge of maybe. I turn my head slowly taking in her whole body.

Her petite ankles prop themselves up on the bath-end. I run my hand along her thigh and tummy, hearing bells from a nearby churchyard. And I know that, in some way or another, they toll for us.

"Melissa," I repeat.

My breath falls haltingly from my stuck chest. I think of her three boys and how I have no base to offer them and I feel hideously inept. But I venture a third time: "Melissa… I'll marry you".

The water stops lapping. The breeze dies down. She looks up at me. She cups a wet hand around my shoulder, sniffs and smiles. Drips run down my back and nestle in the towel I've wrapped around my waist. She weaves her sweet, melancholy eyes to peer into mine, her lips parting, but taut, decision haunting her ears. Her heart "pops". I feel it. She kisses me deeply as I wait for an answer.

Married to Math
Mark Hudson

I was in a café having a drink.
I saw a couple who liked to think.
The woman's finger contained a ring.
They studied math, it was their thing.
Studying statistics, young to be wed.
Math was always too much for my head.
But we need more smart people to marry.
The problems of the world will be theirs to carry.

Meet Me at The Eagle
Moshe Sonnheim

A Philadelphia Story

They met by chance at the Eagle. He was twenty-three; she was nineteen. The concert of the Great Organ drew them together. Was it love? A sharing of laughter and innermost thoughts; an innocent nakedness of soul; one complementing the other; a growing together by shared experiences.

How they shared! Watching a sunset, picnicking in the Wissahickon, visiting Lucy, the Margate Elephant, walking the boards of Atlantic City.

They passed the seasons of the year together, each season enriched by the joy of her presence. But she was not ready. Her mind said yes, but her heart said no. And so they parted.

Heartbroken, he moved to another city, earned a doctorate in Social Work, and became a prominent Professor.

She completed her studies in Medicine, married a Doctor (when her heart and mind were one), and lived not far from the Eagle.

From time to time, he thought about her, especially as he grew older and more lonely. Then, on a whim, he called her from a Conference in Philadelphia.

They spoke as though the years had never dimmed their feelings for each other. There was a sadness in her still-soft voice, and a longing in his.

He had never married, and she had lost her husband recently. Now, she, too, was growing old alone.

"Meet me at the Eagle," she said.

He remembered the tie she liked. She remembered the color dress he loved. They prepared to please each other once again.

John Wanamaker's was no more. Lucy had moved. Atlantic City was a Casino town. The ambience they had known was gone forever.

Only the Eagle and the Great Organ remained.

She awaited him eagerly there.

He did not arrive.

She called the hotel.

He had collapsed in the lobby, and had been rushed to Jefferson Hospital, not far from the hotel.

She had worked there while they were dating.

She rushed to his room, and found him sitting up in bed. He had suffered a mild heart attack.

Gently, she held his hand, as they had done in the past.

He noticed the concern and caring in her face. They reminisced about their shared joys, sorrows, and quarrels.

She noticed the spark of love in his eyes.

Unwilling to lose her again, he proposed. This time, she accepted!

They married at the Eagle. The Great Organ filled the air with music once again.

Mincemeat
Nidhi Singh

Yeah, mincemeat, and he had about 10Kgs of it. He couldn't very well eat it all and he didn't know what to do with it. And he didn't know how he came by it either. He could give it to Farid, but then he would be suspicious and was very likely to feed it to his pigs. Or, he could give it to Karim Chacha, his landlord, who had a large family to feed (Allah be Praised!). But for days his four wives would squabble over how to cook it and the whole stairway in their narrow ramshackle of a building would smell. He could give it to the beggars that lined the noisy street to the mosque, but they would grumble they had nowhere to cook it.

Yet, there the meat lay, succulent, red and fatty, undecided, waiting, redolent; twiddling its thumbs as if, waiting for Kemal to take a call. The early morning flies had begun to discover the juicy dish lying in the huge copper cauldron in his tiny rooftop kitchen, and were fast gathering in a musical hum outside, looking for cracks in the netted window so that they could move in for the feast. Kemal had covered the pot with a newspaper and placed a small pebble atop it—so the meat was safe for now. But the sun was rising, the Maulvi was clearing his throat, and if he didn't decide fast, in the pitiless heat of the summer the meat would soon turn bad as he didn't even own a fridge. Kemal sat at the end of his jute charpoy outside his small rooftop room and gripped his aching head in his hands, and wondered what to do.

As full of ideas as the blank, gaping sky of clouds, or the stuffy day of a merciful breeze, Kemal decided to wash and deal with the problem at Haji's Tea Point over a kick ass breakfast of sooji halwa and poori-sabzi. A practical man, who kept careful, rather secretive accounts concerning customers like Kemal who ate mostly on credit, Haji was sure to know what to do.

"Could you accept 10Kgs of good mince mutton in lieu of my credit," Kemal whispered, out of earshot of a nearby patron who seemed to be leaning in, as Haji poured him piping hot masala chai in a clay teacup. Kemal brought the teacup to his nose to inhale the rich bouquet of cloves, cardamom, and cinnamon mixed with earth, before sipping loudly from it.

"This is a vegetarian establishment, chump," Haji replied, swatting him with a flourish of his sweat towel. "And where did you come by so much mincemeat," he observed, moving on.

"A friend left it..." Kemal's voice trailed, as Haji had already reached behind the sweetmeat counter, where he sat gravely on his seat and became engrossed in swatting flies. *That was that – he wasn't going to get any help from that scourge of the humble housefly.*

"*Subhan Allah,*" Kemal said after finishing the sumptuous meal; caressing his belly, he burped loudly in appreciation of the repast the good Lord had favored him with. Gesturing expansively to Haji to note down his bill, he walked out into the hot day.

****

The street was quickly coming to life: pushcart men shouted out for junk bottles, rags; old buggies and carts worked up a mean cloud of dust, and the clear sky was beginning to cloud up with soot rising from the tanneries and dyeing shops. He sauntered along till he came to the small corner store. The store lady, a widow, who had disappeared behind a maze of sacks and barrels, returned presently with a bag of flour and a broom for another customer who was already waiting.

He salaamed and said pleasantly when she turned to him: "Fix me a paan, Ammi Jaan."

She grinned at him, revealing a row of cracked, betel-stained teeth. After spreading slaked lime, areca nuts, and tobacco on the soaked betel leaf, she deftly folded it and handed him the paan.

"Umm," Kemal mumbled with satisfaction, admiring in a rusty mirror hanging on the sidewall his kohled eyes and under his sharp mustache lips red with the overflowing betel juice. "Your store seems wanting in custom this morning," he observed.

"In custom, or in a particular customer," she quipped.

"*Barak Allah Fik*! May the blessings be upon you! To whom you allude, I know not, but you do jest me this fine morning."

"I do not trifle with my business, Kemal *Mian*—do I tot this up in your account, as usual?" She scowled as he casually reached for a packet of Gold Flake and matches, and lighting a cigarette, replaced the merchandise in his kurta pocket. "Or am I going to see some hard cash here—rare as the moon of Eid?"

"You well know my situation, Ammi Jaan—" he answered, lacing up his talk with the sweetness of gulqand, the preserve of rose-petals that Ammi tucked liberally into her paans. "Eid is just four days away, and that is the blessed day I'm going to seek Fatima"s hand in marriage from that miser of a Maulvi."

"You can't pay me four *annas* for this paan, but you can pay him a fortune in dowry," she rued, tying her hair in a bun and rolling up her sleeves, readying as if, for a scrap.

"I've been saving—whatever a humble clerk working in a leather factory can make. I promise you, Ammi, I will repay you from my first salary after Eid." He paused for a minute. "Would you like 10 kgs of the finest mincemeat instead?"

"Imbecile! What would a poor widow—all alone—do with so much meat! Where did you come by it, by the way?"

"I wish I knew," he mumbled. For the life of him, he couldn't remember how the fresh meat, all chopped and clean and fragrant, came to be in his possession.

"There she comes, "Ammi teased, leaning over her counter, nodding toward three burqa-clad women walking their way, skipping over sleeping mongrels and fidgety cockerels. "The *houris* of paradise."

"Welcome, *Salam Alaikum*," Ammi said, as the women salaamed her and moved on, except for one, who lingered at the far end of the shop, away from Kemal. "What can I get you, Fatima Bi?"

"Some salt... rice, Ammi," Fatima said, tracing the aluminum beading on the wooden counter with a plump white finger. Kemal never failed in recognizing Fatima, though always covered in a black veil from head to toe, from the tinkling silver anklets He'd bought her from the fair and the voice like mellow fluty notes of a brook in the fields.

"How much—or should I guess myself," Ammi asked, grinning.

Fatima glanced, pleadingly perhaps, at Kemal and then nodded, stepping away out of sight of Ammi. Kemal, speechless at this chance encounter, was pinching his pencil mustache and crimping his eyebrows in line. As soon as Ammi disappeared into the dark bowels of the store, he strutted over to Fatima, who receded into a corner set away from the street.

The air suddenly seemed intoxicated with the perfume of green, watered fields and the squalor of the street became suffused with the golden shower that fell from the sky. Fatima giggled; swaying slightly, and the street came alive with the cheeping of birds and the crackling of sunbeams.

"So, how are we this morning...?" Kemal began, edging as close to her as he dared in broad daylight. "How did you know you were going to find me here?"

Fatima shook her head, and bit the edge of her *niqab*. "I know you feed at Haji's on Sundays—and mother wanted—"

"I know, rice and salt—you look so... beautiful... ethereal," he said, grabbing her hand and stroking it. "You are smooth... like the soft underbelly of... "Before he could wax eloquent she snatched away her hand as a *Bhishti*, a water carrier man, carrying a dripping goatskin bag passed by.

"Be wary, what if someone should see me," she said coyly.

"Only I may see you, though you might hide behind miles of shrouds, my *aafreen*. I long for Eid when I visit Abba Jaan and plight our troth. Is everything in place?"

"It is, except, be prepared for a long queue. And... and..."

"I know your infernal tribe of first cousins and rich overlords don't have teeth but will have more wife. Don't worry, I too have saved a fat dowry for you—haven't spent a penny on myself for months. And I'm confident the old man means well for his daughter, he surely will give her hand to me, how many graduates do you know of in this wretched place," he asked, tugging his collar. "Or suitable boys with prospects, might I presume to be the most eligible bachelor in this neighborhood?"

His prospects presently consisted of being surrounded with colorful vats and sprigs of mint leaves that he held under his nose to ward off the pungent smells of soaking and drying leather. His small office lay under a steeply pitched roof and two small smokestacks belching forth huge tufts of smoke, spreading soot over the neighborhood, and befouling the clothing, newly washed and strung on lines on rooftops. While in open fields nearby, newly tanned half hides brown and wet, draped on racks for drying exuded the characteristic tannery odors. But then all that was about to change once Fatima became his, and they would move out to Bombay, or Delhi, where bright young men like himself could eke out respectable pelf.

"And you said *and* – and what," he added, after a pause, realizing she was telling him something.

"And... there is a problem..."

"What?"

"He... he's upset... he may not entertain suitors for his daughter that day?"

"Wha—but why?"

"Something inauspicious happened—his goat got stolen last night."

"Wha—I told you, don't tie it outside your house! Who tempts misfortune to visit his door like that? Proud he was, you'd said—wasn't he, of such a fatted beauty, this was bound to happen!" Kemal kicked a pebble on the street and stomped around in despair. An orphan, a frugal man, all he ever wished in life was to wed Fatima, his lodestar, the one thing that made his crushing loneliness and isolation bearable. "But everyone knows everybody here—who would dare—someone must be out of their mind!"

Suddenly, Kemal froze. Memories of the previous night came flooding back and smack, all became clear: there was no time to be lost. "Don't let him call it off," he urged Fatima, gripping her shoulders. "I'll see you then," he said and rushed off down the bristling street.

****

As soon as He'd turned the corner, Kemal picked up pace. He ran as hard as he could in his leather slippers, panting through the twisted by lanes, past tin-shacks selling recycled hubcaps and sweets shops peddling sesame-encrusted Ladoos the size of golf balls. He dashed through swarms of skull capped men on their way to prayer followed by fat wives in black burqas that rippled in the warm, musky breeze, till he ended up at his friend, Fakir's house.

It was at the top of a building on a street peddling an insane variety of locks, up a steep, stony staircase that opened onto a freshly watered plant-filled courtyard. Fakir welcomed him into the narrow, linear house. His first cousin, the roguish Dawood was also visiting, smoking as he coolly leaned against the wall with his arms crossed before him.

The living room was furnished with a large bed with silk bolsters, a sofa, and two steel cupboards with calligraphy posters and pictures of Mecca. Fakir offered Kemal the sofa while he perched cross-legged at the end of the bed. Bright sunbeams filtered through the blue shutters of a window, forming striped shadows on the frayed carpet. The building overlooked the Hindu temple with its carved domes stretching arrogantly toward the sky, and the temple lane, which marked the unofficial boundary of the congested Muslim living quarters and the spacious, breezy mansions of the Hindus, and the green paddy fields beyond.

A constant uproar of many children crying all at once came from within the house: Fakir's third wife, a girl of fifteen, was still suckling his sixth child. His eldest wife, a rambling lady of generous proportions, her face veil thrown back casually over her gray head, brought them paan and tea and left.

As soon as she was gone, Kemal asked," Brother, what happened last night?"

"Why, don't you remember," Dawood replied, twirling his mustaches and flicking ash on the carpet.

"A little—I think I'd passed out from the rum."

Fakir cupped his mouth in horror. "Don't ever mention the word in this house. *Astagfurallah* – may Allah forgive us!"

"Did it have something to do with the Maulvi's goat?" Kemal left the sofa and sat beside Fakir.

"Why at all should folk tie goats at their threshold for all good men to suffer temptation and risk dire sin," Dawood asked.

"It is the duty of a good Muslim to remove the source of sin that makes mankind betray the righteous path of Allah," observed Fakir.

"Yeah, do away with the sigil of *Iblis* that spells disaster for man by dampening his spirits," added Dawood.

"Luring him to committing what is vile," said Fakir.

"It seemed a seal of Satan with its cloven hoofs, flared ears and a goatee beard," corroborated Dawood, warming to the subject.

"And the Prophet (PBUH) chides us, how many hungry mouths it could feed for days."

"So, what happened then," a bewildered Kemal asked, looking from one cousin to another – both caught up in a spirited sermon on making away with fatted goats of Imams.

"After the three of us finished drinking in your house, we came down to the street to have paan. And as we were walking back, we came upon this goat, this symbol of—"

"Yeah, yeah, I get the symbol of—what happens next," asked Kemal, burrows of worry forming on his forehead now.

"So, we untethered the ram and led him to your house..."

"And where was I all the while," demanded Kemal.

"You were holding up the lamppost, silly, by hugging it," Dawood sneered.

"Then we butchered the ram for his meat, minced it, and divided it equally and fairly among us; and each to his home went, leaving a share for Kemal in his kitchen as he was already fast asleep on his cot," explained Fakir, glancing at his cousin.

"We washed the floor," said Dawood, "and took away the offal and the hide so that when the rain came in the morning not even the hair would be left to tell the tale."

"Why, you could have taken the goat elsewhere?" wailed Kemal.

"Your house was the nearest, and empty."

"I never asked you for the meat."

"Had you been awake, or in senses, you would have; so as fair friends, whom you should show some gratitude, we left you your share."

"But you don't understand, now you've made me an accomplice! You do not realize how important this goat is – or was, to my future plans!"

"What future—what plans," Dawood sneered.

"I intend to betroth Fatima, the Maulvi's eldest."

"Fat chance. Do you know how many eligible suitors she has?"

"Maybe, but she has eyes only for me."

"Is that so, preying in your own backyard, eh?" Fakir thumped Kemal's back and leered at his cousin. "Quite the playboy, eh, we didn't know you had it in you, you quiet operator!"

"Have you the dowry," pressed Dawood.

"I do, enough that he cannot say no, I've been saving up for over three years, ever since I set my eyes upon her."

"Yes, we can see you've been saving," Fakir said, feeling the cheap cotton fabric on Kemal's kurta.

"You don't get it," Kemal protested, rising from the bed, shaking off Fakir's embrace, as it got sickeningly tighter. "The old man is going to call off the Eid feast because his goat is sto—made away by the faithful. It was during the feast he was going to give away Fatima's hand in marriage to the suitors' present."

"You can wait till the next Eid."

"No!" Kemal pointed a shaking finger at the cousins. "I want you both to come away with me this instant and tell the Maulvi, I had nothing to do with all this."

The cousins roared in laughter. "Do not go into denial after burping the biryani, friend, and what are you worried about, no one will ever know."

"Haji would know... and so would Ammi Jaan, the grocery store widow."

"How," the cousins cried.

"Because, as of this morning I told them I had 10 Kgs of mincemeat to give away."

"You fool, what would you do that for?"

"Because I was so hung-over from last night, I couldn't, for the life of me, remember from where the meat came. I blurted out in my innocence."

The cousins glanced at each other in rising panic. Dawood grabbed Kemal's arm and pulled him out into the sunlight-swept courtyard. Fakir closed the door behind them.

"We have nothing to do with the disaster you bring upon yourself, understand?" growled Fakir, his jaw sat. Dawood began to twist Kemal's arm slowly. "Yes, it is your own doing," he snarled.

"Your fate, we're not a part of it."

"We did good by you, feeding you liquor and meat every weekend at your home."

"That's because you two can't drink in your own homes," cried Kemal.

"Exactly, We're respectable family men, not bastards like you."

With a jerk, Kemal freed himself of Dawoods arm lock; "You used me," he said, the pain bringing tears to his eyes.

"You let us." Fakir began to push Kemal toward the staircase.

"Go away."

"We never met."

"We don't know who you are, we don't even know if you're fit for our company, for all you know, you aren't even a Muslim."

"Yeah, who knows, let's find out," Dawood leered, and lunged for Kemal's pajamas; finding the cord, he tried to yank it off.

"Get lost, if you don't want to go down the street naked," Fakir said, restraining his cousin, who'd grabbed a hoe from the lavender bed. "Or before you too get butchered by my cousin here."

"I trusted you, I welcomed you in my home," Kemal cried, backing away.

"We never met."

"We don't know who you are."

"We don't know what you speak of," They shouted after him as he scampered down the stairs.

"What goat." He could hear the yells and laughter as he tore down the street. "Go own up to your doing. Confess!"

"Thief!"

"Scoundrel!"

People paused on the street hearing the cries coming from the rooftop, and hastily separated to make way for Kemal as he scuttled down the street with his arm across his face.

****

He didn't pause till he reached the comfort of his terrace: so wild was his terror. All was lost: his love, his chances, and his easy manner. The lengthening shadows of spires that fell on the roof skewered his flesh like the beaks of crows strung out on electric wires: crows that clawed and fluffed their rage up; crows charred black in the whiteness of the sun; crows with rakish eyes that cawed reproachfully out to him for his crimes; crows sent down by Allah scratching up the ground to show Adam how to hide his brother's naked corpse.

Kemal couldn't bear the rebuke anymore. He spread the evening Urdu newspaper on the roof and poured all the mincemeat over it. Then he laid back on his cot and let the crows sweep down and feast. As he dozed off into an uneasy slumber, the wheel of the sun, clasped in amber clouds, sloped and turned. The sun shook off the bright dust from its parting sheen and made way for the usurping moon. As darkness fell, the crows, not sated with mere cawing, swept into his dream.

"Why, are you not satisfied, that you pursue me thus," Kemal asked. "What bad omen is this?"

"Strange that man should blame us for his dark deeds – that we forewarn the outcome of his evil designs."

"Yet, I am innocent, yet, I'm blamed. Is there no justice?"

The hooded crow made a sound that seemed like laughter in derision. "Crows have a strong sense of justice, Kemal – the rules of natural law bestowed by Allah Himself. We have courts: for when a crow steals a young one's food, do we not scratch his feathers out so that he's as helpless as the little one; when one steals another's nest, do we not tear the nest down and make the thief build another; when one steals the affections of another's female, do we not flock upon the guilty and slash him with our beaks? And do we not then we bury him? Crows have yielded unto the laws of Allah and reached the shores of safety, and so would you!" With that, the large raven flapped his wings and soared into the night in a wake of soot and singed feathers.

****

In the morning, his mind quite made up, Kemal bribed Paro, Fatimas maid to arrange for their rendezvous at the riverfront before dawn.

The next day, when Kemal reached the stone steps leading down to the river, he found Fatima already waiting under the large banyan tree, with an empty milk pitcher at her feet. The river flowed gently, a cool breeze blew in from the paddy fields, and the lazy smell of dewy grass hung in the thin mist. A crimson flower twirled in her fingers, tender and fresh as butter churned in earthen jars. She raised her veil briefly to smile, sending little butterfly wings fluttering against his face where the smile had touched him.

"Don't raise your veil," he said, "for the moon will be jealous. Do not show your hands, lest the wind makes them rough."

She giggled, while little birds wheeled above like parasols, and the mango trees dripped flowers on the village road. "What is it that you bring now," she asked, seeing that he led a fat goat by a rope.

"Here," he said, "take it home and tie him to the gate before your house awakes." He pressed the rope in her hands.

"But—what will Abba Jaan think," she said, shrinking away. "Why are you doing this?"

"So that he doesn't cancel the feast, Fatima, I cannot wait for another Eid to read the *Nikah* with you. Karim Chacha has arranged a handsome opening for me in a leather export house in Bombay. We'll move out of here," he pleaded, "to where there are no separate wells for Muslims. It's a chance we must grab hold of."

"What will Abba say?"

"You tell him the goat had strayed and found its way back on its own. He lacks the light in his eyes – he won't tell the difference if you convince him."

"Where did you come by the goat?"

"I bought it." Grasping her hands, he confessed everything, including the strange dream He'd had of the crows.

"You bought it! It must have cost, what about the *mahr*, Kemal, the bridal money—do you still have it?"

Kemal shook his head and sank on the grass.

"So, you spend our mahr on a goat, Kemal, why? Is your honor more important than our love? You care more for Abba 'Jaans feelings than mine? He will never give me away without dowry: you know that. I could sell my jewelry, he could find out later, but that won't be enough..." she wailed, "*Taawwudh* - may Allah have mercy!"

"Have faith, dear Fatima. Allah ta'ala will show us the way – I... I will think of something," he said, not having the foggiest notion how.

Somewhere the temple gong sounded, reminding the sky to wake up. Village women began to come up from the river, water pitchers gurgling at their hips. Dust rose in the distance as cattle were driven to the fields.

"Please, I beg of you, have faith in Allah... in me... in our love. There's no more time, I will see you on Eid, and Insha'Allah, bring you home with me," he said urgently, handing her the rope, and striding away back to town, as the dawn began to break over the riverfront.

At home Kemal fixed himself a frugal breakfast of tea and savories. Realizing he still had time before the tannery opened for work, he decided to lay down a bit. Racking his brains on how to come with the money by Eid, just a day away, exhausted him and he drifted into an uneasy asleep. His body jerked and twitched as one after another people began to snub him in his dreams.

"I've already given you a hefty Eid bonus," his tannery owner said, cracking a leather whip Kemal had never noticed before.

"You will steal from her mouth," Karim Chacha was saying, waving his ninth infant in Kemal's face.

"Look at this beggar, how will he care for my daughter," announced the Maulvi to the gathered suitors in his house, much to their mirth and delight. As the men laughed and slapped their thighs and flung mince mutton in his face, Kemal found himself dashing out the door, brushing against a fat goat that looked at him with accusing eyes and running out into a brightly lit street where butchers and locksmiths had gathered to hurl abuses and stones at him. "Thief—beggar..." they screamed.

As he fled, he realized he had company, one man ran right ahead of him while another followed close on his heels. He tried hard to shake them off, but couldn't. He turned a corner and sprinted till he reached the mustard fields yonder. There, exhausted, he collapsed on a heap of feed and mulch. His eyes closed as he lay panting, hoping his pursuers were gone. But when he sat up, he found they were still there, perching on his shoulders.

"Who are you," Kemal asked, with a vigorous shudder.

"We're *Hafaza*, earthly shepherds of humans."

"Like *Farishtey*, guardian angels..." he asked.

"More like archive masters, to record your deeds."

"Are you here to help?"

"Verily, Allah will not change the condition of a people unless they change it themselves."

"Then all is lost, for it is beyond me to change," Kemal wailed, banging his fists on his knees, and sinking back in the mound of hay.

****

On the bright, chirpy morning of Eid, Kemal, in an immaculate black *achkan* with a bright red rose pinned to its lapel, a Gandhi cap, and with a small cane with a silvery head, presented himself at the gates of the Maulvi residence: his pockets quite empty of change but his breast quite full of the hope that afflicts the young and the inexperienced. He lingered at the gatepost, caressing with some satisfaction the loose rope that hung there, the crook at its end showing a knot freshly undone. He clasped his hands in silent prayer, looked up toward the skies, and raised his step to cross the threshold.

At that very moment, a bearded man, his face eerily familiar, dressed in bulky sack clothes crossed him and blocked his way. He spread open his cloak to reveal a silver salver covered with red muslin. This he pressed into Kemal's hands and whispered, "Give this to the Maulvi as the mahr."

"But," Kemal began to protest as the man began to make away. Kemal grabbed his arm. "You are the man from last Night's dream, aren't you, the Farishtey."

"This is your chance, man, why do you hesitate?"

The muslin had partially come off the salver in the scuffle. The salver was covered in a pile of silver coins.

"I cannot accept this, this is haram for me. Give me a chance to change things myself, dear Farishtey, and verily, then Allah will help me, isn't this what you'd said?" Kemal thrust the gift back in the man's hands. The ragamuffin gaped but chose to say nothing. He shrugged and vanished behind a sea of brightly painted earthen pots and bead necklaces that hung from the bustling, gaudily decorated shop fronts.

"*Adab*, welcome, Kemal Mian." A woman in burqa had appeared on the door and was beckoning him in. She was giggling and there was a spring in her step as she grasped him by the arm and led him inside. She couldn't be Fatima, he was sure, for she wasn't quite the light that drew him.

Inside the brightly decorated living hall, a long row of men sat on the carpeted floor with plates piled with delicacies before them, while the Maulvi and his remaining daughters stood at the entrance welcoming the guests. Fatima, his eldest, stood right behind him: Kemal could make her out by her plump, fair hands, and the way her head followed him as he advanced tentatively in the queue. She leaned forward and whispered in her father's ear when he came to a halt before them.

A dark hush fell upon the hall, as the Maulvi nodded to his daughter and asked for his spectacles. He perched them on his nose and peered sternly at Kemal, nodding disapprovingly, it seemed, all the time. After examining him from top to toe, the Maulvi's eyes came to rest upon Kemal's hands, quite empty, save for the humility in which they were folded.

Fatima nudged the Maulvi with her elbow, and the old man cleared his throat. "So, you come empty handed at my door and ask for the apple of my eye. Is that fair price for one so beautiful, so accomplished?"

"I crave—"

"I know all about you, your speech and your prospects. Why, I even know about the goat, there are no secrets between daughter and father here. I know what people say behind my back, that I'm a greedy old man who will sell off his daughter for the highest price. Well, son, let me tell you, she's not for sale, no man may put a price on my daughter. Do you think I will give her away to be a third wife in some harem... or risk a blind, wasted, twisted, mutated blind freak—like myself—as my grandchild by marrying her in blood relations? I'm glad you came empty-handed, but with your decency intact. What you offer, as hope and a future for my beloved daughter here, I warmly and humbly accept."

A tear stole into the old rascal's eye and his lips quivered as he embraced his daughter's betrothed.

****

The steam train swayed and jerked on its way to Bombay, plowing through the green and brown Indian landscape, covering its passengers with hot dust and soot. The wooden benches made their backs sore, while noisy fans above blew air that scalded faces and dried sweat running down their backs. Fatima, wearing her bridal suit under her burqa, sat on the window seat, looking dreamily out at the blur of mango orchids and golden sugarcanes. Kemal, with his head nesting on her shoulder, dozed and swayed with the lurching coach.

"Are you awake?" she said when he suddenly sat up erect at a particularly bad jolt.

"Yes, I am now." Kemal yawned and reached out for her hand.

"Don't you have any shame?" she slapped his hand away. "In front of all these people."

"But you are my begum now."

"Do as you please with your begum within the four walls of your house, Kemal Mian."

"Hmm…" Kemal stretched and nestled against his woman.

"Was the story about the silver salver true, Kemal?"

"I believe so," he replied. "Some man gave it when I was standing on your threshold, with nothing but hope in my heart and in my empty pockets."

"Did you know him?"

"No, but he vaguely resembled someone who came in my dream the night before, asking me to keep the faith, and I had nothing but faith that morning."

"Must have been a Farishtey, then," she smiled and closed her eyes. "It indeed is Allah's will. Amin," she mumbled, raising her hands in prayer.

My Nephew's First Love Poem
Mark Hudson

My nephew was a student in the fifth grade,
and he wrote his first love poem to a girl he eyed.
Sounded profound in his first serenade,
I hope the young girl won't injure his pride.
Could they go out and have some lemonade?
Are feelings as a youth a thing you should hide?
I admire his courage, the choice he made,
I trust him that in the poem he hadn't lied.
Childhood is no longer a pinball arcade,
but fifth grade is no time to secure a bride.
I'm glad of girls he seems not afraid,
because there were times where I was terrified.
I hope that this girl knew how special my nephew is,
he took his first test harder than a quiz.

Once Upon a Winter Storm
Margarite Stever

Sleet pinged against the windows making Emma think of thousands of tiny nails hitting the glass. The storm raged outside, and she had no illusions of going anywhere anytime soon. The TV meteorologist said, "Folks, we haven't seen a storm like this one in at least thirty years. So, everyone needs to stay indoors. We will have the latest updates at ten."

Emma clicked off the TV and walked slowly into her kitchen to make some hot chocolate. She was just reaching for the cabinet when her doorbell rang.

"Who could that be?" Emma muttered to herself.

She hurried to the door fearing that someone was in trouble. She swung the door open and nearly fainted when she saw one of her company's independent general contractors.

"Shane Jones, what in the world are you doing here?" Emma sputtered. "Come in before you freeze to death!"

"I'm sorry to barge in on you like this, Emma," Shane began. "The storm took out some trees up the way, and they're blocking the road. I can't get home. You are the only person I know along this particular stretch of road, and I was hoping that you would find it in your heart to let me wait out the storm here with you."

"How did you even know where I live?" Emma asked still reeling from Shane appearing out of nowhere.

"I've known you were here for a while because I saw you mowing your yard last summer. The roads are really bad, and I'm not sure I could make it back to town to stay at a motel. So, can I stay here until they get the road cleared?" Shane asked flashing his expressive blue eyes that always made Emma's heart flutter. With his short dark brown hair, muscular build, and friendly smile, he could pretty much talk her into anything.

"Yes, of course you can wait out the storm here. I was about to make some hot chocolate. Would you like a cup?" Emma asked running her fingers nervously through her long red hair.

"Oh, that sounds amazing! Thanks!"

"Well, make yourself comfortable, and I will be back with chocolaty goodness in a jiffy," Emma said gesturing to the living room as she started toward the kitchen.

She returned a short time later with two steaming cups of rich hot chocolate topped with oversized marshmallows. Handing Shane his cup she observed, "I didn't know you lived out this way. I've never seen you drive by or anything."

Shane took a large gulp of his warm beverage before answering. "I live about five miles south of here on a forty-acre farm. It's nice and quiet. It's peaceful to come home and hear the birds and bullfrogs singing after listening to power tools all day."

"I can imagine. All of that noise would drive me to drink!" Emma exclaimed.

"Yeah, it's pretty intense sometimes," Shane laughed.

"I moved out here last year after my divorce and absolutely love living in the country!" Emma said with a smile.

Shane's face lost his happy expression and his full lips turned down into a frown. "I'm sorry about your divorce, Emma," he said. "I can't imagine any man not being thrilled to death to call you his wife."

Emma laughed sadly and replied, "Well, Danny didn't feel that way. He preferred the company of Brandi, his yoga instructor, to being with me." She gulped down some hot chocolate before continuing. "He told me that Brandi is the love of his life, and I was just a lie that he told himself."

"I can't believe that!" Shane said loudly. "No woman could possibly be as wonderful as you!"

"It's okay, Shane. I'm better off without him. I find that I am much happier now because I can truly be myself," Emma said with a grin. "Danny's betrayal hurts less and less every day."

"I'm sorry that you were hurt, Emma," Shane said softly moving to sit beside her on the couch. He slipped his arm around her shoulders and held her close saying, "You are an amazing woman and deserve the very best that a man can offer. You deserve someone's unconditional love."

"Well, thanks. I like to think that I will find happiness with someone else someday," Emma said feeling quite content to have Shane's strong arms around her.

"Of that, I have no doubt, Emma," Shane said softly.

"You're sweet," Emma said just as the power went out.

"Oh no," Shane sighed. "We've lost power now. I don't suppose you have a generator?"

"No," Emma replied, "but I have plenty of firewood and some oil lamps. We will be fine."

Emma rose from the couch and skillfully made her way to the mantle where she kept an oil lamp and her lighter. She lit the lamp and then opened the glass to the fireplace. She was reaching into the hearth to open the damper when she felt Shane's hands on her shoulders.

She looked up questioningly as Shane said, "Please, allow me to do that for you."

"You are my guest. I wouldn't dream of having you light the fire," Emma replied.

"I insist. It would give me great pleasure to light your fire," Shane said as he gently pushed her aside and opened the damper. His work roughened fingers brushed hers as he gently plucked the lighter from her, and her green eyes widened as she felt tingles run from her fingers to the rest of her body.

Once the flame caught, Shane handed the lighter back to Emma. She lit another oil lamp on the other side of the room, which filled the space with a warm glow.

They both sat back down on the couch at the exact same time and found themselves thigh to thigh. They looked in each other's eyes and neither one moved.

Still gazing into Emma's eyes Shane said, "So, tell me about yourself, Emma Wilson. I only know what I've seen and heard at your office."

"Well, I earned a Bachelor's Degree in Business Administration and started work at the construction firm keeping Hank's books right after college. I've been there for nearly twenty years, and couldn't imagine working anywhere else. Hank keeps me on my toes. I now oversee all four of his offices. In my free time I like to paint, and I read a great deal," Emma explained.

"What about you? What do you do when you aren't building houses and fixing things?" Emma asked.

"Well," Shane began, "I grow corn and soybeans on my farm for a little income. I enjoy fishing a lot. I have a creek running through my land, and I spend a lot of time there. I turned my old barn into a wood working shop and I build rocking horses, clocks, and some small furniture when the mood strikes me. There's a lady with a flea market booth who buys my little projects."

"So, you spend all day building houses and then go home to make toys and furniture? You truly love working with your hands, don't you?" Emma asked on a laugh.

"Yes," Shane answered holding his hands out in front of him, so she could get a good look. "I'm very good with my hands. They are strong and capable. I know how to use them to make beautiful things."

Emma's imagination raced with images of Shane's hands cradling her face, burrowing through her hair, and holding her tightly. She shook her head to clear it, and when she looked back into Shane's eyes, she saw an answering intensity reflected there.

"Emma," Shane whispered leaning closer to her.

"Yes?" Emma answered softly.

"There's something I've been meaning to ask you for a while now."

"What is it?" Emma asked.

"Would you be interested in having dinner with me this Friday night and maybe catching a movie afterward?"

Emma smiled as she answered, "Yes, I would love to!"

"Great! Now, I just have one more question," Shane said.

"And that is?" Emma asked.

"May I kiss you?" Shane asked as he brought his lips to within a whisper of hers.

"I really wish you would," Emma said softly.

Shane closed the distance between them, sliding one of his hands into her hair while the other lovingly cupped her face, and took her lips in a sweet and gentle kiss. He moved his lips slowly and carefully as if she was a fine wine to savor. Emma moaned into his mouth, which he took as encouragement and slipped his tongue past her lips. He tasted her thoroughly before pulling away slightly.

He rested his forehead against hers as he told her, "I have wanted to kiss you like that since the moment I first met you. I have a feeling that I will never get tired of kissing you." Then he kissed her again.

They spent the evening wrapped in each other's arms talking softly, kissing, and enjoying the warm glow of the fire.

"I'm thankful that the storm knocked those trees across the road, so you couldn't make it home tonight," Emma whispered at one point.

"Me, too. I've never been happier to be snowed in," Shane said softly with a sensual smile.

Photogenic
Jason Bleistein

Sitting in the back room finishing lunch, Fred heard the bell above the front door. He was not upset about it because he knew Mr. Johnson would let him take his full lunch break. Mr. Johnson knew Fred worked hard and he had no problem giving Fred the entire hour to do as he pleased. When the bell rang again, Fred knew the customer had left. Having just thrown the brown paper bag that contained his lunch in the garbage can, he was ready to go back to work.

"Fred, are you done with lunch already?" Mr. Johnson asked.

"Time always flies when you're stuffing your face," Fred retorted.

Mr. Johnson laughed heartily at this, though Fred was certain it was a pity laugh. "I just got in a roll of film. Can you take care of it? I have to step out to run some errands."

"No problem."

Mr. Johnson nodded and handed Fred the roll. Fred began to work as Mr. Johnson walked out the door.

Fred ran the rolls through the film processor and went on to various other tasks while waiting for the negatives to emerge. When they were ready, he began to feed them through the printer. Slowly, the pictures began to pop out.

As the pictures printed, Fred flipped through them to check the quality. There were a few pictures of the outside of a house. In the front yard was a sign from a local real estate agent, complete with SOLD declaration.

Fred liked printing pictures. He liked to see what people found interesting enough to capture it forever in time. Fred loved the stories the photos told about what the people were like. He liked to see what was important to people (though some people had a weird sense of importance).

Fred always liked to see the customers pick up their pictures. Some of them he recognized from the pictures. Others, like those who just took pictures of sunsets and landscapes, were more of a surprise. They did not look like what he had pictured in his mind's eye, similar to the way radio DJs never looked the way you picture them.

Fred went back to checking out the pictures. There were waterfalls (and since there were none in the area, it must have been from a vacation) and wooded areas.

Finally, the first picture with a person came out. There was an older man standing in knee-deep water with a backpack over his shoulders. Sun reflected in the man's sunglasses, the bottoms of his shorts wet, and he wore a huge smile. Fred couldn't help but smile as well. The man looked genuinely happy. He was hiking somewhere and seemed like he was having the time of his life.

A customer came through the door. Fred helped him and returned to the pictures. A few piled up while he was helping the customer. As he took them from the rack, he shuffled through those he missed. There was an older woman in the same stream as the man. In the first picture, she was alone, and in the next, the man stood near her. Then a picture of them kissing appeared. Fred again smiled.

A picture of a girl came out, though Fred couldn't see her face. A hand was thrown toward the camera, obscuring it.

The following picture made Fred stop. It was same girl, same curly brown hair, and this time without the hand in front of her face. To Fred, she was the most beautiful woman he ever saw. He could see the way her soft brown eyes captured the sunlight, conveying a deepness he wished to explore. Fred couldn't think of why she would put her hand in front of her face. Her picture needed to be taken.

Fred wanted to meet her. Somehow. Someway. He would wait until she came in to pick up the film. Then, he would meet her. Fred guessed it was her camera, which is why she was only in two of the pictures. Someone must have taken it from her and snapped a couple of photos. Since it was her camera, she would be excited to have the pictures developed and would come in to get them.

Fred finished printing the roll and waited.

When Mr. Johnson came back to the store, Fred barraged him with questions.

"Who brought the film in?" Fred asked.

"I don't know who she was, but her last name is on the envelope," replied Mr. Johnson, stepping into the store.

Fred turned the envelope over and saw Jones written on the envelope in Mr. Johnson's barely legible scrawl. "You said "she". Was she around my age?"

He knew he couldn't just look up the name in the phone book. There were hundreds of Joneses out there. It would take him days—even months.

"I've never seen you like this. Why all the questions?"

Fred opened the envelope and shuffled through the pictures. When he came to the one he wanted, he flipped it over.

"Her," Fred said, turning it for Mr. Johnson to see.

"What about her?" Mr. Johnson asked, stepping closer.

"She's the most beautiful woman I've ever seen."

Mr. Johnson laughed. "This is unlike you. We have a good number of pretty girls come through here. I thought you were dead."

Fred was mildly amused.

"While she is very pretty, I don't know who she is."

When Fred showed up for work the next day, the pictures were gone.

"The same woman who dropped them off picked them up," Mr. Johnson said before Fred even uttered a sound.

"Did you ask about the girl?"

"No, I'll leave the matchmaking up to you."

Fred was a little upset, not at Mr. Johnson, but at the fact he didn't yet know who this girl was. In the six months He'd been working for Mr. Johnson, Fred used the job as a respite from losing his parents his senior year of college. With the large settlement provided by the insurance, Fred didn't need the job. However, after sitting around the house for three months after the accident, he needed something to occupy his time. Mr. Johnson, a family friend, offered Fred a job at his photography studio. Fred took it begrudgingly, but soon began to enjoy the job. Now, there was another reason to come to work.

A week went by and Fred was stuck with only the image of the nameless girl. Again, when Fred was at lunch when the door chime rang. Mr. Johnson took care of it, and when the door chimed again to signal the customer leaving, he appeared.

Mr. Johnson held the film by his thumb and forefinger. "You may want to print this," he said with a smile. "She was in again."

Fred, mouth full of a turkey sandwich, stared at Mr. Johnson in a combination of disbelief and excitement. He snatched the roll and started it in the developer. Impatiently, he went back to eating his sandwich. When the negatives emerged, he began to process them through the printer. He tried to get a peek at the negatives, but they were too small and too little detailed for him to make out anything.

Slowly, even more slowly than usual, Fred thought, the pictures emerged. They were more of the same. There were pictures of the inside of a house, showing empty rooms. Fred was confident in his assumption that they were new to town.

There were more pictures of her. She still looked beautiful. There were even more pictures of (what Fred assumed) were her mom and dad. Fred only cared about the pictures of her. He sighed and put the pictures in the envelope.

The next day, Fred was setting up a display on photo editing when the picturesque girl's mother entered the store. Fred's breath caught when he saw her and all he could do was stare. She looked at him and only Mr. Johnson asking if he could help her broke his trance. Fred just watched her, surprised she was there. The woman smiled on her way out the door. Fred just stared.

"I know," Fred said.

Mr. Johnson laughed and shook his head.

"I hope she comes in again soon."

Fred moped around for the next couple of weeks. Every time he was away, he would ask Mr. Johnson if she dropped off any film. Every time he heard the door open, he ran to see who appeared, hoping he would see Mrs. Jones.

It took two long weeks before she showed up again. Fred did a little better this time, actually mustering up the brainpower to mutter the word hi and avoid being a staring fool.

She handed him the film and he asked for her name. By the time he wrote it on the envelope, she was gone without Fred able to engage her in small talk.

Surprisingly, Mrs. Jones showed up later that same day. Fred never expected to see her, as it was customary for her to wait a couple days.

"Hi there," she said as she stepped into the store and noticed Fred.

"Hello, Mrs. Jones. Your pictures are ready."

"Yes, ma'am."

"Such a polite young man."

Fred blushed and smiled. "Thank you. Here are your pictures. Is that your daughter in those pictures?"

"Yes, it is. Why do you ask?"

"Well, I hope this isn't out of line, and I know it probably is, but she's the most beautiful woman I've ever seen."

Mrs. Jones smiled. "Is that so? I'll be sure to let her know. Have a good day, Fred."

"You as well, Mrs. Jones. Thank you."

"Thank you."

She walked out, and Fred couldn't believe himself. He couldn't believe he actually said something to her mother. He wondered if that would be the last time the Joneses would be in the store to get their film developed. Mr. Johnson may not agree with him, but Fred though it was worth the chance.

Fred was not concerned the Joneses hadn't been in the store in a few weeks. He was still riding the high from his brave conversation with Mrs. Jones. He was secretly hoping the daughter would just come in.

Three weeks after the conversation with Mrs. Jones, they returned. However, this time Mr. Jones brought in the film. Fred, recognizing him from the pictures, was a bit panicked by the site of him. He was not a large or frightening man, but it was the timing of the situation. Prior to this, Mrs. Jones had been the one dropping off the film. Now, the husband was getting involved.

"You're Fred, right?" Mr. Jones asked. To Fred, his voice sounded deeper and meaner than it really was.

"Yes, sir," Fred said. It was all he could think to say at this point. His brain was busy playing through hundreds of different scenarios as to how this would play out.

"You don't have to call me sir. I'm not wearing a tie," Mr. Jones smiled and relaxed a little. "Can you print these for me? The last name is Jones."

"Not a problem."

"Thanks."

"Thank you."

Fred began to develop the film right away while replaying the interaction on an endless loop in his mind. While it was developing, Fred did some other tasks around the store. He straightened up a film display, which was disheveled from little kids touching it. They always seemed to gravitate toward it, so Fred stacked it in the shape of a pyramid. He realized He'd probably have to clean it up sooner rather than later, but it would be fun.

He dusted around pictures on the wall, and when the roll had completely come out of the developer, he dropped everything.

He brought the film to the printer and fed it through, smiling in anticipation. He couldn't wait to see what was on the roll. The printer again seemed to take longer to print than they normally did. Anticipation seemed to be the only thing capable of slowing down time.

The first one popped out, but it wasn't of her. It was pictures of the inside of a house again. There were many pictures of people painting walls. There were pictures of her and a few of her family members, all with paint on their faces and clothes. It looked like they were having fun.

The last picture came out and completely took Fred by surprise. It was not a photo of her. Instead, it was a picture of one of the walls being painted. Someone used a roller to paint "HI FRED" on the wall.

Fred smiled. He showed Mr. Johnson as well. "Sounds like you have yourself a little fan club. Good for you."

Mr. Jones returned, and Fred was still smiling. Mr. Johnson helped him because he knew that Fred was still on cloud nine.

Mr. Jones exited the store and Fred wondered what it all meant.

Fred was unsure what to do. He hoped the mystery girl decided to do it after her mom told her what Fred thought. Because she wasn't in the picture, she would have taken it. Fred thought she might have taken it when no one else was around. On the other hand, maybe her family took it without her knowledge.

As difficult as it would be, Fred decided he would wait and see how it played out. He didn't know what he was going to do.

A week later, he knew it wasn't a fluke. The Joneses dropped off another roll of film. Fred wasn't around when they came in to drop off the film, but he still processed it. The last picture on the roll again was for him. It was another wall and the only thing painted on it was a sad face.

Fred knew he had work to do.

Fred removed the Polaroid from the shelf. He grabbed a piece of poster board and a marker and wrote, Sorry! Hi! and added a smile. He took a picture. When the picture appeared, Fred stuffed it in the envelope and waited for it to be picked up.

"Here you are, Julie," Mrs. Jones said as she handed her daughter the pictures. Mrs. Jones brought the pictures home with specific instructions that she was not allowed to look at them until her daughter did.

"Thanks, Mom," Julie replied, anxious to see what was inside.

When her mom left the room, she opened the envelope and immediately noticed the oddly shaped picture. She removed it and set the others aside. She laughed and smiled at the picture. Her mom was right. He was nice.

They went back and forth with pictures. Every time the Joneses brought in a roll of film, at least one picture on it was for Fred - most times more than one. They learned a lot about each other over the next few weeks. Fred finally learned her name (though he still like calling her the "picturesque girl") and what she liked to do for fun. Fred gave her the same courtesy, and although it was slow going, they really enjoyed themselves.

Fred developed the latest roll from the Joneses. There was only one picture for Fred on this roll. It showed a pamphlet for a local fair. There was a sticky note attached, on which Julie had written Meet me here, eight o'clock Friday night. Fred smiled.

The rain that passed through earlier in the day chilled the evening air, and the seemingly constant breeze did nothing to make it warmer. Fred, wearing a light jacket to keep out the cold, was there before eight o'clock and nervous, which made him feel colder. He paid the three-dollar admission fee and went inside. He scanned the crowd but didn't see her.

He sat on a vacant bench and watched as people filed in. There were people of all ages, but there was no sign of her. Fred looked at his watch and saw she had eight minutes until she was late.

Trying to rid himself of nervous energy, he got up and began to walk around, still keeping the entrance in his line of sight. He took turns watching people play games of chance, checking his watch, and checking the gate.

Someone was in the process of winning a giant stuffed dog and everyone cheered when he succeeded. Fred looked at his watch and saw it was past eight. Did he get stood up?

She was already at the fair when he showed up. She watched him enter the gate and look around. She laughed at the almost obsessive glances at his watch. He was nervous too, and that made her relax. She had butterflies in her stomach all day, but knowing he felt the same way comforted her. She watched him walk around, alternating glances between the entrance and his watch. She watched him gather with the crowd near another game. When he didn't check his watch for the first time in thirty seconds, she walked toward him. The closer she got, the more the butterflies returned. A cheer erupted from the crowd and she was standing right behind him when he looked at his watch.

"I've been here. I'm not late."

Fred whipped around and the roaring crowd behind him ceased to exist. Even more beautiful than the picture, his mouth went dry, and he just stared. He managed to smile at her and she smiled back. The parting crowd bumped into Fred from behind, breaking the trace.

"Hi. I'm Julie," she said, smiling sheepishly. Her breath caught when he turned to look at her. She thought he was so handsome and his brown eyes complimented his soft face and dark hair.

"I'm Fred." He wanted to hug her, but it seemed so weird. Even though they weren't technically strangers, he wasn't sure how it would be received. He waited.

They looked at each other for a long time, embracing a moment that rarely happened, and allowed it to remove the trepidation they felt before meeting each other.

When they both relaxed, they decided to walk around the fair together. They ate the greasy fair food and talked. Eventually, they found a bench where the noises of the fair provided little interruption. They could still hear the screams of the patrons on the thrill rides and the shouts of victory from men trying to win their dates a prize, but mostly, they focused on each other.

He held her hand as they talked. They discussed trivial things as the nerves calmed down. After an hour, when they felt more comfortable with one another, the questions became more personal.

"So, did your mom think I was weird for asking her about her daughter?"

Julie laughed. "No, my mom was telling me about you before you said anything to her. She wanted me to get to know people around here and she said you seemed nice enough to show me around. And, she thought you were very polite—and cute."

Fred deflected the compliment. "I felt dumb saying that to her, but I knew I had to say something. I'm glad she was all right with it. I was a little concerned that I crossed the line because it was a while before she came in again. And then it was your dad, not your mom that came in."

"That was coincidence. My mom had some stuff to do with the house, so my dad brought in the film that day. They all knew what was on it. That's why my dad gave you a little extra time with the film. That was his idea and he was proud of it. He wanted to be sure you had a chance to write back or give me a note of some kind."

They smiled at each other. The clouds had cleared, and the moon was high in the sky. The lights from the fair didn't detract from its romantic aura.

Julie continued to explain to him about the move and all the pictures surrounding it. She loved to take pictures, which is why they were constantly developing film. Julie looked at it as a visual diary.

She began talking about how nice of a night it was and how great it was to be with him. He said he felt the same. He leaned in closer, placed a hand on her cheek, and kissed her softly. There was much emotion in it and only the two of them existed. They went back for more.

Breaking the kiss at the same time, they hugged each other, unsure of what else to do after such a sensual, ethereal moment. The fair was ending for the evening. They had three hours together, but it seemed like a lifetime. They made plans to meet again the next night. As they went to their own vehicles, they couldn't wait to be together again.

Fred went into work Saturday morning, and for the four hours the store was open, he talked about nothing but meeting Julie. The smile on his face would not go away. Mr. Johnson asked a few questions, waiting for the answers with mild bemusement. He would have asked more questions, but Fred would digress for longer than necessary on any given question. When Mr. Johnson asked when they would see each other again, Fred went on about how he couldn't wait to see her again and he couldn't believe how well they hit it off the first night. Fred felt like He'd known her forever.

Fred picked Julie up and they headed to dinner. Fred pulled her chair out for her and she sat down. She thanked him as he seated himself to her left. The host gave them their menus, took their drink orders, and left them to each other.

The candle at the center of the table provided enough light to read the menu. Fred enjoyed watching as the candlelight flickered across her face and danced in her eyes.

"Fred, this place is so nice. Thank you for bringing me here. Everything is so beautiful."

"It's not as beautiful as you," Fred replied and they both laughed. He knew how corny it sounded but he couldn't prevent the words from coming out of his mouth.

The server came back, and they placed their orders. When the server was gone, they held hands and talked for a bit. It didn't last long because the server soon returned with a basket of bread and butter.

They each took a piece and buttered it. As he was eating, Fred looked around. It really was a romantic atmosphere. He couldn't have imagined a more perfect setting. His date was radiant. He couldn't believe he was here with her. First, he only knew her from a picture and now he was sitting here with her.

"What's on your mind, Fred? You look like you're deep in thought," Julie said.

Fred smiled. "Before I knew your name, I just referred to you as the "picturesque girl". The first picture I saw of you, your hand was in front of your face as if you didn't want your picture taken. I couldn't believe you wouldn't want your picture taken. I was so glad there was another picture of you. I thought you were beautiful. Then I meet you in person and you are even more beautiful than your picture.

She smiled and bowed her head in embarrassment. "Thank you, Fred. That's very sweet."

"It's true. And you look beautiful in that dress."

"Thank you. You had more to go on than I did. I only knew what my mom told me. I was so nervous that night at the fair because I didn't know. I didn't know what to expect or how to feel. Fred, you are the sweetest, most polite, and compassionate person I've ever met."

It was Fred's turn to shy away. "Thank you, Julie."

"I could hardly sleep last night. The time I spent with you last night was so perfect. I wanted the night to go on forever. This one too."

"I didn't either. I bent Mr. Johnson's ear today at work about how last night was and how I was looking forward to tonight."

The server brought out their entrees, momentarily breaking the natural back and forth of their conversation. They began eating and talked between bites.

"So, you were looking forward to tonight?" Julie asked, returning to the conversation.

"Of course, I was. I had such a great time last night and there was a certain quality in the air. As you said, it was perfect. I felt as if I were walking in a dream."

Julie was no longer eating. She had stopped when he began speaking, hoping he would say that he, too, was looking forward to this evening. Julie couldn't stop talking to her mother about Fred (of course, sparing her some details) and how much she couldn't wait for tonight as well. A single tear fell from her left eye—Fred saw it shimmer in the candlelight—and cascaded down her cheek.

"What's wrong?" Fred asked.

"Nothing. This is all just too amazing to me. I can't believe this is happening, Fred."

"Neither can I, but I'm glad it is."

Through the rest of the meal, they said little, only staring at one another, very aware of the emotions between them.

Fred took Julie home and walked her to her doorstep. The porch light was on and to Fred it seemed like everyone was sleeping.

"Thank you for a fabulous night, Fred."

"You're welcome Julie. I had a great time. You looked wonderful tonight."

She kissed him. It was though the emotions of the night culminated to that single event. They were alive with things they never felt before.

"Goodnight, Julie."

"Goodnight, Fred."

As the months went by, Fred and Julie we inseparable, seeing each other every day. One Sunday, they met for brunch, saw a movie and walked around the mall, shopping for nothing in particular.

They started talking about things. Fred told her about his parents, speaking more in depth, telling her the story of the accident and everything that happened afterward. He explained how he came to work at Mr. Johnson's store because of it, which was ultimately, how he met her.

Julie explained her history of moving and why she still lived with her parents. Her parents, while doing other small jobs, made large profits on flipping houses. They liked to buy older homes and remodel them. Then, they resold them at a profit. It was their way of playing the stock market. They had quite a bit of money saved up for retirement this way. Julie helped them out with taking pictures and documenting the renovations of all the houses.

It never occurred to Fred what this may mean. He was too intrigued by her, too lost in the way she spoke to foresee a problem.

They went in a few stores, just to look around. They were just trying to spend as much time with each other as they could.

Fred took Julie home. The sun was just setting. They sat on the porch and talked a bit more.

"Julie, please tell me this feeling will never go away."

"What feeling?" she asked, her heart caught in her chest.

"The feeling of us. There is so much between us it's amazing. I hate to repeat myself, but I don't know how else to describe it. It is truly incredible."

"Yes Fred, it is. Sometimes, it leaves me speechless."

"Julie, I love you."

"I love you too, Fred."

As time moved on, they became closer. However, Julie seemed to be in low spirits. Fred picked her up and as soon as they got in the car, he asked what was wrong.

She began crying. Fred, not knowing what else to do or what had caused her tears, hugged her.

"Fred, we have to talk."

Fred had heard those words before and knew they never preceded anything good. "What's wrong Jules?

"We're moving again. My parents found another fix me up about 16 hours from here. They've already visited it once and they want to buy it. They're going back in about a month to close on the house and get all the paperwork through. My dad said it'd probably be about two months before we move."

Fred didn't know what to say.

"I don't want this to change anything, but I don't know how it can't. We are going to be so far away from each other. I don't know what to do. I've been crying ever since they told me. I don't know what to do Fred."

"Julie, it will be okay. I promise. Everything will work out." He wanted to believe that, but at that moment, he was having a difficult time.

They spent the rest of the night outside of Julie's house, sitting in the car. They didn't say much to each other, but there was plenty on their minds. They kissed and parted ways, knowing that the situation would never be resolved that evening.

Fred tossed and turned, trying to think of a way they could be together. He was up all night trying to find a way to keep the perfect relationship alive. As the sun woke, and he was just drifting off to sleep, he knew what he had to do.

They saw each other as often as they could. While Fred knew what had to be done, he needed some time to complete the plan. In the meantime, he consoled Julie when she needed to be consoled and told her that everything was going to be all right.

Two weeks after he found out that Julie was moving, Fred went to Julie's house. It wasn't to see Julie; it was to talk to her dad. Fred was nervous.

Mr. Jones answered the door and welcomed Fred. Walking through the house made Fred sad. Though he knew - hoped - things were going to work out, it was still difficult to accept. Boxes, some empty, some full, were in every room. Crumpled newspaper lay beside boxes holding fragile items. Fred sighed.

Mr. Jones led Fred to the living room and told him to have a seat on the couch. He sat down in the recliner. They began talking about the weather and sports. Mr. Jones humored him for a bit, and after chatting for about fifteen minutes, Mr. Jones spoke up.

"Why are you really here Fred? I know you didn't come here to talk about the weather. I've never seen you so nervous. What's on your mind?"

Fred swallowed hard, knowing that this was a big step. "I came here to ask you a favor. I know you're moving very soon. I can see all the boxes around and Julie has told me. I have known Julie for a couple years now and she is the most incredible person I know. I can't stand the thought of being so far away from her. I've thought long and hard about it and I know it's the right thing to do." Fred swallowed his mouth very dry. He wished he could have a drink. He was very thirsty.

"Go on."

"Well, I wanted your permission to ask your daughter to marry me."

Mr. Jones sat there. Fred couldn't quite read the expression on Mr. Jones' face and his stomach turned. For what seemed like an eternity, Mr. Jones just looked at Fred.

Slowly, Mr. Jones began to smile. He got up for his chair, stepped over to the couch, and offered Fred his hand. Fred shook it. "Julie's mom and I had been wondering if this was going to happen. The two of you seem to complement each other so well. We figured it was bound to come up, especially after we decided to move. Believe me Fred, I wish we didn't have to. Would you mind telling me your plans?" He grinned.

Fred smiled. "I'm going to keep you in suspense." They shook hands again and laughed.

"The missus is going to be very happy to hear this. And I'm sure Julie will be too."

"Let's hope so."

Fred and Julie planned their annual trip to the local Fair for Friday night. Instead of meeting each other there, they rode together. They parked the car and walked toward the entrance, talking again, about how their first meeting was a dream.

"You seem quiet. Are you alright?" Julie asked.

"I'm fine. I'm just remembering."

They walked on, paid their admission fee, and began walking around. They ate more food and then progressed to their bench. He was still quiet, and she decided to let him be for a bit.

Fred knew she wasn't having much fun. Well, she at least wasn't having as much fun as she should have been. He wasn't sure he knew what he was waiting for. He was trying to be fun and not think about what he was going to do, but he was so nervous. He was almost sure she would say yes, but there was that shadow of doubt there.

He wanted it to be perfect and he wanted it to be here, where they first met. He was concerned about all the people that were around. He didn't do well with an audience

He looked at her knowing he had to do it soon or she wouldn't be very happy with him. He loved her.

She knew her departure date was getting closer and she was sure that was weighing on his mind as heavily as it was hers. She was closer to him now and that made her feel safe and secure. She was still worried about him and concerned about his thoughts. She knew she had to say something to put her mind at ease.

"Fred, are you worried about me moving? I know it's going to work out. I'm not sure how, but it just has to."

She saw him smile a bit. She felt better when he smiled. He reached in his pocket and handed her a picture. In the photo, he was down on one knee. She looked at him with curiosity. Then he got up.

He saw the look of confusion envelope her face when he got up. He thought the picture was a nice touch, seeing as that was how they met. He was sure she understood it, but he doubted she really comprehended it.

He stood there looking at her, admiring her beauty like he has so many times before. "Julie, I remember when we first met here two years ago. It was the most wonderful experience of my life. Since then, you have become my best friend. You are someone I confide my hopes, dreams, and fears in. I can't fathom being in this world without you. I can't imagine doing anything without you." Fred reached into his pocket, grabbed the ring, and got down on one knee. "Will you marry me?"

She looked at the ring, then at him. Her eyes were filled with tears. She reached for him and embraced him strongly. She pulled back, looked at him again with tears streaming down her face, and hugged him again.

"So, is that a yes?"

She pulled back again and smiled at him. "Yes! Yes!"

A small crowd gathered, and they applauded when they heard her accept. Neither of them knew anyone was there. Anxious to tell family and friends, they left to pats on the back and words of encouragement.

When they pulled up to Julie's house, the light immediately went on and Julie's mom was on the doorstep.

"Hi, Mom," Julie said, acting like nothing exciting happened.

"Hello Julie. Hello Fred. How are the two of you this evening?"

"We're fine. And yourself?" Fred asked, chiming in.

"Terrific. I just wanted to make sure the two of you had a good time." Mrs. Jones was practically bursting with anticipation.

"Want to see what Fred won me at the fair?" Julie was holding her hands behind her back.

"Yes."

Julie pulled her right hand from behind her back and showed it to her mom. "It must be the other hand."

Everyone smiled. Julie brought her hand around from behind her back and displayed the ring for her mother. It sparkled brightly in the porch light. Mrs. Jones began crying and hugged her daughter. Then, she hugged her future son-in-law.

"This is so great. You guys will be so happy together."

The wheels were set in motion to plan the wedding. Fred and Julie wanted to get married in the time before her parents move. They decided on a small ceremony with only family and close friends attending. The Joneses suggested the backyard of their current house.

They began making phone calls and sending out invitations. In one month, they would be married.

The backyard of the Jones" house looked immaculate. Countless measures had been taken to ensure the yard looked magical.

It was the morning of the wedding and Fred snuck over to survey the scene. He was feeling nervous, excited, and scared, but all these emotions went away when he saw the setting.

Julie and he would be standing in a gazebo at the back of the lot. Fully bloomed rose bushes lined both sides of the property. There were three rows of five chairs on each side of the aisle.

Fred left, filled with a sense of calmness from what he had seen. Momentarily, he forgot about all that had been going on. The sight of the backyard, even though it was related to the wedding, calmed him. He knew he was making the right decision to be with her.

Julie hardly slept. She was half-awake when the sun rose on her wedding day. She was nervous and excited. She lay in bed for a bit, reflecting on what had passed, and what lie ahead. She thought about how the two of them were together and she saw nothing but a bright future ahead.

She got out of bed, stretched, and shuffled toward the window. When she pulled back the curtain, her breath caught, and she was more awake now than she had been all week.

She was overlooking the backyard, seeing the same things Fred saw only moments earlier. She began to cry tears of joy.

As Julie began walking down the aisle with her father, tears filled Fred's eyes. In fact, there was not a dry eye to be seen. Fred had never seen her look so beautiful, not in the first picture and not on the night he proposed. He knew she would grow more beautiful as the years went on.

After pausing for Mr. Johnson to take a picture, they made their way toward Fred. Julie's father hugged him and then gave Julie's hand to Fred. They were married. Together they walked hand in hand down the aisle and rode in a limo to the reception.

The reception was just as beautiful as the wedding. The place was wonderfully decorated. As Fred and Julie shared their first dance together, they talked about how things got to this point. Neither of them could believe that their whole relationship started because she was so photogenic.

The day was over. They were married. Everything was picture perfect.

Piece by Piece,
It Leaves and Returns
Chereze Booysen

It lives and it dies.
It strives and it fails.
It guides but is lost.
It finds but keeps seeking.
It contains hope, but strains in tears.
It screams trust but encases suspicion.
It howls love but gives birth to detestation.
It bellows honesty but steals integrity.
Love is a difficult emotion defined by all.
Few get the opportunity to experience love.
Those that do not know how to describe it.

Pursuit at Dawn
Billy Malanga

That's a raspy barn owl, I said.
It's a mourning dove, she said.
We lay quietly, stainless like soupspoons
while the restless male exposed himself,
eager to find a lover to pass his seed,
to choose a secure nest in the shadow
of daybreak.

Then his calls faded into the morning
blast of machines and busy folk,
where the sun greets the bold
and turns Autumn to gold.
He reminded me, I should've flown
straight to you long ago,
down into the bare hills
where your tender Appalachian soul
fluttered, instead I corkscrewed
like a fool.

But his time is our time,
I press hard into my Angel and can see
my whole valley, her wings stir
the air and her fiery sword ignites
the room, guides my body
more surely to paradise.

Reach for the World
Joseph Murphy

June passes
And you have left
Speechless At your table
A last few Sunlit moments
Weaving These well-shaded streets
As my thoughts Turn To that ghost
Your touch
Lost somewhere
Behind the moon
While I imagine The brightness of our hope
One morning As we wake
Just eyes Just children Looking out
From the distance of another world

Reflections
Joseph Murphy

Here By the shore Things seem easy
I chant to the four quarters And to the mouth of the river In
remembrance Of our sighs
Many shades of clover Sing here in the wind
But it seems The light they cast Is hollow
But when I recall Your lips
The constant roll of pebbles Beneath insects" hooves Does not
frighten me
And I have these words What's more This pen Beaming in the dark
That lingers Within each well-lit Hope
I still sometimes seek A hiding place A distant moon's Darker side
At other times feel Like the barrel of a gun
In those times Money has been good I buy myself A foothold Beg to
rest Beneath your skin
Not to harm you But to be a holy man Just for you
If only I could find A hilltop to fortify A map To aid us
But I know Old masters Have told me
When this river was a mountain All our hands were joined
None were homeless And this planet Was our tongue

Ribbon
Gavin Meggs

There are strands which run through our lives and bind us together
Fundamental elements which when viewed from up close seem
disconnected But from a distance their substance assumes meaning
Like staccato strobes passing in and out of view
Until you begin to feel the beat and Understand their flow
For me the threads are most often sensual Feelings of togetherness
which retain their connections Across the divides between us
A catalogue of imagery and music so intricate that it carries our
combined DNA Perhaps from this world into the next A tactile
moment, often imagined Which brings depth and understanding in
moments of fear
And yet, I do not feel bound by these ribbons
I feel free to love and to be loved And I pray that this loving can last

Seascape
Sandeep Kumar Mishra

My love, my dream! Come with me,
We will blanket the lea, beyond the sea,
Build a palace among the stars
Far from earthly strife and wars;
Look at the rainbows, the white rivers,
Slaty mountains, red roses, brown sparrows,
Bright glow worms, golden eagles, black bees,
Yellow sunflowers, scarlet macaw, green trees;
Showers drench the morning, nights glow with dew,
Posy noon to dose, then evening linnets in view;
Winter with warm sun, moonlit cool nights,
I admire thy grace; thy touch razes my frights;
When your raven-blown hair radiates—shades,
I repose in your lap, night comes, day fades
Your wondrous, hazel eyes keep me at ease,
We will love till there are stars, skies, seas.

Serenade Andante
Joseph Murphy

I could hear your voice Within mine Moving I was the tide And
hopeful Waiting again With fire
All the saints are waiting In blue houses Where halls of little birds
Will kiss you Kiss the leaves As teachers Little portraits of Buddha
Beaming On the branch
I will see you Light and roving On the chest of hours As I hold you
Naked As I kiss you Like the sea Kiss you Like the fruit Of stars

She Walks in Rhyme
Sandeep Kumar Mishra

When my eager-eagle eyes saw thee,
I found a thrall in the veins,
A stop in the labor heart pumping the red;
Like a day of golden sun in summer bright,
She comes as morn's refreshing breeze,
A live garden forever in bloom;
Half shy of thy own glory
Fair than the fairer, a shine that never fades,
Her aspects best of dark and light;
Her lips are coral red,
Cheeks are roses red and white,
A valley in the breasts, deep and steep
A smile that wins a thousand realms,
Her charm that pleases but
Might waste thy youth in sighs;
Her airy hair swings spider" silver line,
Mild voice fades like an old opera tunes,
The perfume of her soul feels you vigor,
As she walks in rhyme on blank verse path
A thousand nameless graces moves;
When she dances with autumn leaves
A soft whisperings vibrate in our spirit,
She shakes earth beneath and sky above
For she is a deity, an incarnation,
I can only see through my close eyes

Such Is Love After Lovelessness
J. J. Steinfeld

I buy my dreams, she says softly
and offers me wakefulness
such is the promise of love.

Reach for the lightning, she encourages me
mistaking me for that unforgotten lover
abandoned at the edge of the sea
before high tide, before the unforeseen,
near or at transmigration's unfurling.

You said to me, she recalls,
I cannot think here, I cannot leave,
everyone here dies without thrashing,
praying for another hour.

We never spoke before, I want to say,
to drown in honesty
but I run from the sea
in memory and in passion.

Lying there, warm with tears, her words are not a lover's:
Compare the lives of loves who have died
attempt to recall flesh and foolish words
forget the fears, wondrous as they might be
get to the endings bleeding into beginnings.

Lying there, cold with uncertainty,
my thoughts are not a lover's:
What a formidable escape artist
what a result of too many madnesses
of walking along demanding streets, fully clothed
wishing for nakedness, for a hint of the indisputable.

Then the morning comes
with the surprise of unintended wisdom
I remember my name
and ask to visit the edge of the sea.
Another less disarranged day
I will write her name not with misgiving
but with leniency and piety
and the serene calligraphy of desire.

I buy my dreams, she shouts
and stabs me into the best of sleeps
such is love after lovelessness.

Surprise 20ᵗʰ Anniversary Party
September 1976
Michael D. Jones

Once upon a time might surprise once
Like miniature franks wrapped in bacon
Or wrapped in crescent roll dough
Or helplessly swimming in BBQ sauce
Sooner or later it's the expected appetizer.
Surprise pales with familiarity.   Yet, we
Frequent occasions for Loves expression
Knowing that once, just once, a surprise party
Is surprising- for everyone; the honoree
The guests, and the hosts (which were us
although not old enough to drive a car)
Working the room with hors d'oeuvres
Dark as ambush, stealthy as covert operation
As sleight of hand magic; your Best Man
And Maid of Honor, friends from the club
Former business associates, pot-luck group
And their invisible spouses materialized
Infinitely pleased with cheese and crackers
Attempting to cut Surprises" dark tension
With cheap wine and colored toothpicks
And our love, hot like miniature franks.
One of many ways love leaves a strange
Desire for Spearmint gum, surprising us all.

Tale of Woe
Mahinour Tawfik

My heart is weighed down and I can't tell
For you won't comprehend and I don't know
How much misery -in a heart-can dwell
Dare not look deep, there are tales of woe

Ahead of titles, engraved "Farewell"
Every smile sows seeds of throes
Jaded with wondering if it's heaven or hell
So here's my heart, darling- I bestow

Will you hold it tight or let it hail
After you have become another tale?

The Breakdown of Love
Rebecca Ruth Gould

"You must tell me if you ever feel unloved," he whispered as he ran his fingers through her hair. They had known each other for only six days, yet love was rapidly spiralling around them. They had lived through the process before, and were wary of activating the familiar oxytocins again. Their flesh was heavy with the smells and tastes of former affections.

"If you ever feel unloved, you will tell me, okay?"

"Okay," she said.

"Promise?"

She promised, unable to imagine ever feeling unloved by him, the most affectionate man she had ever known. For the past six days, his hands had not parted with her skin. They had met in Paris, in arrondissement thirteen, at the Hotel Belambra on Rue Corvisart. They had been introduced to each other through email by one of his friends, Sam, who was trying to help Jacques break with his past. Sam had met Melissa at a conference that had been convened to honour her former husband, who had died in a car crash, three years earlier. Although she would never forget him, she told Sam over too many glasses of wine, she was ready to move on, to find another man. The problem was, there was no one to fall in love with, no one not already committed. "Well," said Sam, "I have a friend who is also looking for a woman to love."

As it turned out, Sam's friend was Jacques, who happened to be a friend of her friend Jessica. Hence, they were connected by two degrees of separation. Sam told Jacques that his friend Jessica had a friend named Melissa whom he might be interested in. Jessica introduced them by email. "You two are a match made in heaven," Jessica whispered in Melissa's ear as she escorted her to the train station. "I predict You'll be drawn to each other and will never let go."

She got lost on the way to the hotel, but was able to find him easily by asking at the reception in what room he was staying. He came down and they greeted each other like old friends. Breakfast went well, and extended into lunch. Lunch soon became a dinner neither of them wanted to end. Jacques could not summon the courage to kiss her on the first night, although he wanted to. They fell asleep in separate beds. The sense that something was about to happen was palpable. She appreciated the delay, as it gave her more time to savour the anticipation, the waiting for his kiss. It only goes downhill after that, she told herself, weary with memories of the past lovers from her pre-marriage years. Early on the morning of their second day together, immediately after breakfast, he asked if he could come to her room. He started telling her about a novel he was reading, Stoner by John Williams, a classic work that had been neglected during the author's lifetime. Then suddenly, he stopped in mid-sentence and kissed her on the lips. Their bodies had been magnetically linked together ever since.

Jacques would not have been her first choice, had the choice been put to her in this way. He was a civil servant in a vast European bureaucracy, and a theoretical physicist by training. What could be less promising than a man with no professional ties to the arts, whose job did not require him to live the life of the mind? She had had her fill of scientists in her private life. As a class, they struck her as emotionally barren, narrow-minded, vulgar, and unable to speak about anything not directly relevant to their field of expertise.

Even worse: he appeared to have abandoned his research after he failed to obtain an academic position. So, he entered the civil service, selling his soul to the government. A sell-out! How could they possibly share their passions, given the different choices they had made with their lives? His job that brought in a good income and job security, but it could never fill his life with meaning. Her vocation that paid badly, yet it nourished her deepest spiritual needs. What if he doesn't understand my passions? she mused. What if he's intimidated by me, as men tend to be? Notwithstanding her doubts, Melissa trusted her friend's instinct, and persisted with the assignation.

Jessica's instincts had been right. After the breakfast that became a kiss, they continued talking all through the afternoon and deep into the night. They canvassed the city, oblivious to their surroundings. Shakespeare & Co, the bookstore that had hosted Joyce and Hemingway, became an occasion for sharing every book they had ever read, as they sat side by side on a dilapidated sofa in the back room on the second story and picked books off the shelves. Rue Lepic became the plays of Chekhov. Rue Saint-Antoine became Dostoevsky. Rue des Rosiers became the films of Krzysztof Kieślowski.

They spent three days wandering around the catacombs and in and out of the Pantheon. They recast the alleys and boulevards of Paris in the images of their beloved writers, poets, and filmmakers. While meandering through one alley way, he invited her to travel back with him to Brussels, to pass the rest of the vacation with him in his recently acquired home. "There will be lots of space, and a room just for you in case you want to be alone," Jacques explained. It was winter vacation for them both, and his son was spending the Christmas break with his mother, so they could extend their date across the entire Christmas holiday and celebrate the New Year together. 2015 had been a year of partings and deaths. 2016, they decided, would be a year of union.

They took the Thalys train from Paris to his Brussels home locked in each other's grip. The sensation of touching someone in that way, with such repeated intensity, had long been forgotten by them both. He immediately escorted her to his library, and proudly pointed to three bookshelves filled with an assortment of DVDs,

Blu-rays, and even some videos. His collection of films as well as of books was vast, covering all times, places, and genres.

The middle of the second bookshelf was dedicated to the films of Fritz Lang. Lang was his favourite director, Jacques explained. He told her the story of Lang's escape to Hollywood the very day that he had been offered the position of head of the national German film studio by Joseph Goebbels himself. Lang's wife refused to accompany her husband and chose instead to remain behind with the Nazi regime.

The two lovers decided to organize a private festival of Fritz Lang's films in the basement of Jacques" four-story home, which doubled as a screening room. They watched two films per night, one from Lang's German period and one from after his migration to America. During the second film, her hand would gently caress his penis until it was entirely erect. Sometimes they would continue watching the movie to the end, and sometimes they would stop right there and make love.

The night when he insisted that she tell him if she ever felt unloved was the third day of their private festival. *M* from the German period had been followed by *You Only Live Once* from Lang's American era. They ate bougatsa, a cream-filled Greek pie, together, and licked the lemon sauce topping off each other's lips.

They went to bed that night as they had had done on each of the three days they had been together: locked in each other's arms. He woke up sweating, wrapped his arms even more tightly around her, and interwove his legs into her body. The combination of conversation and physical intimacy brought tears to her eyes. Her body had hungered for such contact for too many years.

Soon after becoming a widow, she had fallen in love with a married man who had not loved her back. His affection was elsewhere committed, and nothing she could do, he informed her, would ever change that. She was ashamed to admit it, but it was true: her love for the married man had devastated her even more than the death of her husband and the end of her thirteen-year long marriage. Meanwhile, Jacques had been raising a child with a woman who revealed that she had stopped loving him. In the final year of their relationship, she repelled his embraces and told him she hated the sound of his voice. Melissa by contrast was passionate, too passionate for him to fully reciprocate. Yet in the early stages of their love, they were able to adapt to each other's idiosyncrasies.

One flaw was gradually becoming more and more evident with each conversation: he was tone-deaf to poetry. After they had catalogued all the novels, plays, and short stories they had ever read, she asked him about the poets. "Aren't there any poets you love to read?" she said. "About poetry, you will have to teach me," he answered. "It's a mystery to me why people devote themselves so intensely to this art. Poetry reminds me of gardening. Sure, it doesn't do any harm. But what good does it do? Perhaps you can convince me otherwise."

Words were her life, and poetry was her most complete form of sustenance. She felt a twinge of pain as he spoke, but it soon became submerged with other emotions as they indulged their shared passions.

Five days into her visit, she found herself thinking every day: this is as close to paradise as it gets, as much like Eden as the earth permits. She felt blessed, and on the path to happiness. She told herself that she was, at long last and after a year of drought in her emotional existence, in love.

II.

A week after their interlude in the passage of time, she went home to Exeter, the city to which she had moved three months earlier in order to take up a position at the university. Back in Exeter, she resumed planning her lectures and correcting the proofs for her book. She began to regret that she had chosen the senior job offer extended by a university far from London over a more junior position at the University of Kent in Canterbury, within an hour's commuting distance to London. Although Exeter had much to offer that Canterbury could not, living and working at the University of Kent would have placed her along the Eurostar line, which would have meant a shorter commute to Brussels and greater proximity to her beloved. Had she worked in Canterbury, she could have lived in Ashford, within two hours commuting distance to Brussels.

Weeks became months. They spoke every night, for at an hour or more, recounting every moment of their separate lives. How they slept, what they ate, what they wore, the commute to and from work, the contents of their conversations with family and friends: everything was shared, until, inevitably, certain details were slowly, but systematically, omitted. The omitted details tended to be those were most revealing of and important to her inner life. Her inner life mattered less to him than did the places that she shopped, the number of hours she spent teaching, what she ate for lunch, and the make of the refrigerator in which she stored her food. By contrast, she couldn't care less about such details, whether they pertained to her own or to her beloved's life. Their conversations were too trivial for her taste. With every hour of interrogation, she felt increasingly alienated from the man she wanted to think of as her beloved.

The phone conversations were his initiative. She sensed they were important to him. He wanted to "do things together," as he put it, and it seemed that daily phone conversations were a necessary element in this togetherness. Flattered by his persistence and the loyalty it implied, she duly complied with his demands on her patience and time. These nightly conference calls cut into her routine—sometimes severely, causing her to lose sleep and to lose contact with her friends—and created stress. But she did not want to threaten their relationship at such an early stage in its gestation. Besides, it was nice to have someone in her life who made a ritual of talking to her everyday, whether or not she enjoyed it.

After three weeks of such exchanges, and partly to introduce a new rhythm to their interactions, they decided to reconvene in London. She had a three-day training course coming up on the topic of how to engage with government, and he was long overdue for a visit to London's theatres. He bought his Eurostar tickets and requested a few days of leave from work for the beginning of the week. She extended the hotel booking to double occupancy. They spoke with anticipation about this second rendezvous, hoping it would revive the Paris feeling, if in a different key, and with a greater degree of mutual familiarity.

Just as at their first meeting in Paris, she arrived two hours late. Along the way, she had told herself that her delay wouldn't matter much. He would be able to go directly to their hotel, and they would meet there instead of in the centre of London as planned. She had underestimated the effects of her lateness. He greeted her complaining about the hours he had lost with his son as a result of her tardiness. She tried to soothe his wounds by touching him tenderly in the places that used to trigger a reaction from his body, at least while they were in Paris and Brussels. He turned away from her, and explained he didn't feel up for sex.

The night they spent together was full of acrimony. The openness that had come to them so spontaneously in Paris seemed to have entirely vanished. The first problem was deciding on where to eat. Every place she chose was too low-class for him. He accused her of being cheap and of having no appreciation for good taste. Finally, she decided that she would not voice any preference with regard to food and would agree to any restaurant he suggested. After all, he had come to London to see her, and she ought to treat him like a guest.

Her assent drove him as crazy as did her resistance. He told her he needed to leave her for an hour, to cool down and reduce his anger. She began to touch him again, hoping through her fingers to revive their former intimacy. Because they could not agree on a place to eat, they decided to see a play first and then to resolve the issue of where to have dinner afterwards. As they walked to the Duke of York Theatre on Moor Lane, keeping clear of each other, she wondered to herself: Where did it go, that upsurge of affection that once swept over me? Why did it disappear so quickly?

The play was short and intense. Called "The Father" and translated from the French, it told the story of an aging man stricken with memory loss. Each time the father saw his daughter it was as if she were a different person, and partnered with a different man. Alzheimer's and the situation deteriorated with every new scene. Ultimately the daughter decided to shift her father to a nursing home in Paris and promised to visit him every week from London.

Jacques and Melissa sat in the front row, holding hands during the entirety of the performance. It was the first moment of genuine closeness between them since he had arrived in London, and was perhaps enabled by their reliance on gestures rather than words. She was sorry when the play ended. They would have to start speaking again. She feared that they had nothing more to say to each other. Three weeks of love, going on four, and there seemed to be nothing more to discuss.

They survived dinner with their relationship in tact, but something had changed. Every word seemed to release a toxin into the air that putrefied their entire evening. They went to sleep without having sex. It was the first sexless night they had spent together over the three months of their acquaintance. Before going to sleep she told him that he had ceased to figure into her sexual fantasies and she was worried what this meant for their relationship. He moved to the other side of the bed.

III.

They woke up the next morning uncertain how they would spend their day together. London theatres were closed on Sunday. After arguing for several hours in bed about where they would go, they decided to simply explore the city. They walked through Hampstead and up along St. John's Wood to Maresfield Gardens. To their surprise they ended up in front of the Freud museum. Here Sigmund Freud had spent his final years after leaving Vienna, and here his daughter Anna had passed the remaining decades of her life. The museum would have held great interest for them both on another occasion, but every moment they passed by each other's side seemed to release new toxins into the air. They walked back to the Tube in silence.

Then came the battle over where they would eat dinner. Finally, he burst out with a master critique of her, in the highest possible decibels. "All you care about is your career and money!" he shouted. "I've had enough of you! I'm through!"

He then stomped away, leaving Melissa watching him, her jacket wrapped tight around her suddenly diminished body. She felt small and defenceless, and feared returning to the hotel at night alone. As she moved forward into the night, she tried to persuade herself that their argument was a blessing in disguise. To say that they were getting on each other's nerves would have been a wild understatement. Hatred was brewing, and its origins were obscure. They were driving each other crazy, and were more miserable together than apart. Simple decisions, like where to have dinner, had become occasions for shouting matches conducted at a decibel never attained even during the most heated arguments with family or friends. Every argument generated more violence, and it was increasingly coming to seem like silence was the only option. How could he speak like that to her, he wondered, if he loved her?

So, when he came back to their hotel room, around eleven at night, she did not greet him. Nor did he greet her. He set about searching through his email for correspondence with his ex-wife over their custody of their son. She continued reading and typing. When the time came for bed, he asked her to stop typing. She ignored him. He sat up and repeated himself. She continued to ignore him. Finally, he stood bolt upright and came lunging towards her, threatening to destroy her laptop and to call the police. "This is my room," he insisted. "I paid for it with my credit card. And I can kick you out onto the street."

From there, he launched into a series of attacks. He called her a horse, who only looked straight ahead, and never noticed what happened around her. She was inconsiderate and rude to people on the street and in the Freud Museum where they had purchased tickets. She was incapable of caring for anyone other than herself. And, finally, he declared: "It's finished. I regret so much that I ever opened up myself to you. Meeting you was the biggest mistake of my life. I'm booking a room and leaving you tonight. Have a good life."

Perhaps because she was in shock, she didn't think about the things one is supposed to think about when one is breaking up. She didn't, for example, think about her love for him, which she had felt to the depths of her being on more than one occasion. She didn't think of what would become of that love once they were no longer together. She thought about what she would tell her friends and family, and how she would explain the sudden cessation of a relationship that seemed so promising in its beginning stages. And she thought about her books. How would she return them to Exeter? Would she have to hire a moving company, or would he agree to ship them back? Do I love him? She asked herself. Why am I asking myself? He's the one who's breaking up with me. Maybe I'm protecting myself from my true feelings.

The accusations dragged on for nearly ten minutes. She did her best to play mute. "You relish insulting me," was the most she said. Even that did not stop him. Finally, at the end of the tirade, she approached him in bed. They fell together into a drowsiness that augured the beginning of sleep. She tried touching the backside of his knees, as a kind of experiment, to see whether he had really meant what he said, and whether he was serious about breaking up. He remained still. She could not tell whether this was because he was sleeping or whether he had really intended to end their relationship. She would have liked to know the answer. Even if he didn't intend to breakup forever, she reasoned, even if thinks that we can be together after this argument, staying with him would mean accepting his attacks. Loving him would be self-abuse. I am no masochist. I must refuse. Something has died between us, regardless of what he says.

When they woke up the next morning, she began packing. She was moving to the more luxurious hotel booked by the training organization, and he, she presumed, would book another night in the hotel where they were now. They were on the verge of a permanent separation.

She packed for fifteen minutes while he fiddled away on his laptop, presumably trying to book a night for himself in the hotel, alone. That would have signalled the end to their relationship. And yet when she had finished packing and sat down next to him, he seemed to have made no progress with his booking. What was preventing him? Pride? Did he mean what he had yelled to her the night before, in the heat of anger? Perhaps he regretted his aggression and violence towards her?

She could not say. When she sat down next to him, he looked at her calmly, with his big deer-like brown eyes. It was impossible to imagine that the violence she witnessed last night could have been associated with these eyes. These were the eyes she fell in love with: gentle as a deer, soft, and open to anything and anyone. There was no acrimony in them anywhere to be seen. She wished she had never had to witness his eyes in any other mood.

They lay down together and talked. They rambled around the world of events, while carefully avoiding any reference to what had happened the night before. Then they touched. He took off his clothes, and they made love as they used to do, in Paris and then in Brussels, as if nothing and no one existed for them at that moment outside each other. "I want you to come," he said to her. "I want you to make this your task. I won't come unless you do first."

When they finished, he wrapped his arms around her shoulders and said: "Let's go to your hotel." No reference whatsoever to what had passed between them on the night before.

That night, for the first time she they had arrived in London, they didn't argue about what or where they would eat. They had lunch at a sushi place nearby, just off Russell Square, and then went to Skoobs, London's largest used bookstore. Here they did exactly as they had done in Paris, where they had fallen in love. They skimmed the shelves for books, comparing notes along the way, asking each other for advice on what to buy, and making endless lists of all the books they wanted to have. While engaged in this activity, they seemed made for each other: the worlds" two most impassioned book buyers. It was like Paris all over again.

They had almost given up on finding a worthwhile production for that evening when he suggested that they look at the playlist for a new theatre off West End: Almeida, in Islington. They checked online. To their surprise, Uncle Vanya was on that evening. Two tickets were available, just behind a pillar, so at a heavy discount. Chekhov had brought them together in Paris, and now, it appeared, he would bring them together again, in London, in the aftermath of their separation. She called the theatre immediately and booked their seats.

The show was negatively reviewed in the mainstream media due to it its length, but that didn't scare them. They were true lovers of Chekhov, and the longer the better, as far as they were concerned. They rushed to the theatre hand in hand, and sat down behind the pillars. He whispered to her between the acts, praising the acting, and she nodded her head. He bought ice cream for them both, extravagant as always, two cups for every intermission: salted caramel, raspberry, vanilla bean, and hazelnut.

She could tell how pleased he was with the performance by the way he leaned back in his chair, his large deer-brown eyes awash in peace. After the show, there was a question-and-answer session with the actors. They sat through it quietly, holding each other's hands. Love was wrapping its tentacles around them again, making the violence of the preceding night seem like a dream and conferring an aura of reality on the domestic peace they felt while watching the revolving stage. The real and the imaginary had become inverted, thanks to Chekhov.

When the question and answer session ended, they looked at each and kissed. It was the first time they had kissed in that way since Paris, utterly oblivious to their surroundings. She could not speak for what was going on inside him, but for her part she knew that her passion at that moment, and her willingness to overlook all that had gone wrong the night before, was connected to her dawning awareness that what had started between them was doomed to end. They might see each other again, but the next time they encountered each other, it would not mean what it had meant before.

They had lived through the birth and death of love. The love might return, but it would always be mingled with that night of acrimony and hate. The hate they had given voice to would permanently change the dynamics of any future relationship. Violence had infected their love, creating a new emotion that neither could ignore.

They spent the night naked together, intimate, without tension. As earlier that day, he told her that she had to have an orgasm, and refused to come until she came first. He did not want sex just for the sake of his pleasure, he said. He wanted to be part of her fantasies when she masturbated alone.

On most nights when they slept together, she would sleep with him for an hour or so until he fell asleep. Then she would go to the restroom or another adjoining room where she would work for a few hours longer on her laptop, often greeting the dawn. Then she would return to bed, to sleep by his side, after he had already turned his back to her.

This night was different. Conscious of its finality, she wanted every moment to last. So, she did not go to the bathroom, and consequently did not set her alarm. Instead, she fell asleep in his arms. The hotel reception had promised to give her a wake-up call at eight o'clock. She decided she would leave the many emails she was due to write to another day, and soon fell fast asleep.

They woke up two hours late, having slept through the wake-up call. He had missed his train. She had missed the first session in her training course. The first wave of disoriented panic was followed by the awareness that she would not be able to say goodbye to him in the way she intended to while falling asleep in his arms on the preceding night. By the time she turned around he was already on the computer, trying to replace his ticket as quickly as possible. From her past experience with him in stressful situations, she knew that it was better not to speak to him at a moment life this. She left, without saying goodbye.

For most of the walk from the hotel to the Euston Tube station she stared at the ground, afraid of what she would see if she lifted her eyes. The sight of couples in love at the edges of her vision was particularly painful. "Love," she said aloud, "What a joke."

The performance the night before had stirred memories of all her past encounters with Chekhov, which had mostly taken place through reading his stories. She recalled one story in particular, "Lady with a Lapdog," that she had read during her first year at the university. The story had struck home at so many different levels, even though she had yet to have an affair of the kind described in the story between Gurov and Anna Sergeevna. What struck her about the story most of all was the division Chekhov had proposed between real life, which is conducted under the cover of night and in secret, and fake life, which defines our work days, our professional relations, everything we do in daylight hours, and which is usually all that the world knows about us. For Chekhov's hero Gurov, his real life took place only when he was with his beloved Anna. Yet their love was burdened by falsity and deception because it contravened society's law. When she arrived at Euston Station, she decided to read "Lady with a Lapdog" again. Even if the story could not resolve her predicament, it might enable her to see it in a new way.

IV.

As Melissa waited for the train that would take her to the training course, she reflected on the catastrophic vacation she spent—or better stated, squandered—with Jacques. *Why do we hurt the ones we love?* she asked herself, feeling like character in a Chekhov play. *Why do we insult them in ways we would never insult strangers? How can words be so full of hate?*

She boarded the first car, searched for a vacant spot, and sat down. The italics in her head seemed to her to mark the birth of a story. About what precisely, she did not know, but she guessed that Chekhov would figure in it somewhere. The story would be about Chekhov as interpreted by Jacques, Chekhov read through the eyes of her former beloved. Although he had been blind to so many movements of her heart, they also shared many loved in common. Chekhov was one of them.

She spent the rest of the train ride trying to imagine their relationship through her lover's eyes.

"One thing I always notice about Chekhov plays," Jacques had said during the first intermission, "is that the characters are always in love with the wrong people. Whether it's Sonya and Michael or Vanya and Elena, these people don't know What's good for them, so they end up hurting themselves."

Henceforth, Melissa decided, Jacques would become a fiction to her. She would become Sonya, the girl in Uncle Vanya whose only hope lay in the peace that would follow after her death, and who seemed destined to become a spinster, managing the estate alone. She would set Jacques free, free to find himself, free to find love. She would seek these very same things, without ever expecting to find them. It's the search that counts, she reflected, paraphrasing Sonya, not what you find when you reach the end of the road. If they both ended up empty handed and alone in the aftermath of their searches, she would at least know that that they had belonged to each other during the days that they passed in Paris, and that their souls had merged briefly, while walking hand in hand along the Seine.

She would never forget his deer-brown eyes, or his tender, overly anxious plea, that she tell him if she ever felt unloved. During those first days of their acquaintance, that passed without leaving time for reflection, his time had belonged to her and her time had belonged to him. They had shared together moments that could not be repeated, by anyone, anywhere in the world. Those moments belonged to another chapter in her life, a chapter in a book that was reaching its close, but it didn't invalidate the love she had once felt for him. Goodbye, Jacques, she whispered, kissing the air, and stood up to change trains.

The First Time We Met
Lisa M. Scuderi-Burkimsher

I worked as an administrative assistant in a brokerage firm, when I first met him. At one o'clock I had walked to my friend Josie's cubicle to meet her for lunch. There he stood. Assuming they were discussing business, I kept walking with my head slightly turned in Josie's direction.

Josie's head popped up from her cubicle. "Lily, where are you going?"

I turned on my heel and walked back. "I thought you were in the middle of a work discussion."

Josie laughed. "No, we were discussing where to have lunch. This is Robert. He just transferred to the Compliance Department from Registration."

Robert's broad physique and striking blue eyes gave off an attractive appearance. He stood very tall and confident, his brown hair parted to the side. It had been difficult not to stare. I offered my hand.

"Hi, I'm Lily. Welcome to Compliance."

He shook my hand.

"If you two are done shaking hands, let's go to lunch. I didn't realize the time. It's almost one-fifteen. I guess we'll have to head downstairs to the cafeteria and go to the café another day." Josie sighed.

I walked next to Robert. "That's fine with me."

Robert smiled in agreement.

After we bought our lunches, we took a table near the window overlooking Battery Park. The sun shined and not a cloud appeared in the sky. Too bad we didn't have time for a walk.

"Where are you from Robert?" I asked, realizing I had been tapping my foot under the table and stopped, hoping I didn't annoy him.

He swallowed his food before he answered. A gentleman.

"I'm from Howard Beach, Queens, but I live in Suffolk County, Long Island. Mount Sinai to be exact."

We had something in common. "Oh, I have cousins that live-in Selden, Long Island, Suffolk County."

"What a coincidence, that's only ten-minutes from where I live, and I also have cousins that live-in Selden."

"What are the odds." I stared into his eyes.

"Hey, we're going to be late. We have to head back now." Josie interrupted.

That had been the first day I met Robert. Several weeks passed and we continued to have lunch, discuss our families and Long Island. Soon after he asked me out on a date. I lived on Staten Island at the time and he drove two-hours on a Saturday to take me to dinner.

Did I mention he was eight-years older than me? My parents weren't thrilled at the age difference. Their twenty-two-year-old-daughter, dating a thirty-year-year-old, didn't sit well, but as soon as they met him and had conversations about family and Long Island, they realized he was genuine.

I chose Alfredo's Italian Restaurant, one of my favorites, to have dinner. Robert ordered lasagna and I ordered chicken marsala. I'm sorry to say I didn't remember what we spoke about, because I couldn't take my eyes off his clear porcelain skin face. Not to mention we were both enjoying our dinners. We spent several hours at the restaurant and ordered an outrageously delicious Italian cheese cake for dessert and coffee. When we finally finished, he drove me home.

I fumbled through my purse for the house key and Robert gently touched my hand. He whispered in my ear if he could kiss me. Before I could answer, I leaned in and kissed him hard. His lips were strong and warm. Embarrassed, I pulled away, but he put his arm around my waist and pulled me toward him. He kissed me gently on the lips and I could feel the warmth of his body against mine. We put our arms around each other's necks and held the kiss. When our lips parted, he whispered into my ear again.

"You are beautiful."

I didn't know what to say, so I just smiled, unlocked the door and went inside. He followed.

From upstairs my mom yelled. "How was dinner?"

I quietly chortled. "Great. Lots of food."

It doesn't take much to figure out we married and remained the best of friends.

It's not an overly sentimental romantic love story, but it's my love story.

The Inexplicable Reality of Love
Gavin Meggs

Think of it and it will become
Believe in the possibility of flow
Let love wash over your being
And soon heartily you will know
Feel the pulse in each instant
Breathe as though you are free
Open yourself to the possibility
And together my sweet we will be
As one with each thought and intention
A dream on the cusp of real life
Swollen through the depth of interaction
Sharpness beyond that of a knife
Recognition of each other's need
Forgiving of life's splendid turns
Slow motion in action across wavelets
Knowing touches as we each yearn
To feel this is to exist hon
So blissfully blind that we see
The inexplicable reality of our love
Defining the way that we be

The Secret Garden
Moshe Sonnheim

In a secret garden
At a table just for two
I'll be waiting, darling. Waiting there for you
We'll lock the gate behind us,
The world will never hear,
The whispered words "I love you,
Love you truly, dear"

We've shared our lives together
For nearly fifty years
We've seen our children growing
Through happiness and tears

We've watched the flowers blooming
And the saplings growing tall

But now our flowers faded
And our trees are old and bare

And when I look around me
You are no longer there

But in our secret garden
At a table just for two
I'll be waiting, darling, waiting there for you
The gate will now be open
For all the world to hear
The whispered words, "I love you,
Love you truly, dear"

The Secret Locket
Julia Benally

Thomas" mouth hung open as he gazed at Melissa, the girl with the short black bob and green contacts. Long nails glittered on a slender hand gliding across the math paper. Those penciled eyebrows furrowed in deep thought. Thick lashes lay like feathers upon light brown cheeks. About that shapely neck hung a small locket glinting like an evening star beneath an altar of kissable, red lips.

Thomas squeezed his ears. Never would he feel that little mouth on his for his heart's desire possessed a fiendish boyfriend shrouded in mystery. What sort of mongrel could captivate such a radiant pixie? If Thomas could know, he could steal her.

"Thomas," Mr. Doolittle boomed in his ear, "what are you looking at?"

Thomas dropped his pencil, the math test fluttered to the floor. "N-nothing!" He got to work on the paper with gusto. Smirking, Mr. Doolittle waddled across the sniggering room like a ball with legs. A few strands of gray hair trimmed the sides of his shiny bald head.

The bell rang. Thomas scribbled his name and slapped the paper down on Mr. Doolittle's desk. Tongue hanging out, he followed after his dream girl. The other wenches wore gaudy pretensions of fashion compared to his Melissa's loose-fitting overalls, blue and white blouse, and small puffed sleeves. Her cute little pigtails bounced happily along with her steps.

"Thomas," Mr. Doolittle called with a smirk on his old mischievous face. Those eyes behind his thick glasses seemed large and insane.

Thomas stared wistfully at Melissa's shrinking form as she meandered down the hall. Her bedazzled overall strap winked at him. The love-struck sufferer's feet danced in agony as if he needed the toilet, then he stumbled to Mr. Doolittle's desk where the aroma of stale coffee and meatballs met his nose.

"Is your name Melissa?" the teacher said in that craggy voice of his.

Thomas's heart seized up. "What? I... uh... what are you talking about?" The boy slapped the door shut lest anyone hear.

Mr. Doolittle chuckled, slid his math test to him. Where Thomas was supposed to have written his name was "Melissa" instead. The tortured boy turned redder than when his pants fell off in class last week. The pudgy old man guffawed as the shuddering teen erased the beloved name.

"You like her, Thomas," Mr. Doolittle said. "Why don't you ask her out?"

Thomas shoved up his black-rimmed glasses. "I... I can't." He scrawled his own name.

"Why, does she have a boyfriend?"

Thomas nodded dolefully. "She has him in her locket."

"I didn't know Melissa had a boyfriend." Mr. Doolittle took the paper from him. "Who is he?"

"I don't know."

Mr. Doolittle grunted in disbelief. "You mean you follow her around like a dog and you've never even seen him?" Thomas yanked on the hem of his gray polo shirt in mortification, but the brazen wretch went on. "Then how do you know she has a boyfriend?"

"She talks about him all the time!" Thomas' throat choked up. "She says he's always helping people, and he can fight really cool, and he stays out all night whenever he wants to and... and I can't." Thomas sighed heavily. He went to bed at nine, did his homework on time, and was basically a dork. "And he's really rich." A poor dork, too.

"Well," said Mr. Doolittle, observing Thomas' tall slender frame with its too long limbs that did no justice to his neat clothes. Pimples accentuated the scar on his left cheek bone. He had combed his hair like Christopher Reeve's Clark Kent. Too bad no Superman existed under that rickety facade. "Well, we can't all be cool. You're going to be late." The old goat was no help at all.

Lunch time rolled around. Thomas spotted Melissa heading to the cafeteria with one of her friends. *FLOP-FLOP-FLOP* went his shovel feet as, like a grotesque spider monkey, he slid into line behind them. The divine scent of Sweet Pea caressed his senses. Closing his eyes, he inhaled, transported to his Elysium where Melissa pranced in a silken gown through pink roses.

Her friend wrinkled her nose and promptly turned her back on him to face her superior. "You going out with Bruce again tonight?"

Melissa giggled, fingered the locket. "Yeah. He's so cool!" Her voice was as the chimes of Aphrodite's bells, the sweet tinkling of a bubbling brook. "I like watching him walk. Oh, my goodness, his stomach—aaaahhhh!" Her gorgeous eyes crinkled; Thomas shivered with oncoming madness. Would that they did it for the miserable, clunky wretch who could only worship from afar? He glared at the locket.

"I bet he's not as cool as she thinks," he snarled.

"Thomas," said one of his classmates behind him, "who the crap're you talking to?"

Laughter rang through the line. Thomas' cheeks inflamed up to his ears. Had he really said that out loud? Indeed, who was he talking to? Some lunatic in his brain that held sway over his every move, That's who. He glanced at Melissa; her green eyes swept over him as if he were in his birthday clothes. A sad excuse for a smile trembled across his lips.

Melissa's friend rolled her eyes. "Don't you have to sit by hIm next hour?"

"Yeah." Melissa turned gracefully around, still fingering the golden locket.

Thomas gripped his skinny arms, stared at his great flat feet. Even the floor had no compassion on him because it wouldn't swallow him. But as the line began to move, Melissa's pigtails waved at him. The chuckles faded into the background. He knew exactly what she would choose. As she picked up her lunch, he paid no attention whatsoever to his own choices. Somewhere along the line he grabbed what looked like a chicken sandwich.

Heart puttering with the rhythm of her bouncing pigtails, he followed her to a table, but huddled at the other end of it in blissful worship. She bit the sandwich. How exquisite were her jaws as they chewed! With the stupidest smile ever conceived, he chomped down on his sandwich. It was fish. He threw up.

Melissa's head snapped towards him. "Ew, gross!" Students jumped back, pointing, laughing, gagging. Thomas' only comfort was that Melissa had noticed him. He ended up in the nurse's office and missed next hour, which meant he missed his last chance to see Melissa. He was a dejected little dork when he finally came out.

****

Thomas paced his room like a madman. Why couldn't he be cool like Bruce? Who the crap was this wretch who had his woman's heart? He was probably a criminal and Melissa was too innocent and good to realize it. Stomping to the mirror in the tiny bathroom like a man on a mission, he lifted his shirt to see what state his abs were in. He cringed.

"They look cheap!" He marched back to his room, his mind a whirl of schemes. Melissa said she liked Bruce's abs, well, Thomas could have abs too. He laid his spindly frame on the floor and tried to do a sit up. His tiny muscles squeaked in pain, but these little problems would not deter him. Kicking his spidery legs with angry groans, he sat up. Beads of sweat formed on his bumpy forehead. "YEAH!"

Victory won, he headed for the next assailant: the dreaded pull ups. He set the bar on the door frame and… hung there in dorkdom.

****

Thomas slid into his junky gas-reeking car. Every muscle in his stomach twinged. Even his fingers ached. What had he done to do that? Perhaps it was hanging on the pull up bar? As he sputtered on to school, he switched on the player and Demis Roussos started to sing "My Friend the Wind."

"Melissa's like the wind," he mumbled in love-struck anguish.

And then, he saw them: tiny bobbing pigtails beckoning to his tormented soul. A pink backpack glittered with sewn-on jewels. The sole possessor of his writhing heartstrings strolled along the sidewalk. How cute was she in the short yellow dress with the small puffed sleeves and baggy jeans underneath! Could it be that fate had made her miss the bus? He slapped off the music.

Mouth open in glee, Thomas pulled up next to her and reached over to roll the passenger window down. His stomach burst in pain and he fell on the seat. Scrambling for the handle, he succeeded in opening the door. To his horror he could not sit back up.

"Hi," he said as dashingly as he could as he leaned on his elbows. He just sounded jittery. "Do you need a ride? I mean... uh... I'm not meaning to kidnap you... I mean... I'm from school, too. Um..." He grinned.

Melissa bestowed a dazzling smile. "I know you."

Thomas flushed. "You do?"

"You sit next to me in History." Melissa moved to come inside. Thomas shoved off the seat, pretending with all he had that his muscles weren't howling. She didn't sit down at once, but dusted the crumbly seat off. Thomas covered his face in shame. His whole car carried the city's dump in it.

"Thomas," Melissa said, "what are you doing?"

He bumped his head on the ceiling. The houri had gotten into the car despite the crumbs. "What?"

"Are we going?"

"Oh yeah!" Thomas hit the gas and nearly smashed into another car. Melissa squealed in glee, but Thomas heard nothing but the blood pumping through his brain. The divine aura of Herbal Essence and Sweet Pea wafted through the vehicle. What a cruel fate that destiny had bestowed! Now that the beauty of ages was there, he had reason to look at her with impunity, but he couldn't tear his eyes from the road. He might burst into flames if he looked at her.

"Do you have music?" Melissa said. "Hey, you have a cassette player. My grandpa had one in his car. Then he changed it to a CD player. I don't know if he's gonna upgrade anymore or not."

Thomas flinched. Even the old man was more high-tech than he was.

"Do you have cassettes?"

Thomas wanted to die as *My Friend the Wind* lyrics rushed through his head. Thankfully, the cassette case was safely hidden in the glove compartment.

"No. So..." He glanced at the golden locket around her slender neck. "What's in the locket?"

"Bruce." Melissa's face glittered at the mention of that overrated brute.

"I've never seen him." Thomas could hear his voice shivering, but he couldn't lose it now. He had to make a good impression.

"Yes, you have." Melissa turned, rested her elbow on the top of the seat. "If you haven't, you're living under a rock or something." She giggled; Thomas gripped the wheel until his knuckles turned white.

"I haven't seen him," he repeated as calmly as possible. "Can I see the picture?" He would hunt the wretch down and... and... DO something to him!

Melissa twittered and shook her head. Those pigtails bounced and winked... giggled. She held the locket between tapered glittering fingers. Thomas' lips shivered with the mad desire to kiss and caress them. His eyes swallowed up the locket.

Since the boy never looked her in the face, and clearly had trouble breathing, Melissa freely observed his weirdness. Her green eyes grew round and mischievous.

"I have a date with Bruce tonight," she said. "You can see him then."

"You mean, you're inviting me on your date?" Thomas could hardly believe such crassness. "Do you think he would care if I came along?"

"Bruce is very serious." The mirth drained from Melissa's oval face, except the glint in her eyes. "Besides, you don't invite people to your dates. That's nuts! You can get a glimpse of him if you can find me after school. I have to hurry and meet Bruce so I can't meet you."

"Oh..." Thomas stared at the road. The light turned red, but the other one further down stayed green so he kept going. Horns and angry shouts followed them, but Thomas didn't have time for petty trivials such as car crashes and law breaking. "Wait... you mean I get to see Bruce just like that? I thought he was a great secret. You're sharing a secret with me?"

A grin spread across Melissa's face. "Only if you can catch me."

Thomas' heart hammered until the friction burned him all over. "Oh, I'll catch you."

"It's hard to catch Bruce."

Thomas didn't care. What would he do when he found her and Bruce? What sort of person was Bruce? He felt like a fool, but he had to warn her. "Melissa, are you sure Bruce is alright? I mean, what if he's some kind of nut? What class is he?"

"He's out of school already." Melissa twirled the locket in her fingers.

Thomas started; his car swerved into the next lane. "Wait, you mean he's like in college?" Somebody shouted obscenities.

"He's out of college." She sounded so maddeningly calm about it.

"Melissa, you can't do that. It's dangerous." The car climbed the curb, drove along the sidewalk and parked on four spaces in the school parking lot. "Does your dad know about him?"

Melissa giggled. "Bruce has the most awesome abs." She jumped out of the car. "My last class is in Hamblin's. Thanks for the ride!" And she skipped away with her pigtails bobbing goodbye.

"Melissa, wait," Thomas cried, but by the time he had manually locked the car, the nymph had glided out of sight in an ocean of sniggering students, exasperated teachers, fancy vehicles and smelly buses. Thomas groaned. Even if it meant death, he would have to save this damsel from certain ruin. Now, where was Hamblin's class again? He was the art teacher. What sort of a grade was Melissa getting in there? He clearly remembered his D+. D for dork, plus for extra special dork.

The day passed in agony. His life would soon be over, but he would die for his Melissa, which was the best cause that he could think of. Finally, the last hour loomed its sleepy head.

Thomas' knee bounced up and down as the clock ticked on. Five minutes after the hour... fifteen... He broke his pencil in half at the half hour mark. He twisted his paper into a cone. Fifteen "til... ten... Thomas shut his eyes, stuffed his head in his arms. He looked up. Two minutes. One minute... fifty seconds. His heart pounded in his throat, beads of sweat broke out on his forehead. Thirty seconds. Fifteen... ten seconds. He seized his bag, flung it on his back.

Ding-ding-ding!

"I want everyone to stay after a little," Ms. Perkins droned. "I have more things I want you to know—Thomas!"

Thomas sped from the room like a boy possessed. Hunting like a hound for Melissa, he spotted her up ahead. And then she vanished through the double doors. He barreled students over and burst outside. She stood at the top of the steps before the band room as if she had been waiting for him. She waved her delicate hand, beamed like a drop of light separated from the radiant sun. He screeched her name.

She vanished around a corner. By the time he got there, she was gone. Frustrated shrieks twisted him all up inside, but some of his senses returned in time to save him from certain humiliation. With a miserable groan, Thomas meandered through the guffawing crowds towards his trashy car without so much as a glance at any of his mockers and got in. The whimpering lover drove right past the object of his madness. She just laughed.

****

"You totally missed me yesterday," Melissa said as she sat beside him in History.

Thomas looked up as his heart leaped. There were the glossy pigtails, the puffed sleeves. Today they were white and her overalls ended in a skirt instead of pants. She had earrings on!! Chills curdled his blood, yet his heart pumped with the electricity of her resplendent presence.

"You were running or something." He sounded so sulky he wanted to slap himself.

"And by missing me, I mean missing me with your car."

"What?"

"You almost ran me over." Melissa beamed as if it had been the most wonderful thing that had happened to her. Thomas had a heart attack of overpowering passion. "Do you want to try again? I'm meeting Bruce again. You'll think he's so cool!"

The edges of Thomas' mouth almost reached the bottom of his chin. "I doubt it. But I'll save you from him if it's the last thing I do." He bit his tongue, eyes went wide.

Melissa's cheeks turned bright pink.

"Oommggpf." He covered his face. "Kill me now."

"D-don't be ridiculous. Bruce does all the saving." She shoved her face into her school book as if she had never read about Christopher Columbus before.

Despite this, Thomas scrambled to Hamblin's room at the end of the day where he missed Melissa again. The next day and the next—was she running from him? Why wouldn't she after what he had said? The crushing blow came when she switched seats with a friend in both math and history class. He stared at her as if someone had ripped out his spine. Mr. Doolittle said something to him, but mere gibberish to the torments of Thomas' shattered soul!

The weeks sped by. He plunged into school work and his after-school workout to get his mind off of her, but she gazed at him from every math page, looked at him in the mirror when he brushed his teeth, sat in his chair as he exercised. Were his teeth white enough for her? Did he wash his butt ten times so she'd never smell him? How were his muscles coming along?

One awful night he measured his arm and found it had become no bigger than before.

"No! No!" He collapsed on his bed, his reeling mind a fever of emotions. When did he fall asleep, he did not know but the pigtails came that night. They hopped around him like disembodied spirits as they dangled the locket just out of his reach.

"NO!" Thomas jerked awake.

"Thomas," his mom shouted, "what is wrong with you?" She

burst into his room. "You want that girl, go get her! Stop being a coward!"

"I-I don't have a crush on n-nobody," Thomas sputtered.

"Everybody knows. I'm tired of this!" And she threw him out, a disheveled, unwashed mess with wide sleepless eyes and drawn face. How in the world did his mom know? He was an expert secret keeper. She had some weird telepathy or something.

History came around once more to torment him with unreachable love. Why couldn't he just snatch Melissa up? He didn't have to know who was in the locket. And he wasn't a coward...at least, he didn't think he was too much of one. He glanced at Melissa who stared at her desk. Thomas' head tilted sideways, mouth open.

I'll catch her in Hamblin's room, he thought as a surge of determination welled within him. I'll get Melissa. I'll make her mine! I'll... I'll kiss her! Cold fear froze the pit of his stomach and he had to go to the bathroom to barf.

Once again, the final hour before his doom arrived. Every second the clock ticked seemed louder than the last. Faster and faster the minutes raced as if they were on a relay team. Thirty real time seconds went by, but the clock had gained fifteen minutes on it.

"Oh no," Thomas moaned.

"What, Thomas?" said Ms. Perkins.

He scratched his scalp. "N-nothing."

"Focus, Thomas."

Five minutes until the bell. Thomas' stomach churned. The girl next to him made a face.

Ding-ding-ding!

Thomas stared at the clock. His hour of death was at hand. What would Melissa do? His legs moved on their own as he stood. Somehow his backpack made it on, he was out the door. Students swirled in a fog that formed a tunnel leading to Hamblin's dreaded art room. Suddenly, a light shined and raced towards him as if the devil were after it. Tears glassed its beloved eyes, even the dear pigtails quivered with emotion.

"Melissa." Thomas gripped the little puffed sleeves. "What's the matter? I'll rip off his head who made you cry." His face reddened. "I mean... oh boy."

Melissa turned as pink as her sleeves. "I lost my locket." She grew frantic. "I don't know where I dropped it! It fell off my neck! I looked all over Hamblin's room but it isn't there."

"Alright, let's backtrack. We'll find it, Melissa." Even if Bruce's picture was in it. The chump probably wouldn't even care about the locket. But Thomas did.

"Somebody might steal it."

"Don't worry, we'll find it. And if you miss the bus, I can give you a ride home." He cringed. "Unless..." He would kill Bruce if he was giving her a ride home. "...you're meeting Bruce?"

Melissa wiped her heart-rending eyes. "Not right now."

And so they went searching. They couldn't find it anywhere, and then Melissa said, "P.E. got nuts. It might've fallen in the gym."

Racing to the gym, they scoured it for the precious, but vexing, locket. As Thomas hunted around the bleachers, a golden glint caught his eye.

"The locket," he hissed. He glanced around for Melissa. She couldn't see. "Open!" His stiff limbs flailed towards the shine; his wide hands clamped over the small evil thing as his muscles screeched in protest. With feverish shaking fingers, he snapped it open. His jaw dropped in astonishment.

"Oh, you found it." Melissa ran across to him. "You opened it." Her mouth screwed up in horror.

"Yeah... uh..." Thomas didn't know what to do. "Batman?"

Melissa smiled sheepishly. "Bruce!"

"Your boyfriend?"

"I said he was out of college and rescued people and stayed up late and had the most awesome stomach."

Thomas' eye twitched. "But all your friends say you have a boyfriend."

She replied simply, "I lied to them."

"But your dates." Thomas stared at the ceiling. Melissa was no one's girlfriend.

"I play video games," said Melissa. "And I have all the cartoons. I said if you could catch me you could see Bruce." She looked at her pink converse shoes. "But I guess not now, huh? You think I'm weird?" She sighed as if about to cry. "I knew you thought I was. You stopped coming to Hamblin's class." She started walking away, but Thomas seized her wrist in a heated grasp.

"What do you mean? You switched seats on me."

"We had a new seating chart."

Thomas' ears burned. "Oh... w-well I don't think you're weird. You're beautiful." He almost swallowed his tongue, but he couldn't back out now. "And—and... yeah." He could have kicked himself. Why couldn't he make up a flowery speech of everlasting love? Here it was, the moment of truth, and he sounded like a Neanderthal. He was even hunched over like one. He was supposed to be looking deep into her eyes; he was supposed to kiss her. Why did he have to throw up for?

Struggling for breath, he did the only thing he could do. He opened her small warm hand and placed the locket in it. Melissa didn't pull away or shudder at his touch, but smiled into his face. Before Thomas knew what he had done, he had pressed her fingers to his lips. Warm streams from Nirvana replaced the very blood in his veins—and then he realized his madness. Was he supposed to have done that?

Before he could sputter an apology, Melissa leaned into him, arms circling his middle and her head rested on his chest. The strength abandoned Thomas' body; his heart hammered against Melissa's ear. A grin spread over her face and she pulled back, eyes scrunched up just for him.

"Let's play Batman," he said, struggling to control his quivering voice.

Melissa gave an excited nod. "Okay." Slipping the locket into her overall pocket, they left the school side by side, hand in hand.

The Wedding of Queen Victoria and Prince Albert

Mark Hudson

(February, 1840)

Victoria was eighteen when she succeeded to the throne,
her uncle thought she should not be alone.
Her German uncle named Leopold,
wanted to find a man for this eighteen-year old.
When she first met Albert, she already knew it,
the couple were happy playing piano duets.
It was actually Victoria, who proposed,
and Albert said yes, it was supposed.
The couple were singing, dancing, and kissing,
and when apart from each other they were missing.
The wedding was to occur in February
the first marriage of a queen since Bloody Mary
three hundred years before to that date,
the marriage procession came to the gates
of Buckingham palace, with some carriages,
to accompany the couple to their marriage.
She had on a diamond necklace and a sapphire brooch,
she led Prince Albert around like a pooch.
The wedding cake weighed three hundred pounds,
the guests couldn't be contained on the grounds.
And photos were taken in black and white,
the first photos ever of a wedding night.
Nine children were conceived one by one,
till Albert died young in 1961.
When Albert died, Victoria cried,
she had loved being Albert's bride.
To each other the couple was loyal,
and old England never was so royal.

This Isn't a Dream
Rachel A.G. Gilman

Honey took the key from her seashell key ring to unlock her family's Cape Cod cabin in North Truro. Dropping her bag next to the umbrella stand by the entry, she stepped into the living room. She and her brother, Zack, spent almost every weekend there in high school while their antique-shop opening parents were at caravans, and they always brought their best friends, Lizzy and Jacob Sibbald. It still had the smell of sunscreen and salty air. They had all planned to meet up this weekend. Honey noticed the little red light blinking on the cabin's landline answering machine. Pressing the button, Honey sat down at the kitchen table. There was a coffee ring on the wooden top, undoubtedly Lizzy's from a year ago.

"Hey, sis," Zack said. "Look, I know the plan was for all of us to meet up, but…"

"We're engaged!" Lizzy's slightly obnoxious trill of a laugh felt even more annoying through the phone. "Yeah, Zacky popped the question, and now We're getting married." Honey heard them kiss into the speaker. "So, sorry to have you make the long trek up there, Honey, but We're home to tell your parents. Get some sun. Love you!"

Honey got a sponge to scrub at the coffee ring. "Honey" was the stupid nickname Lizzy and Zack had given her after they had met but before they became a couple the Christmas of their junior and Honey's freshman year. They had thought her biblical name was boring, ignoring the fact Elizabeth and Zacharias are also boring biblical names. Lizzy said she couldn't understand why anyone would want a name meaning sheep. Honey couldn't grasp how a nickname associated with the gooey stuff Winnie the Pooh adored was any better.

Giving up on the stain, Honey returned to the living room. Her eyes scanned the photos on the wall she and Lizzy (but mostly Honey) had added to every summer. They felt like a timeline, showing the years before Lizzy and Jacob, and everything after, too. That was how Honey divided time: things before the Sibbalds and things after. The siblings had moved to Peabody before Honey's freshman year of high school from farmland Ohio, and had never been to the beach until they met Honey and Zack.

Honey lingered on one snapshot of her and Lizzy from their first summer together: Lizzy, about five feet tall with pin-straight, chocolate brown hair, blueberry colored eyes, and fair skin, and Honey, not quite half a foot taller but fifty pounds heavier, trying to keep her mangled blonde curls out of her sort-of green eyes. It was like Lizzy used to say: "Oh, Honey, it's just you're the girl all the mothers think is cute, but not the one the boys want to screw. It's okay, that's why I love you." Honey realized her allowing Lizzy to say this said just as much about her as it did about Lizzy.

Honey focused on a picture of her and Jacob from the previous summer.

The two of them were on a sailboat. He had thrown his arm around her, probably because Zack had prompted him to. The burgundy letters on his worn MIT t-shirt, faded and shrunken from too many washes, peeled away from the cotton. It was the summer after she had graduated high school and before his year of being a teaching assistant before going back to get his Masters in computer engineering.

Honey saw everything in that photo she had fallen in love with on a summer Saturday morning five years ago after meeting Jacob, the things that had shaped her high school fantasies of making out in his Jeep in their driveways: his one blue eye and his other that was more gray-green, his shaggy, sandy brown hair poking out underneath his Cleveland Indians cap, his narrowly pointed nose, the way his slightly-too-sharp canine teeth rested on his thin bottom lip when he smiled. He was cute, though a bit of a tan and washing his hair more frequently would have likely pushed him beyond.

That photo of her and Jacob was the only one where it was just the two of them. It wasn't as if she were Jacob's girlfriend. Lizzy had always sort of turned her off of making a move, saying he was focused on school or interested in girls his own age with mile long legs and hobbies like hiking, even if he, realistically, didn't have a chance with those kinds of girls. He thought of Honey like a little sister, or so Lizzy told her.

Honey figured Zack had had the decency to inform Jacob of his plan to propose so he did not waste his friend's time, which left her on her own. That was the way things worked. She took her suitcase back to the single bedroom and set it on the bed to start unpacking. When she opened it, a handful of condoms fell on the ground. Lizzy had given them to Honey when she had left for Cooper Union last year, when she was furious over Honey's decision not to attend college in the Boston area with everyone else. There were exactly eight. For the past year, Lizzy had jokingly asked how many Honey had left, knowing the answer was always going to be eight.

Honey had hoped moving to New York would mean she wouldn't be the girl in those pictures on the living room wall anymore: the loser who drew pictures of the city, Lizzy's quiet, undistinguishable best friend, the girl absolutely in love with Jacob. She was supposed to move on, but she hadn't really wanted to, and therefore, she had not. Maybe she hadn't felt like she was done with it yet.

Honey heard a car. Out the window, she saw Jacob's Jeep with its Cleveland Browns license plate holders pulling into the driveway. He knocked on the door a moment after.

"Honey?" Jacob said after Honey had nervously opened the door. Her nickname sounded so much nicer in his nasal, higher-pitched voice, giving her some thin hope. A royal blue t-shirt peeked out from under his zip-neck gray sweater, and he wore jeans constructed of more holes and paint stains than denim. His Indians cap sat on his head. It was neater than his usual crappy t-shirt and elastic waist shorts — definitely bordering on "adorkable," as Lizzy might say.

"Oh, hi," Honey said, straightening her posture. She had thought of lots of things to say. Awesome, clever things that probably would have made Jacob smile and laugh. But did she say any of them? Of course not. Instead, she smoothed her bangs down on her forehead, trying to cover her tired eyes and sunburned skin. "Here for the group weekend?"

Jacob nodded and set his things next to the couch. "I got Zack's voicemail when I was already halfway here. Didn't really see the point in turning around."

Honey nodded. "Sorry, I kind of took over the bedroom. We can switch."

"The couch will be okay." Jacob carried a large, brown paper bag from their favorite seafood shack on Route 6A into the kitchen, along with a six-pack of Heineken. "When I heard it'd just be the two of us, I picked up dinner. That okay?"

Honey nodded, though she wanted to tell him that it, he, "the two of us," was perfect. Getting out the brightly colored ceramic plates and sea glass-colored cups, they sat down at the table to eat.

"How's New York? You still doing charcoal pieces?" Jacob asked.

"Some days are more productive than others." Honey sipped from the bottle of beer Jacob had uncapped for her despite not being much of a drinker, only liking how he had thought of her. "New Yorkers are snobby." She paused, chewing. "I can't look at the Manhattan skyline without thinking about being on the George Washington Bridge with you, pointing out the important buildings."

Jacob smiled and stroked the small patch of reddish facial hair he had been trying to grow out on his chin since Honey had first met him. "That was a good day." He played with his necklace, fingering the big, silver pendant with his family tree on it between his thumb and index. The clasp on the leather chain would go to the front a lot. Honey wanted to lean over and adjust it so she could touch him, feel the pressure of his body. The longer you love someone, she figured, the more ridiculous the things you want to do become.

They looked at each other. Honey could tell he did not understand how easy it was for her to get lost in his eyes that could not even manage to be the same color. The moment broke when Jacob grabbed his cell phone from his pocket. It made Honey question if what Lizzy had been periodically gushing about for the past six months was true, if Karen was, indeed, Jacob's girlfriend. Honey had never met Karen, or even heard Jacob really talk about her, but she knew Lizzy had already started planning that wedding. Apparently, the two had met when Jacob was the teaching assistant for Karen's electrical engineering introductory class last semester. According to Lizzy (who'd met her half a dozen times in passing), Karen was gorgeous: thick, black hair, almond eyes, and the dainty, eloquent bone structure of a ballerina. She had grown up in New York, gone to prep school and all that, so obviously she was brilliant, too. You did not get into MIT without being brilliant.

"You know, you can just call Karen on the landline," Honey said, pointing to it.

Jacob tucked his phone into the pocket of his jeans before starting another bottle of beer. "So, you want to drive into town and see What's open? Maybe hit the movie theatre?"

"I did that on my way in. Whatever was open closed at like, four. The movie theatre is under construction. That only leaves the bars in Provincetown," Honey said.

"Well, what about a movie here? There's a DVD player, right?"

"VHS," Honey said, dipping her spoon in and out of her soup. She could not snap out of the bad mood thinking about Karen had put her in, which made her feel foolish.

"I'm sure we can find something." Jacob checked his phone again then took out his laptop. "Shoot, I forgot my chargers." He never swore, despite being twenty-three and perfectly able to get away with it.

They finished dinner. Honey washed the dishes although Jacob protested to leave them. She liked cleaning, the control of it. It helped when she was jumpy or nervous. They went to the armoire where things like old movies ended up, the place where the junk drawer had started and eventually taken over, filled with: a set of Ping-Pong paddles from before Zack had broken the table circa Honey's sophomore year; board games with most of the parts missing so you had to play Clue with Monopoly pieces and use a combination of checkers and Old Maid cards to tell you "who'd done it"; various blow up swimming toys in the shapes of frogs and ducks, etc.

Sitting down on the floor, pretzel style, Jacob set his beer next to him and shifted around until he found a plastic crate of VHS tapes. "Oh boy, Richard Simmons work outs, recorded episodes of MASH, and," looking closely, "three copies of The Bridges of Madison County?"

"My mom's favorite, and she's not the best with remembering things."

Leaning his head in, Jacob pulled out a book tucked between beach towels and handed it to Honey. She sat down and ran her hand over the embroidered gold anchor on the denim front cover. "What is it?" Jacob said, scooting closer.

"It's a photo album Lizzy and I started before we expanded onto the living room wall." Honey opened it to the first page with Polaroids from their first sleepover.

"Was that her seventeenth birthday?" Jacob asked.

Honey nodded.

"Wasn't that when she met Zack?"

"Yeah...wait, how do you know that?"

"Lizzy can't keep anything to herself." They both laughed a little. "Hey, there's me and Zack in our old Cheesecake Factory uniforms. That is where we met. Isn't it weird you and Lizzy became friends, too?" Honey had gotten over the weirdness factor a while ago. "Wow, you guys even have when I started MIT." His thumb dragged down the page, fingering a parking pass pasted to the burgundy paper. "We moved here because my dad got the job. That's the only reason I got into MIT, because of him."

"Oh, that's crazy," Honey said, but it wasn't. It had been an ongoing but relatively unspoken thing that Jacob and Lizzy's father was a smart man who liked to flirt with his students, which put him out of the house a lot and sort of made Jacob feel as though he was the male adult. After all, he shared the same name as his dad. Lizzy claimed that was why he was so serious about school, why he had lived at home.

The next page had pictures of Zack and Lizzy, their arms around each other, their noses pushed into the other's cheek. Honey noticed Jacob tensing up. "What, is something wrong?"

"No, I'm ecstatic about my sister getting engaged," he said, sarcastically.

"You don't want my brother to marry your sister?"

"I just don't think they're ready. I'm two years older and I'm not even ready."

"Well, don't tell Lizzy. She's already planning your wedding."

Jacob scrunched up his face. "To who?"

"Karen, obviously."

Jacob rolled his eyes and kicked his feet out amongst the pile of old toys and forgotten Tupperware bowls. He had a hole in the toe of his black socks. "She's a friend," he said. Jacob continued to flip through the book, smiling and laughing at some of the pictures. "Hey, do you remember why we took these?" Jacob pointed to a page of photos where Zack had a lampshade on his head and a feather boa around his neck, as Lizzy appeared to be singing into a hairbrush while standing on top of the coffee table.

Honey remembered it perfectly. "Yeah, we'd been playing that game, Two Truths and a Lie. We used to do that a lot." It was one of those things Lizzy and Zack easily dominated. It always turned into the two of them trying to beat each other to have the most ridiculous hidden secret. They had usually been drinking. Not Honey, though, always volunteering to be the sober one in case things got too crazy.

Jacob closed the album and stood up, stumbling. He was always clumsy, but it was accentuated after two beers. "Why don't we play now?"

"Um… because it's lame."

"More lame than driving around a ghost town full of drag queens, or doing Richard Simmons work outs?" Jacob raised his eyebrows and bit the corner of his lip. He did not know Honey wasn't able to say "no" to him when he acted in this adorably boyish manner, but she still felt like he was trying to play into it.

"Fine, but I don't want to tell lies. I never saw the point in it." Honey did not lie, just hid things. That was completely different.

"Then we'll just tell truths," Jacob said, picking up the junk on the floor and quickly shoving it in the armoire, shutting the door before it had a chance to fall out again. He carried the photo album out to the living room couch. "Okay, I'll go first," he said. "I had a black pet rabbit as a kid. I was able to hide from my parents for a week."

"Wow, what a rebel," Honey said. Jacob gave her the shit-eating grin he always got when he was being a brat, a grin that made her smile and blush. "I have a scar on my tongue."

"Really?"

Honey stuck out her tongue to prove it then felt awfully ridiculous.

Jacob smiled and kindly laughed. "I once let my sister highlight my hair."

"I've never highlighted my hair."

"I guess you don't need to."

Honey wanted it to be a compliment, but that would be making something out of nothing.

"I'm legally blind without my contacts," Jacob said.

"So am I."

"That feels like cheating. You shouldn't be able to take my truths."

"Sorry."

Jacob flipped to a new page in the album. "It's okay, I'll let you slide." He combed his hair back from his face and under his cap. Honey liked when he combed the back of his hair down with his fingers, probably because she wanted to be able to tangle her own hands in it. Being alone with him was so hard for her. "I wanted to be a cowboy when I was little."

"Did you have the hat?"

"Yeah, and one of those horse heads with the sticks on the end, too."

"I thought I was going to be a princess."

"You still have time." They laughed. Jacob crossed his ankles then uncrossed them, flexing his feet. "You roll your eyes too much, especially when you're being sassy."

"Oh, so We're saying truths about each other now?"

"I don't know, maybe," Jacob said, biting down on the tip of his tongue and winking.

"Well, in that case, you need to buy more than five shirts. You've had the exact same wardrobe as long as I've known you."

"What's wrong with being comfortable?"

"Nothing, but there's also nothing wrong with variety."

"I think I own more than five shirts."

"The one that says something about sarcasm on it, the one from an old basketball tournament in Ohio, the one from MIT, the one from New York City, and the one you are wearing now. I don't count plain white t-shirts."

"Maybe you just pay too much attention." Jacob flipped to the last page in the album, a group photo from their last day at the cabin last summer, all four of them sitting in the sand. Lizzy and Zack had their heads pressed together, Lizzy looking at the camera but Zack looking at Lizzy. Jacob and Honey sat on either side of their friends, slightly pained and saddened expressions painted across their mouths and eyes. Jacob had taken it. You only saw part of his right arm because he was holding the camera.

Honey could remember exactly how She'd felt when they'd taken the photo: happy to be leaving but scared of what it meant. She had not thought she would be no further along in understanding any of it over a year later.

Slowly closing the album, Jacob said, "If I tell you a secret, will you tell me one?"

Jacob would not stop looking at her, sitting by her side calm and collected and clearly unaware. He was so oblivious, oblivious to the way she felt, oblivious to the way he made her feel. He was so smart and so dumb all at once. Honey nodded, tentatively.

"Last year wasn't a gap year. I had to make up some classes I hadn't passed."

"Why hadn't you passed them?"

"I got too busy with work, trying to keep the house up, everything else. I guess I let them get away from me for too long. I was so embarrassed about it." Jacob was still embarrassed, looking at the ground, moving his head a lot, his sure signs of humiliation. "They said if I was a teaching assistant, they would let me retake the courses. But it was mortifying having to go through the whole process, being Professor Sibbald, the almighty "Dr. Jacob Michael senior's," son and unable to graduate."

They were quiet, the sound of Jacob's breathing filling the air. Honey wanted to ask if Karen knew, but it somehow did not feel appropriate. She felt like she should reciprocate, though. She had a big secret, other than the obvious, one she hadn't told anyone, an important secret she felt maybe she could share with Jacob.

"Okay," she said. He did not reply and yet she went on, sighing and breathing and refusing to be the girl who drank one beer and cried. "I hate school. Seriously, I'm miserable."

Jacob sat up. "You are?"

"Yeah." Honey crossed her arm over her body to rub her left shoulder with her right hand. "I was in... a bad place."

"What does that mean?" Jacob's breathing got even heavier.

Honey had always wanted to make Jacob breathless, but she had not wanted it to come out of pity or worry. She looked out the window. She had talked about the situation on so many couches before, trying to figure out a way to define it.

"I was alone. I was an insomniac. I couldn't finish pieces without destroying them twice. When I got tired, I started to think about where I'd put things, and if I couldn't remember, I began to think I'd lost something, and that made me crazy and sad. I started to spiral, screaming at people in the elevator, crying myself to sleep every night. I guess I just wanted to be home, with my family, my friends, and I couldn't have it." Honey closed her eyes. She bit her lip. "I can't believe I just told you that."

"You could have called me," Jacob said. "I would have talked. I would've driven there."

"No, you wouldn't have. You say that now, but it wouldn't have happened." Honey breathed in then slowly out. "You, of all people, were the last one I wanted to see me like that."

"Why?" Jacob ran his hand through his hair again, pulling up his cap.

"Nothing, never mind. It'll just make you uncomfortable."

"Honey, c'mon." Jacob smiled gently. "I care about you more than I care about me."

Even if it was a lie that was part of the reason Honey loved him.

Honey looked down at the photo album on the couch, the visual of everything she both loved and hated about her life. Her chest kept tightening and relaxing a little too quickly. She had not planned to be alone with Jacob that night. She had not planned on much of anything at all.

"I-I love you." The first words came out stubborn and garbled. "I love you in a way I can't imagine ever feeling again. I always have." Once she started, more awkwardly fell out. "Sometimes I think about what it would be like to find someone from the city, the kind of guy who curls up on the couch with a chai latté and a book of poetry, but doesn't know a handsaw from a hammer... It's just, I've wanted you for so long—"

"How long?" Jacob said.

Her tongue dodged around her mouth, debating whether or not to give up the truth. "Well, honestly?" He nodded. "Since the first time I met you." She looked up at Jacob, the big, helpful eyes and sleepy smile that usually accompanied his snarky sense of humor gone, replaced with an expression that felt like it was looking through her more than at her. "Forget it; forget I said anything."

Jacob placed his hand over hers. She had wanted this, but not like this. "Why?"

"Because it's embarrassing, and you have Karen now and... and all of it!" Honey looked at the ground. Jacob scooted closer to Honey on the couch, squeezing her hand too tightly. He was warm and pink, like her old woolen mittens from middle school. His thumb started to circle his thumb around hers. "I hate thinking about you holding me in your arms or trying to grab my hands during a movie or helping me grocery shop. I know That's not going to be the reality. We can only survive in dreams." Honey pulled away, bringing her shaking hands inside the sleeves of her sweater. "It's so stupid. God, this whole thing is stupid."

Jacob stood up. "Come on, let's go outside." He picked up the blanket from the couch.

Honey felt childish, as if he was only doing this because he did not want to deal with having been the person to make her cry, but she followed him anyway. They went and sat in the same stretch of sand where they'd taken the photo last year. Jacob covered them with the blanket, pulling it to their chins so their toes were exposed. Honey had never noticed Jacob's bare feet until then, gangly thin and covered in dark auburn hair. She loved them, too.

"You don't have to do this," she said into the collar of her sweater. He did not answer. She looked out at the ocean, the dark waves reflecting the setting sun. The sky was a blast of purples, blues, and oranges, making a sexy, blurry mess. Rolling over slightly, she faced Jacob. He was looking at her, his mouth flat but his eyes wandering over her face. "Lizzy told me about Karen, okay? I get it. I don't want to deprive you of having her."

Jacob put his hand on Honey's shoulder. "Can't you chill out?" he asked. He had never touched her there, at least not when they weren't joking around and shoving each other. He seemed to realize it, too, smiling. "Look, I don't know who told you I'm dating Karen," he said. "She's just a person in my life, but I don't like her like that, like, like her like her. Okay?" He brushed his hair under his hat again. His hand crept down Honey's arm then back under the blanket. "Can I ask you one more thing?"

Honey nodded.

"Did you ever have a plan to tell me? Or were you just going to hide it forever?"

"When you moved me into school, I thought I'd tell you. I brought you to what was supposed to be my very favorite place and I didn't even have the balls to kiss you." Jacob laughed a little when she said "balls." "When you were walking away, I was going to follow you down Stuyvesant Street calling your name, tell you everything, and knot my hands in the back of your hair and—"

"Kiss me?" Jacob finished.

Biting her lip, Honey nodded.

Jacob leaned closer to her, his normally heavy breathing even heavier. He closed his eyes. She leaned in, too, watching his lips as they started to part slightly. Her teeth let up from their bite on her skin. Jacob pulled his arm out from under the blanket, putting his hand back on Honey's shoulder as he kissed her. The last and only time she had been kissed was last year at some trashy party in the East Village, by a guy so piss drunk he had mistaken her for his girlfriend. This was not the same.

****

When it got dark, they went inside. They held hands, Jacob getting the door.

"Do you want to turn music on?" Honey said, pointing to the CD player in the corner of the living room. She had to let go of his hand. It felt like she was missing something, which was perfectly ridiculous. Without waiting for an answer, Honey went over and shoved in Lizzy's mix CD from a few years back. A violin version of

Jason Mraz's "I'm Yours" started to play.

She walked into the bedroom and saw Jacob sitting on the bed, bent over, one by one putting the condoms she had dropped earlier back into the box. He pointed to her suitcase, which he had knocked completely to the ground. Smirking, he said, "I thought you didn't know I was coming for sure?"

"Shut up," Honey said. She felt stupid, but she kind of felt like he did, too. They stood there looking at each other. She leaned in the doorway, crossing her arms in front of her chest, very self-conscious.

Jacob got up from the bed and took his hands out of his jeans" pockets, wringing them in each other. "So..." he said, stopping about two feet from Honey.

She took a step toward him and placed her hands on his bony shoulders.

"What are your intentions?" he asked.

Honey pushed him a little in his chest, rolling her eyes, but Jacob pulled her back by her waist. He dragged one of his hands down her spine. She could feel it shaking a little when his hand returned to her waist and slid it inside her sweater, touching bare skin.

They kissed again, his lips rough but warm. Honey found herself pushing Jacob back toward the bed, more impulse than actual knowledge. Through stumbling hands, they pulled off each other's clothes: Honey's sweater, then Jacob's shirts, followed by their jeans. Honey took Jacob's Indians cap and set it on the nightstand before getting under the covers.

The pillows were cold against Honey's back. She looked at the dorky blue sheets with the anchors, feeling overly annoyed.

Jacob hovered above her, still in his gray boxer briefs. His chest was moving up and down as he continued breathing heavily. When he exhaled, they were chest to chest, his wiry, pale body making contact with her sun-kissed, chubby one, grazing the lacy fabric of her light green bra, his protruding pelvis gently tapping her leg. Honey felt so embarrassed.

"Are you okay?" he said, leaning up a little. He smoothed his hair down and tried to catch his breath, unsuccessfully.

Reaching up, Honey grabbed his shoulders again to try to stop herself from trembling. "I've never done this," she said. She wanted to cry, not because she was scared but because she felt stupid. "God, I'm so sorry..."

"No, it's okay," Jacob said, his voice lowered to a whisper. "I haven't either." Honey looked into his face. His eyes were big and soft, but not dishonest. "I'm going to stop."

"No," Honey said, quickly. She wanted to do it, not only to finally lose it, but also to do it with the person she loved. "But..." She pointed to the condoms on the ground.

Jacob got up. Once back in bed, he slipped in next to her with the box, trying to remove his underwear under the sheets. After a moment, he dropped the gray Hanes to the side of the bed, and turned and smiled, laughing a little, though Honey wasn't certain as to why. She pulled off her own boy shorts and unclasped her bra, throwing them into the pile of clothes. Was it silly they were removing it all under the sheets, would a real adult would have told them it meant they were not ready?

Jacob leaned over and pressed the upper portion of his chest into Honey's, kissing her a little hungrily. It was awkward, but good, to be touching him with nothing interfering. Pulling away, he picked up one of the condoms.

"Um, I actually don't really know how to do this. I went to Catholic school. They didn't show us the whole banana thing."

"I'm in the same boat, buddy," Honey said. "I went to Catholic school, too. The only sex education we got was 'don't'."

They both laughed, trying not to feel ridiculous for having to read the directions. Jacob moved his lips when he read, making her further fall in love with him.

After three opened foil packages and failed attempts, Jacob managed with the fourth. He moved back on top of Honey, pulling the blankets tighter.

"You ready?" he asked.

She started to nod then noticed something. "Wait!"

Jacob's back stiffened. He almost fell on top of her. "What?"

Honey reached up to his neck and touched the pendant on his necklace. It was warm from being close to his body. Just moments before, she had felt the metal pressed into her own breast. Gently, with clumsy fingers, she adjusted the clasp to the back of his neck. Jacob gave her a confused look. He probably thought she was crazy, but not crazy enough to not want to do it with her, though he could have been thinking more with his penis than his heart or head. Honey told herself she did not care. She was happy, placing her hands on his shoulders as he pushed inside of her slowly.

****

It had only taken twelve minutes. It would have taken Honey longer to clean out her sock drawer. She wondered if they had done it wrong. It was not at all what she had imagined, but she could not imagine it being any better with anyone else. Part of her wished She'd had someone to talk to before going into it, someone to warn her how strange and invasive it was. She could only think to compare the feeling of him inside of her to what it would feel like if her vagina had swallowed an entire Thanksgiving dinner whole, and even that didn't feel adequate.

Honey had delicately traced zigzags across Jacob's back. Jacob had made an odd, cracking noises with his voice and nuzzled his head into Honey's neck, his breath hot and wet on her skin. Honey did not tell him how badly it hurt, or how much she wished he would stop. She figured he was being as gentle as he knew how to be. At one point, she had looked down to see if she was bleeding or something, but there was nothing, just Jacob's parts next to her own.

Near the end, Honey had asked Jacob to talk to her as a distraction, and Jacob had started to mumble against her neck about computer programing. Honey didn't understand an ounce of it, but hearing him stumble over words like "algorithm" and stutter on ones like "debugging" made her feel better. She loved his stutter more than she liked sex. It all helped her to arch her back and get a breath to ease the pelvic pressure. She laughed when he stopped mid-sentence about something he was trying to code as he finished.

Now, Jacob was wheezing, a stupid grin on his face, a grin she did not expect to be there. It made the discomfort in her lower half worth it, somehow reassuring.

"There's something I've been meaning to tell you," Honey said. She tilted her head toward him and dragged a finger down the side of his face, able to feel the stubble of facial hair growing in, the thing that had been tickling her own face and neck when He'd kissed her.

"Okay..." Jacob took her finger and held it in his hand before interlocking all of hers with all of his. He used his other hand to put his Indians cap on her head.

"You have the hairiest legs I've ever seen on a person."

Jacob dropped her hand and waved his in the air in mock disgust. "Oh, well, excuse me!"

"No, don't, I kind of like them," Honey said, giggling. She whispered, "They're kind of a turn on."

Jacob grabbed her and pulled her closer, placing Honey's head on his chest and dragging his fingers through the waves in her hair until she eased against him. They listened to the music still playing in the living room, Maroon 5's "Sunday Morning."

"This could be our song if today wasn't Friday," she said.

Jacob laughed, his Adam's apple jumping in his throat. "I don't know. I still kind of dig it." He started to sing, completely off key, bobbing his head offbeat with the music. "That may be all I need... In darkness, she is all I see... Come and rest your bones with me!"

"Stop, stop!" Honey lost her breath in laughter. "I didn't realize you were tone deaf!"

"You're just jealous!"

Their laughing subsided as the song changed. Jacob's fingers lightly traced Honey's shoulder blades as she rolled onto her stomach.

"Do you feel different?" Honey asked him.

"Maybe," Jacob said, twitching his nose.

Honey bit her lip. "Are you happy I was your first?"

Jacob breathed in deeply then slowly out, moving his hand off her shoulder. "I'm happy you had me as your first," he said.

"I still feel like that loser who holds Lizzy's hair back when she gets drunk at bonfires."

"I don't think you were ever really that girl."

Honey held Jacob's waist tighter, as if pulling them closer would bridge their emotional gap. "You know, I've never drawn you."

"Well, do you want to? Like, right now? Have you studied nudes?"

"Yes, I mean, I don't know," Honey said, giggling. "I've studied nudes, yes." She dragged her fingernails along his upper thigh. "But I'm worried it might ruin some of the magic, you know? It might make me realize I have a blow-up image of you in my head."

"You're so silly," Jacob said, drumming his fingers again on Honey's shoulder, a little behind the beat of the music. She really was, she realized, but maybe being silly was the only way she had managed to not lose it entirely. She thought love should be a little silly. "I had no idea you liked me. You know that, right?"

"That's because you're an idiot—an oblivious, marvelous, wondrous idiot. The bigger miracle is that no one ever told you anything."

"I mean, Lizzy joked about it." Honey wished she knew exactly what Lizzy had told him, how much damage she had done. Lizzy wasn't much of a "best" anything at all. Jacob flicked her shoulder, breaking the thought. "You should have told me," he said.

Honey dug her nails (perhaps too roughly) into his leg. "Lizzy said you thought of me like a sister, and no one wants to kiss his sister. She already said I was the girl none of the boys wanted to mess around with, and she was right. None of them did. I don't know...it wouldn't have made a difference."

Jacob leaned back against the headboard. Honey wanted him to say something, to refute her, but he didn't. He just wore a contemplative look, his mouth at the side of his face and his eyes off to the side in the opposite direction.

"I love you," she said, only to realize it wasn't right. "No, I mean, yes, I do, but look, I never thought I was the kind of person who was allowed to be happy. I thought I was supposed to be the person who didn't experience happiness. You know, so the happy people would always be able to fully appreciate what they had." Honey brought her hand back up to Jacob's face. "I thought I would have to be happy enough with watching you fall for another girl."

Jacob coughed. "Maybe no one's happy. Maybe We're just figuring out how to survive."

She knew she was happy in that moment. She wanted him to be, too.

"I'm trying to figure things out, Honey, okay?" Jacob pulled his arm away from her and she felt something dip down in her stomach, something that hurt a lot more than having him inside of her. Jacob dragged his hands down through her hair. It did not feel the same. "You've been thinking about this for five years. I've had a few hours. Give me a few more."

****

When she woke up, Honey found Jacob in his MIT t-shirt and jeans fixing breakfast in the kitchen. His hair stood up in the back and he had circles under his eyes his glasses could only partially cover, though his cheeks were rosy as if He'd had sun. She wondered if she had done that to him. The small hickey behind his right ear was definitely hers. It was not exciting, as she had always expected from a hickey.

Jacob was the same guy to her, not nearly as breathtaking. It wasn't that she didn't love him anymore, but rather she could now see how his hair needed trimming, how his breathing became distracting, and how his overall scrawny body was not as dreamy as She'd made it out to be—just a simple "nerd," more dork than "adorkable."

"Morning, Honey," he said, handing her a plate of pancakes with a side of bacon. "Figured I'd make you something before I took off."

"You're leaving?" Honey looked down at her feet, not feeling very hungry at all.

"Don't you have to get back to the city, too?"

The city only offered her emptiness, which Honey now knew was not necessary and therefore did not want. She did not know what Jacob offered, but she figured it had to be better. Jacob put his arms around her shivering shoulders. "We'll see each other soon. Here, take this." He handed her his sweater from the night before. She tried to read into the gesture, but he cut into her thoughts. "I'm glad you told me everything you did last night. Really, I am. It's just, I don't know. I'm confused. And I'm trying to un-confuse myself."

Honey rubbed the soft, gray fabric to her face. The sweater smelled like his basic soap, the cinnamon air freshener in his car, and maybe a little bit of unsweetened iced tea. He was so messy. Even his thoughts came out messy.

"Should I call you when I get back to Cambridge?"

Honey wanted to make a quip about Karen, but she realized it would not help him with whatever it was he was trying to understand. "Call me when you're ready," she said. "When you think you've figured it out." It was not what she wanted to do. It felt disappointing. She wanted to put up a fight, get something definitive, but that was not her. She had tasted happiness, if only briefly. "Just make sure you drive safe."

Jacob finished putting the dishes away before he picked up his bags. He never cleaned up. Honey figured that meant something more than he was just a nice guy, doing the right thing. She followed him out.

"Bye, Honey," he said.

They did not kiss, didn't hug; they just waved. But, God, did Honey want to, just tell him she loved him one more time, give him another hug and feel the way his back moved under her arms when he breathed against her.

Once his Jeep was out of sight, Honey pulled on his sweater. It made her feel even younger than she was.

Going back inside, she started to eat the breakfast, looking out the window at the mist starting to come down. She found Jacob's Indians cap on the nightstand. It was a mistake for him to have left it. He was not calculated. She placed the cap on her head, and then took it off, feeling silly, before deciding she did not really care and putting it back on. For now, it was hers. Maybe, just maybe, Jacob had wanted it that way, even if he did not understand why he would want such a thing.

Her body felt stiff. Her heart felt a little sicker than she had hoped. When she had imagined having sex with Jacob, it had not included his leaving the morning after, but then again, it had not included him being so clumsy and making her physically uncomfortable either. When she had imagined telling him she loved him, she did not think he would say he was confused. It was a ridiculous response.

The house phone rang. Honey saw Zack's number but did not pick up.

"Hey, Honey," Lizzy's voice said, "is everything alright there?"

A car engine roared outside. Looking out the front window, Honey saw a Jeep Wrangler with Cleveland Browns" license plate holders slowly pulling back into the driveway. She wanted to jump up and meet him but stopped herself, waiting for him to ring the doorbell.

Jacob stood there, ruffling his hair and half waving his hand at her. "Hi, um…" His voice trailed. "You know, I actually need the sweater back." Honey was paralyzed until she noticed the corner of his mouth turning up into a smirking grin. "No, uh, look, I-I don't know wh-what I'm doing-ing, but I, I just have this w-weird feel-eling like, I don't want t-to leave yet, I-leave you yet. And I don't really g-get it." Jacob dragged the toe of his sneaker across the front step, pushing his hands into the pockets of his jeans. He only stuttered when he was nervous. "Want to go for a walk or something?"

Honey adjusted his cap on her head and nodded.

This Rain-Unending Weather
J. J. Steinfeld

I've been standing in the rain
all these thirty-five days
maintaining an accurate count
weather is not ordinarily my vocation
but these are extraordinary times
and the rain seems unending.

A woman appears at my side
as if by magic
but magic would be too easy
of an explanation.

Speak to me, mysterious one,
I request courteously
as if the miraculous
had not occurred
and this rain-unending weather
was normal for this time of year.

She smiles and I have no words
for the beauty and mystery
wondering if five more days
is enough time to fall in love
or sail magically away.

Two Roads
Rosanne Trost

Oh, what a hectic morning, thought Jeanne. Time for a nap. She looked at the stack of books next to her bed. Her eyes rested on one of her favorites, Robert Frost's, The Road Not Taken.

She picked up the book, but did not open it. She began reciting, "Two roads diverged." Her mind wandered a bit. All those years ago.

Back in high school, it had always been David. The boy with the sweet smile. What fun they'd had; football games, dances, studying after school. So comfortable. No thoughts of the future. They were enjoying the present. After graduation, she left for college, same state, different city. David was going to step into a very good position in his father's insurance business. Of course, they promised to visit each other, and they did, but only the first year of college. After that, they drifted apart. Bittersweet, but not necessarily painful.

After she married Chuck, Jeanne only thought of David, occasionally. When Patty, her daughter, entered high school, Jeanne remembered thinking, I hope Patty has a David in her life. Chuck was more concerned about Patty's academics.

Jeanne and Chuck had a good life together. At times, she thought they focused too much on Patty, and neglected their marriage. Also, she had to reconcile feelings of abandonment, when Chuck became distant and shut her out. His distance might last a week or two, sometimes longer. The good times far outweighed the bad, and for that she was grateful. During those happy times, they worked so well together, that she was able to lay her sad feelings aside. When Chuck said, "Jeanne, you are my world. I love you," she never doubted him. Patty graduated from college, and married. Her parents celebrated with their own second honeymoon.

Jeanne always believed that she and Chuck would grow old together. They never discussed what if. They exercised, ate relatively well, and loved traveling together. A drunk driver ended everything. Chuck was hit head on, and died at the scene. For weeks, Jeanne could not bear to be alone, but also craved aloneness. Nothing, nothing helped. There was no closure for her when the drunk killer went to jail.

Now ten years later, she is taking a nap or trying to rest a bit for this evening. Her mind is racing. What if she had not taken that tour of the wine country in France two years ago? I came so close to canceling and losing my deposit. She did take the trip, and everything changed. In Paris, where the group gathered to meet, all she saw were couples. She tried to reassure herself. I am outgoing. I'll meet people. It is only two weeks. She had brought several books for the alone times. The books never came out of her luggage.

There he was, older of course, but that same smile. "Jeanne, is it you?" David asked. They hugged. She giggled. After a welcome by the tour director, there was a "get acquainted" happy hour. Somehow, they missed getting acquainted with the other tour members, and caught up with each other's news. His wife had died, after a very long illness. "I did most of my grieving after we heard the devastating news. In many ways, it was a relief when her suffering ended." David had heard about Chuck's death. "I did not have your address to send a note, Jeanne."

As it turned out, two weeks was not nearly long enough, for they had years and years to discuss. That discussion has continued.

Tonight, another road will begin, or perhaps, a return to the earlier road. David's grandson will be best man, and Patty will walk her mother down the aisle. Tomorrow, she and David will return to the wine country, where this new chapter began for both of them.

Unrequited
Danial Francis

Sight in twilight 'twas beauty be seen
endless and finite love o'er me
quietly reciting thine heart's poetry
" Tis me, tis me-thy leavings of me "
remaining upon yon balcony

An angel befitting heaven t'was sent
striking and sitting mid elegance
brusquely admitting to suffer relent
" Relent, relent-thine heart's discontent "
against thy will what sorrow is meant

Alas laid to waiting for love brought intern
embers abating from fires yet to burn
feelings belated nor mannered return
" Return, return-thy rapturous yearned "
feignly I stated unrequited love spurned

Untitled One
A.J. Huffman

In the rare moments that I think
I might someday want a family
of my own, it is you I imagine
as my other half, my safe haven, shimmering
like an angel, answering the million wishes
I have whispered into fountains and after falling stars.

Untitled Two
A.J. Huffman

Last night I dreamed
I was a flower and you were a newborn
butterfly, perched to drink.
I inhaled the scent of wind from your wings
and shuddered as you released
into flight.   For a moment, I could not breathe.
My body numbed with the knowledge
that your absence would haunt me like an earthquake,
and I doubted if I wanted
to survive the aftershock.

Winter Heartbreak
Dmitry Blizniuk
(translated by Sergey Gerasimov from Russian)

It's harder to lick wounds of your heart in wintertime.
The whole city looks like a computer program
Devoured by the weak-sighted virus of snow.
Blue shadows freeze in paper cups.
The waterline of twilight becomes fuzzy.
The white, pink, orange darkness draws near.
Sumo wrestlers shake their cold blubber
On the pavements, awnings, benches.
The snow rustles, the blizzard swishes,
Snakes settle in old newspapers...
And you've found three pairs of gloves
While cleaning up the shelves.
Now that you are alone again,
Who could you give these nights to --
The lilac triangles of love and warmth,
Of light snoring and sleepy kisses?
It's only winter that hugs you,
And loneliness puts its heavy paw on your breasts.
It's not January but a factory for sewing silvery covers.
God's moving house from this planet to no one knows where,
Packing belongings into boxes, into Styrofoam of snows:
Fracturable things, lives, orchards, ships.
He puts them on foam rubber, wraps the dishes in paper,
Careful not to break to smithereens
The fragile Christmas bauble with people on it...

You Live in Me
Dmitry Blizniuk

You live in me.
Every morning you come to my eyes
From inside my head. They look like French windows –
Their clear cast glass extends down to your feet.
You stretch yourself on tiptoe and look out
At the green, breathing waterfall of the new day,
Staying yourself.
You stare at the well-known but unfamiliar world
At the city waking up in lilac pebbles…
I've given you a bright drop of immortality,
I've let you live in the red forest of my heart
like a bird of prey, tawny owl…

I used to kiss you,
Inhaling the sweet smoke
From the clay mouthpieces of your breasts.
I absorbed the brackish essence
Of your translucent clavicles and neck.
My fingers rubbed the moire glow
On your shoulder-blades.
I held your consciousness
In my hand like a fluffy dandelion.
It was enough to blow tenderly in your eyes
To puff away all your seeds
And send them slowly waltz around the bedroom
Like a thousand and one swan needles…
After that, we used to sleep, hugging each other.
Sometimes I started in my half-sleep like a fridge,
And you gently stroked the nape of my neck.
Our flat was ropy with wires.
It needed a renovation

Like a poor fakir needs
A new basket for his dancing snakes.
We didn't have either a magic fish capable of granting wishes
Or even the sea,
Only a monumental view from the window,
Looking like a (removed by the moderator.)

I was a kid inside a ship,
And you were my mysterious sea.
I fought against the light of your candle;
No one wanted to give in,
To lose to the scalding darkness growing between us.
I whispered "off",
But your love glowed softly.
Little by little you were becoming a part of me;
You nestled inside my brain
Like a blade nestles inside a pocket knife handle,
Like the rib outgrowing Adam...

My love,
I've become a hostage of good habits
I'm plagued by the universal hunger:
Everyone I remember becomes me.
We find the extension of our soul
In a worthless stone found on the seaside,
In a woman, in an idea, in a tree or a theorem,
In a rural dullness, in the thickets of science,
In the eternal, glimmering orchards of art,
In the tiny warm palm of a baby,
In any other straws we grasp...

You Should Know
Ashley Collins

I fiddle with the station, trying to find a song that matches my disorientated mind but every lyric I hear is wrong. I shut it off.

"This isn't working."

The light is red for a while and I'm so out of it that I forget I can make a right turn, the red Honda honks. I blink, realizing where I am and make the turn. I watch, in my rearview mirror, the red Honda turn into a garage.

"I don't know if I can keep doing this."

The street is somewhat familiar. I drive further down the street and remember the house.

An empty spot comes to view and I take the opportunity.

"I just don't know, anymore, okay!"

I take the key out of the ignition, lean back, and fall into the heart of my hand. Suddenly my phone glows and I see that it's Ayla.

"I'll be out in five minutes"

Before I can put it down, another message comes in, this time from a well-known sender.

It's a desperate promise, its unlike him.

"You're not gonna walk out on us, Liv. I'll be damned, if I let you go."

The phone jumps into the passenger seat and my mouth softly leans on my poorly made fist. My finger lightly strokes my upper lip as I try to gain control of the fountain that spews from my sight.

"Hey babe, you ready to go?"

Suddenly tonight becomes real, as if it was just some walking nightmare before. If only it was just that.

"Alivia?" he quickly descends the stairs before slowing down when he realizes I'm not paying attention. I'm standing by the French doors that lead to the backyard.

His hands use my arms for slides, as they start from the tops of my shoulders and end at the bottom of my elbows. He leans down to my ear, "Hey."

Outside is no longer outside, instead it's the reflection of us both, and I study him through it.

"What's wrong?" I politely smile before looking down, not ready for the words to follow. I move out from his gentle grasp, creating space between us.

"I'm gonna pick up Ayla by myself," I say. He chuckles a bit to himself, probably at my sudden weirdness.

"Okay," he pauses, taking a step forward. I take one back. Something's off. "Did I... Did I do something?"

I don't say anything at first. Unsure if what I'll say is what I really want.

"Aliv-"

"This isn't working," is all that comes out. My eyes are mildly entertained by the small dust buddies on the wood flooring.

I could only imagine what his face looked like then, I could only wonder if he understood what I was saying.

He decides to be optimistic, "What isn't working? The AC? There's a guy coming by on Monday." If smiling could make a sound, I could hear it, I could hear him smiling at his desperate joke.

"No Tucker," I sigh. "I don't know if I can keep doing this anymore."

He's silent for much longer this time. I know he knows what I'm trying to say, I know he does. But, I also know him well enough to know he won't let me off so easily.

"Keep doing what?" His voice is flat, he's not smiling anymore.

"I don't know," I stutter. "I don't know if I can—" I begin. He shifts, folding his arms.

"You don't know what?"

Frustration spikes. I finally look him in the eye. "I just don't know anymore, okay!"

He shakes his head, "No, Alivia, you don't get to just say that, and not tell me what you mean," he pauses, as I glare. "So, come on, already, you can't keep doing what?"

I roll my eyes, upset. "I can't keep doing this relationship. I can't keep doing us, I can't do "this", anymore," attitude trails throughout the spaces between the words.

He studies me at first before turning around, running his fingers through his short and blonde, icy blonde, hair. The other hand rests on his hip, he looks out into the backyard. This time the reflection is different, he's the only one in it.

I want to say that I'm joking but I won't find the words.

"I don't understand. Why are you saying this?"

"We hardly see each other anymore," at this he mutters, and looks to the ceiling. "I mean think about it Tuck. You're here and I'm there—," he turns around. He can feel it, feel that I'm lying.

"You're gonna pull the distance card, seriously Liv? You're what? An hour away? That's nothing! You know how many guys wish they were only an hour away from their girl? Nah Alivia, I don't buy it."

"Well you really should, because that's what it is."

That statement goes over his head, "What is it, huh? Another guy?"

I roll my eyes, "Oh because I don't want to date you anymore, it has to be because of someone else—"

"Answer the damn question, Alivia!"

"Seriously? It's not because of someone else, I'm not cheating!"

"Okay so what? You don't love me?— because if it's 'no', you're not only lying to me but you're lying to yourself," he's not really asking. "And last time I checked, love didn't mean 'within five minutes of each other'," he mocks.

"Oh my gosh Tucker. I never said that—"

"Okay so tell me, Liv, what exactly are you saying. It isn't someone else. It's not that you don't love me. What is it? Are you running? Because it sounds like to me you're giving up because it's getting hard, because it isn't so easy like you thought it would be in your little fantasy world—"

"So, what if I am?! Huh? What if I am giving up? What if I don't want to only see you every now and then? What if I don't want to stay up late at night wondering what you're doing or who you're with? What if I want to be able to hear your laugh in person and not through the stupid phone? What if I don't want to hear about your day through one-worded, lagging answers? What if I don't want to choose between you and the life I'm making for myself over there? What if I don't want dumb occasions, like coming up to see Ayla in another play, in order to see you? What if I want you, here and now with me? So what, if I want it to be easy?" My eyes work up the water, and it travels down my dark skin.

He stares at me in disbelief.

"I don't want this anymore, okay, I don't," I have trouble convincing myself.

"No, no. I know you. And I don't believe you. You're running. And, and you're scared," he clenches his jaw as he walks back and forth. "I just don't understand why, why is this all of a sudden?" I don't say anything.

His voice changes, "I mean you don't think I don't wonder about you, that I don't think about you every waking moment. Do you know how boring it is over here without you?" he shakes his head. "I love you. Don't you understand that? I look forward to crappy FaceTime calls and the dumb occasions we get to see each other. I enjoy the pockets of time we get to talk for hours, like nothing has changed. I look forward to the end of the day because I know none of the other guys get to talk to my girl, I know that no one else loves your heart like I do. Don't you know that? Don't you know that I would never dream of being with anyone else that isn't "Alivia Laurie Cartwright". I treasure every moment that I have with you, I don't have time to think about all of the things that could be easy, because easy means I don't have you. And I want you,

Liv, I want us."

The tears are slower now, and I find myself regretting what I say before I even say it. My hand embraces his hand to pull it away from my chin. "Well it's not enough."

"Bull." He shakes his head. "I don't believe you for a second. And I know you don't mean that."

"I do," I confirm.

"How— how can you look me in the eye and say that? After all we've been through, after everything we've done together. Are you honestly going to say that this isn't enough," he pauses.

"That I'm not enough." I can't muster up the courage to say that he wasn't enough, but I couldn't tell him he was either.

I turn away, grabbing my keys that rest on the counter. I pull the front door open and walk through. As if everything else that he was saying wasn't right, there was one thing he knew more than anything. I was running.

"Alivia?" I walk further along the stone walk away, remembering to count three steps down before I'm on flat ground.

"Alivia," he calls. I unlock the doors to the car, sliding into the plush seating, the door closes me in.

"Alivia!" He's in the doorway now, his mouth parted in disbelief.

The only key that matters, finds its way into the ignition and the car starts up, "Alivia don't do this. Don't do this," my hands rest on the wheel. "Don't give up on us. Don't."

My eyes find him looking me dead in the eye through the glass. His blue orbs are brimming with the clearest water known.

They're pleading, they're begging.

And as if I couldn't be anymore heartless, my eyes float to behind me as my hand finds the strength to pull the gear shift into Reverse, backing out of the driveway. As I speed off, I find him in the rear-view mirror, his hands intertwined on top of his disheveled hair.

I hear his last and final call, "Alivia!"

The sound of vibration pulls me out of the thought drift. I pick up my phone and I'm greeted with seventeen messages from Tucker and one from Ayla that reads: Where are you?

I put my phone in the cup holder and look out to see Ayla walking out of the house and down the sidewalk, I'm across the street and a few cars down. I rub my cheeks to remove the white, narrow stains before rolling down the window, slapping a smile on my face and honking the horn. Ayla instantly jolts up and glares at the perpetrator.

"Not funny," she scolds. I smile, but not truly. She squints, most likely at the fact that the passenger seat is empty. She was expecting Tucker, when were we ever apart is what I suppose she would of said.

"Ayla!" a boy calls from the steps of the house that she had come out of, "Wait up!" I can't see him but I can hear him running. Ayla fights a smile before telling me to hold on for a minute as she turns back on the sidewalk. The boy comes into view, a familiar face, probably one of the guys in the play earlier tonight.

"Hey Caden," she greets the tall boy in a way that I've never heard her greet a boy before. It was less of what she said, more of how she said it.

"You uh, forgot these," he pulls out the bouquet of flowers that Tucker had picked out for her after the show.

"Oh my gosh," she exclaims sheepishly as she takes them from his hands. His fingers instantly kiss the dark hairs on the top of his head before they rest at his side, fidgeting. "Thank you, I totally forgot about these." I just know her dimples are making a scene.

"Yeah, no problem. I uh, I— you were really good— I mean great tonight," he's tripping over his own words. Ayla has an admirer.

If her skin didn't prevent her from blushing, she would of been a porcelain doll, "Thank you." Okay, so Ayla has a crush.

They stand awkwardly in front of one another and I forget how high school used to be. Awkward. Ayla opens her mouth to say something but Caden beats her to it.

"Well, I, I guess I'll see you on Monday," he says.

She smiles, but I know her better enough to know that she's disappointed, "Right. See ya Monday." His tower like frame returns to the house and Ayla only shrugs her shoulders as if to say, "Better luck next time."

"Actually. Ayla," Caden calls. An eyebrow of Ayla's raises up.

"Yes," she sings. He laughs.

"Um there's actually something I've been meaning to tell you," he begins. He watches her but Ayla's expression doesn't change, she's protecting herself.

"I," he chuckles to himself, "Sorry, I can't believe I'm finally going to say this. I—," he claps, he can't find the courage to say it. "It's been a long time coming, but I think you should know."

"Are you—" she's interrupted.

"I like you. A lot." Her eyes widen at his boldness. "I didn't want to graduate with any regret and not telling you that seemed like a big one."

Ayla doesn't say anything at first and Caden sticks his hand in his pocket and the other rubbing the back of his neck.

"Okay well—" he starts, trying to remove himself.

She instantly hugs him and he slowly closes the embrace as she whispers, "I like you too." They remain like that for a while, in each other's arms, whispering phrases I can't pick up.

"Do you want to hang out for a little longer?" he asks as they pull away, she nods. He looks over to the car I'm in.

"Don't worry Alivia—" Didn't know he knew who I was, let alone that I witnessed the whole thing.

"I'll only be an hour more," Ayla finishes for him and just like that she's off, back into the house, and I'm left alone.

I ignore the fact that mom would kill me for letting her go off with a boy at this time, even though it was only nine, and there were a billion parents in that house. Instead something comes to mind, a memory of why this street is so familiar.

It was some sort of banquet in the house's yard and Tucker and I were sitting at the same table. As soon as he said hello, he was teasing me, all night, and every day after that. He was

annoying and for the life of me I couldn't understand why all the girls were obsessed with him.

As our paths kept crossing in school, I slowly started to understand why. But at that point we were going back and forth with each other like animals, I knew there was no way of there being an us. But then suddenly it was different.

Graduation day, we were waiting for the ceremony to begin and he said something stupid like, "I like your shoes." The usual sass unleashed and I preceded to face forward, we were about to go out onto the football field and I didn't have time to understand his games. But as the ceremony ended and our caps came raining down, he was the first face I saw.

"What are you doing?" I questioned, as he came forward.

"You should know, I like more than just your shoes."

I'm driving, the radio's on, and all I can hear is the drum inside my chest. There's no one on the street and no one behind me to remind me to make a right turn. The house is still, not at all how I left it. The garage door is halfway open and I can hear the tools rumbling inside. I climb out of the car, tucking the shorter strands behind my ear to join the rest of them.

I walk up to the garage door and push it up, to find him staring at me with clear goggles on and wood chips on his old football shorts. He turns off the table saw and removes the goggles.

There's nothing but silence between us, a first for us, we always had something to say.

"You were right, I am—I was running," I confess. "And I'm scared." I chuckle in disbelief as I realize I have to admit something that I no longer believe, "You scared me." He only blinks.

"When I first met you, Tuck, I couldn't understand what was so great about you, why all the guys cared about what you thought or why the girls were obsessed with you. All I knew, was that some jerk was teasing me every day in class, and he wouldn't leave me alone," I paused.

"But suddenly it was different. Suddenly, it's senior year and you're confessing to me that you want to be more than what we are and I was so surprised and so. So happy.

"I had been waiting for so long, that I, I didn't think it was real. And sometimes, I still don't. I still don't think we're real, sometimes I think I'm gonna wake up and we never happened. That that day was all made up. I keep thinking I'll wake up to you saying you can't do the distance or that you don't love me. And I hate feeling like that all the time, I hate thinking about you like that.

"That dumb play had me thinking about us, in a way that I put off. Like what if we are too good to be true, what if you are. What if at the end of all this, we're just another couple gone sour. And that, honest to God, scares me. And I was scared that if I didn't do it now, then I would be the one hurting," I laugh at the wetness of my cheeks. "But it looks like that theory was wrong, wasn't it?"

It's hard not to feel stupid now when he was right. How many people wish they had what we had, what we had was easy compared to people who actually have problems. Problems that they can't control, not problems they make up. A cowardly move, a move that isn't me and yet that's exactly who I was an hour ago. And as he watched me, I realize the only distance we've ever had was right now in this moment. And I hated every moment of it.

The way Ayla looked when Caden said her name, man, it made me remember the feeling.

The feeling every time Tucker surprised me at school or the weekly letters, on top of talking to him every day. It made me remember all the times I couldn't think of something to spit back when he teased me. All the times he made me speechless. The compliments I never picked up on until after we were together. It made me think about the purity of our relationship and how we were satisfied with where we were because we knew that one of these days, it would be more. So, as he watched me from a far, I knew I had to tell him. My mouth parted to continue but his movements prevented the sound. That's the thing about Tucker, he already knew.

He pulled me close, kissed my temple, "Your theories are always wrong. Always."

Yours and Mine
Danial Francis

Love is deeper than the seas
and taller than the tallest trees
love is gentile, love is kind
love is yours and mine

Love is wider than the sky
and higher than the highest high
love is perfect, love is why
love is yours and mine

Love is greater than all else
and more giving of ourselves
love is loyal, love is free
love is you and me

Contributing Authors

Julia Benally

     Born to the Bear Clan of the White Mountain Apache Tribe, Julia enjoys writing about her people and her area. She has been published in online and print venues such as *Sanitarium*, *The Wicked Library Podcast*, *Mantid Magazine*, and more. Her story *64 Dresses* is upcoming in *The Wagon Magazine's* next issue, *Love Notes* will be featured in *Liquid Imagination* and *Devil's Hour* will be read by *The Wicked Library Podcast* in October. When not writing, she loves nature walks, cross-stitching and playing the piano.

     You can follow her @SparrowCove.

Jason Bleistein

Jason Bleistein is a yet to be published writer and a not very good beer league hockey player. He resides in Arlington, TX with his wife, two children, and a greyhound.

Dimitry Blizniuk

Dmitry Blizniuk is an author from Ukraine. His most recent poems have appeared in *Dream Catcher, The Ilranot Review, Reflections, The Courtship of Winds.* He is a finalist for 2017 Award *Open Eurasia, The Best of Kindness 2017 (*USA). He lives in Kharkive, Ukraine."

Shayna Boisvert

Shay Boisvert is a sophomore at Saint Francis University in Loretto, Pennsylvania. She is majoring in English Literature and Philosophy and minoring in French Cultural Studies and Communication. She was inspired to become a writer after reading the Harry Potter novels at age eight and began writing in high school. Besides writing short stories, she is now an editor for her school's literary journal *Tapestries*. Currently she is studying abroad in the south of France while working on her first novel.

Chereze Booysen

2012: *City Varsity* – Film and Television Production Techniques

2016: Published the first article in the *Advertiser; First Female Doctor to Open a GP Practice.*

2017: Published *Standing In Awe* in an international magazine called *Swan song Le chant du Cygnet* this was the final issue of *Mauvaise Graine-* Publisher: Walter Ruhlmann

2017: Published in a US Literary journal with Grey Wolfe Publishing, *Piece by Piece.*

Susan Burdorf

Susan Burdorf is the author of several YA Contemporary novels as well as numerous short stories in a variety of anthologies. She is thrilled to be part of this Grey Wolfe Publishing production. A resident of Tennessee she is often found hiking the trails on the hunt for waterfalls.

Susan can be reached on her Facebook page at www.facebook.com/susanburdorfauthor and twitter at @sburdorf.

Ashley Collins

At the age of twelve, Ashley Collins wrote her first book on Wattpad, a website for authors to gain an audience, and has successfully gained over a million reads. As the years progressed, she was the first to write a consecutive serialized fiction story for her high schools' newspaper, awarding her with the Editor-in-Chief position the following year. Now that Ashley is attending college in Southern California, she is only training her craft and searching for her next big story.

Shelby Curran

Shelby Curran graduated from Florida State University with a degree in English: Editing, Writing and Media. Her work has appeared in *The Miami Herald, Snapdragon Journal, Panoplyzine* and *Jumbelbook*.

Ian Dixon

Ian writes prose and screenplays and his films have been distributed and won awards internationally. He has directed television for *Neighbours, Blue Heelers* and SBS TV (his episode, *Wee Jimmy*, won a best director award at the San Francisco International Film Festival). Ian Dixon's debut feature film *Crushed* (writer/director) screened at Cinema Nova in 2009. Ian has also been funded to write feature films for Screen Australia and Film Victoria. Ian's novel *Loving the Amazon* is currently seeking publication.

Ian completed his PhD Doctorate on the films of John Cassavetes at The University of Melbourne, Victorian College of the Arts in 2011 where he also studied a Post-Graduate Filmmaking Degree. Ian has also delivered academic papers (including a plenary speech for CEA in USA) and published academia internationally and currently lectures in filmmaking, semiotics and screenwriting at SAE Institute, Melbourne and Deakin University, Burwood.

Ian also spent over twenty-five years as an actor (he took over from Guy Pearce to play the lead in Grease). In television, his performance work can be seen on: *Underbelly: Squizzy, Rush, City Homicide, Guinevere Jones, Martial Law, Blue Heelers, Stingers, Heartbreak High, Shadows of the Heart* etc.

Pamela Q. Fernandes

Pamela Q. Fernandes is an author, doctor and medical writer. She writes romantic suspense, speculative fiction and Christian nonfiction. Some of her published romances are, *Seoul-Mates*," and *Under A Scottish Sky*.

You can find her on Twitter @PamelaQFerns or on her website **www.pamelaqfernandes.com**

C. Flynt

C. Flynt is the writing team of Carol and Clif Flynt.   Each is the principle writer of some stories and consultant, critic, first reader and polisher of the other's stories. We spend hours debating plot points, character motivations, likely (and unlikely) events, doing research and critiquing each other's text.

The end result is truly a collaboration, although the primary author's voice does show.

Clif is a computer programmer, technical author (*Tcl/Tk: A Developer's Guide, Linux Shell Cookbook*) and filk-song writer. He's been active in science fiction convention circles since the 1970s, has proven himself inept as a fencer, and no longer raises guppies.

Carol is a bookkeeper, report writer and musician. She's been involved in science fiction fandom, madrigal singing, Civil Air Patrol and gardening.

Rachel A.G. Gilman

Originally from Woodstock, NY, Rachel A.G. Gilman is a rising senior at NYU's Gallatin School of Individualized Study concentrating in creative writing and gender studies. She is the General Manager of WNYU, NYU's student-run radio station, where she produces the award-winning talk show *The Write Stuff*. She is also the Creator and Editor-in-Chief of NYU's first feminist arts journal, *The Rational Creature*. Additionally, she is a staff columnist at *Washington Square News'* arts blog *The Highlighter* and a staff writer for *Popdust*. Her work has been featured in *Adelaide Literary* and *Minetta Review*, among others.

Find out more at rachelaggilman.com.

Rebecca Ruth Gould

Rebecca Gould's books include *Writers and Rebels: The Literatures of Insurgency in the Caucasus, After Tomorrow the Days Disappear: Ghazals and Other Poems of Hasan Sijzi of Delhi, and The Prose of the Mountains: Tales of the Caucasus.* She teaches comparative literature and translation studies at the University of Bristol in the UK.

Mark Hudson

Mark Hudson is a regular Grey Wolfe contributor, who writes for them all the time. As far as the passion pages, Mark once had a female pen pal from Taiwan who said, "You write a lot of good poems. But you never write love poems." Mark replied, "That is because I'm not in love." Mark has a passion for writing and art, and spends most of his time doing it. So marriage sounds like a difficult idea to him-but he's bumbling through life barely making ends meet, dazed and confused, but at least he's got a sense of humor about it! He believes that love does exist-and the best love is the love of God for his whole creation. He believes God loves everybody- but why is a mystery. He feels the holy spirit's love of him.

A.J. Huffman

A.J. Huffman has published thirteen full-length poetry collections, thirteen solo poetry chapbooks and one joint poetry chapbook through various small presses. Her most recent releases, *The Pyre On Which Tomorrow Burns* (Scars Publications), *Degeneration* (Pink Girl Ink*), A Bizarre Burning of Bees* (Transcendent Zero Press), and *Familiar Illusions* (Flutter Press) are now available from their respective publishers. She is a five-time Pushcart Prize nominee, a two-time Best of Net nominee, and has published over 2600 poems in various national and international journals, including *Labletter, The James Dickey Review, The Bookends Review, Bone Orchard, Corvus Review, EgoPHobia*, and *Kritya*. She is also the founding editor of *Kind of a Hurricane Press*.

www.kindofahurricanepress.com.

Jen Hughes

Jen Hughes is a writer from Ayrshire, Scotland. She has been furiously scribbling ideas and writing elaborate stories since she was seven. She has worked as a school assistant and a support worker for the past year, and will be starting university this month. She'll be studying English Literature and Film & TV Studies. She has been published on various online journals such as the *McStorytellers, Oletangy Review, Minus Paper and Pulp Metal Magazine.*

If you liked this story, then check out her own website, dearoctopuswriting.wordpress.com. There you can find an up to date portfolio of her short stories, flash fictions and poems. You can also show your appreciation by giving her a like on Facebook (Dearoctopuswriting), Twitter (@dearoctopus4) or on Tumblr (dearoctopuswriting.tumblr.com)

Michael D. Jones

Michael D. Jones is spending a great deal of time lately celebrating his family (his wife and four children). The love he experiences is largely familial, brotherly and divine… in short, Agape. He has two collections of poetry, *Unlikely Trees* (2014) and *Overtime and The Dance* (2017), two Pushcart Prize nominated poems, and a third collection forthcoming (2020). Recently his poems appeared in *Legends Literary Journal 2015, The Garfield Lake Review, Third Wednesday and the Kerf*. He holds a Master of Arts degree from Oakland University and a Bachelor of Arts degree from the University of Michigan. He and his wife, Joanne, live and work in Holland, MI.

www.michaeljonespoetmi.com

Billy Malanga

Billy Malanga (M.Sc. in Criminal Justice) is a first-generation college graduate, U.S. Marine Corps veteran, and the grandson of Italian immigrants. He played college football and worked for many years in a state prison system. All of these influences have undeniably shaped his way of thinking about his art. His poetry reveals his small victories and his struggles in redefining masculinity in an effort to better understand the beauty and brutality of the world around him. His poetry has been published/or is forthcoming in:

The Adelaide Literary Magazine's 2017 Award Anthology; *The Dead Mule School of Southern Literature; Indolent Books; Aji Literary Magazine; Burnt Pine Magazine; The Journal of Formal Poetry; Wraparound South Literary Journal; Spindrift Art & Literary Journal*; and numerous on line literary journals.

Gavin Meggs

Gavin Meggs lives in London, England and has been writing poetry since he was a child. Inspired by life in all its forms, Gavin seeks to share his perspectives on life in a way that will live on in the hearts and mind of those that read his work.

Gavin finds his inspiration in simple things which are often overlooked and enjoys the surprise that comes from the detail of life—like recognising the daily growth of an innocuous plant on a familiar walk - or a young child attempting to lick raindrops from the inside of a car window whilst his parents bicker over the sat-nav in the front seats.

The majority of Gavin"s work is, as yet, unpublished. Those that have read it say that it belongs "out there—he hopes you agree.

Sandeep Kumar Mishra

Sandeep Kumar Mishra is a writer, poet, and lecturer in English Literature. Last year his work published in more than fifty national and international magazines. He has edited a collection of poems by various poets - *Pearls* (2002) and written a professional guidebook -*How To Be* (2016) and a collection of poems and art- *Feel My Heart*(2016)

http://www.sandeepkumarmishra.com/
http://sandeepkumarmishra5574.blogspot.in/
https://en.gravatar.com/sandeepmishra551974
https://twitter.com/sandeep551974
https://www.facebook.com/sandeep551974
Email- sandeepmishra551974@hotmail.com

Joseph Murphy

Joseph Murphy has been published in a number of journals, including *The Ann Arbor Review, Northwind and The Sugar House Review*. He recently had collection of poems published, *Crafting Wings* (Scars Publications, 2017); his second collection, *Having Lived*, is forthcoming from Kelsay Books.

He was awarded Eisner Prize for poetry, the University of California Berkeley"s highest award in the arts, while an undergraduate. Murphy is also senior poetry editor for an online literary publication, *Halfway Down the Stairs* and a member of the Poetry Society of Colorado.

Michael Noder

A Love Extinguished is Michael Nader's first published piece. He is a dedicated father and proud to be included in this *Passion Pages* Anthology as the proceeds go to the *American Heart Association*, which he has a personal interest in supporting.

Gabriel Parker

Gabriel Parker is a senior at Southwest Covenant Schools in Yukon, Oklahoma. He enjoys acting in and directing the school plays, playing football, and in his spare time writing.

Lisa M. Scuderi-Burkimsher

Lisa M. Scuderi-Burkimsher was born and raised on Staten Island, New York.

Her love of writing came from her love of reading. She took online writing courses to hone her skill and is currently involved with an online writing critique group and a fiction book club. Her flash fiction story, *The Big Duke*, was published in September of 2015. She had several micro flash shorts published the same year, including *The Plunge*, and also has flash stories in the *Winter Writes, Halloween Musings & Amusings* and other Grey Wolfe Publishing anthologies.

Lisa currently resides on Long Island, New York with her husband Rick and her little dogs Lucy Lu and Breanna Sue.

Kayla Simmons

A native of Kansas City, Missouri, I've grown up my whole life a part of two very distinct worlds. I was raised near a metropolis, with the values of a farmer. I prefer the solitude and the peace that the beautiful natural landscape of Missouri has to offer as opposed to the hustle and bustle of downtown Kansas City, but I still hold the city near and dear to my heart, as it is a labyrinth with fantastic cultural and historical sites.

My heart belongs to my family first and foremost, secondly to my furry family (which grows every year), and thirdly to my creative passions, headlined by my love for language and literature. Currently I am attending Northwest Missouri State University as a graduate student pursing an English Master of Arts.

If I'm not gardening, snuggling with my cat, or wandering among the endless grottos of the Missouri landscape, you can most likely find me shamelessly binge-watching movies on my living room couch.

Nidhi Sing

Nidhi attended American International School, Kabul, before moving to Delhi University for BA English Honors. Currently, she lives with her husband in Yol, a picturesque cantonment, which was a British POW Camp housing German and Italian soldiers during the World Wars.

More than 50 of her short stories have appeared internationally in Military Experience and the Arts, Grey Wolfe publishing, Expanded Horizons, Vagabondage Press, Rigorous, TQR, SPR, Fantasia Divinity, Fiction on the Web, Storyteller, TWJ Magazine, Indie Authors Press, Flyleaf Journal, Liquid Imagination, Digital Fiction Publishing Co, LA Review of LA, Flame Tree Publishing, Four Ties Lit Review, The Insignia Series, Inwood Indiana Press, Bards and Sages Publishing, Scarlet Leaf Review, Bewildering Stories, Down in the Dirt, Mulberry Fork Review, tNY.Press, Fabula Argentea, Aerogram, Fiction Magazines, Flash Fiction Press, The Dirty Pool, Asvamegha, Thurston Howl Publications etc.

She has also authored several translations of the Sikh Holy Scriptures.

Moshe Sonnheim

Dr. Moshe Sonnheim, a native Philadelphian, lives in Jerusalem, Israel.

He is married to Jolene, a Dutch Child Survivor of the Holocaust, and they have two married daughters and nine grandchildren.

Dr. Sonnheim is a retired Senior Teacher of Social Work with several academic publications and two short stories---"Somewhere Else" and "Lacunae" to his credit.

At the age of 83, Moshe has finally returned to his "first love"---creative writing

His latest stories include "Jean Jacques," "The General"s Leg." "The Forest Beast." and a poem, "Listen" (Legends: Paranormal Pursuits 2016).

Passions Anthology 2017 includes "The Secret Garden" (a poem), and "Becky," "Meet me at the Eagle: A Philadelphia Story."

J.J. Steinfeld

Canadian fiction writer, poet, and playwright J. J. Steinfeld lives on Prince Edward Island, where he is patiently waiting for Godot"s arrival and a phone call from Kafka. While waiting, he has published eighteen books, including Should the Word Hell Be Capitalized? (Stories, Gaspereau Press), Would You Hide Me? (Stories, Gaspereau Press), An Affection for Precipices (Poetry, Serengeti Press), Misshapenness (Poetry, Ekstasis Editions), Identity Dreams and Memory Sounds (Poetry, Ekstasis Editions), Madhouses in Heaven, Castles in Hell (Stories, Ekstasis Editions), An Unauthorized Biography of Being (Stories, Ekstasis Editions), and Absurdity, Woe Is Me, Glory Be (Poetry, Guernica Editions). His short stories and poems have appeared in numerous periodicals and anthologies internationally, and over fifty of his one-act plays and a handful of full-length plays have been performed in Canada and the United States.

Margarite Stever

Margarite Stever grew up in a tiny Missouri town of just over 200 people. She currently lives in a larger Missouri city with her family and beloved fur babies. She writes stories and essays that touch a person's heart. Her work has recently appeared in the 2017 issue of *The Crowder Quill*, 2016 issue of *The Crowder Quill*, the Fall 2015 issue *of The Maine Review, Mamalode Magazine's 2015 Better Together*, and *Writer's Digest 2014 Show Us Your Shorts Collection*. She has placed in several contests, and insists that writing is her true passion. She has a Bachelor of Arts in English and is the treasurer for *The Joplin Writers' Guild*. She works for a community action agency where she is instrumental in assisting low income people achieve more energy efficient homes.

Mahinour Tawfik

Mahinour Tawfik, a 24-year-old Egyptian senior medical student born in Saudi Arabia. She was educated in an English school and fell in love with the language and literature. In her teenage years, she suffered from depression to the point that she almost gave in and became suicidal. That is when she decided to create her own light instead of giving into the darkness. Poetry became her way to relieve the pain.

Her first anthology " Dark Secrets" was released April 2016 in USA by KCL publishing company in South Carolina. She was one of the participants of the 9th international poetry festival in India September 2016.

She was featured in the local Indian daily newspaper besides the former features in multiple anthologies and online literary Magazines {Creative Talents unleashed – Ripen the page – International forum of literature and culture of peace}.

She received a certificate of appreciation from world poetry Canada , Vancouver. She's currently working on the 2nd major publication, "once upon a dream".

Rosanne Trost

Rosanne Trost is a retired registered nurse. She lives in Houston, Texas. Since retirement, she has realized her passion for creative writing. Several of her pieces have appeared in journals, including Chicken Soup for the Soul, Seeing Beyond the Surface and Cell2Soul.

Christopher Woods

Christopher Woods is a writer, teacher and photographer who lives in Houston and Chappell Hill, Texas. He has published a novel, *The Dream Patch*, a prose collection, *Under A Riverbed Sky*, and a book of stage monologues for actors, *Heart Speak*. His work has appeared in *The Southern Review, New England Review, New Orleans Review, Columbia* and *Glimmer Train,* among others. His photographs can be seen in his gallery.

http://christopherwoods.zenfolio.com